The Memoirs
of Lottie Hill

A Novel by

Meredith Kennon

This book is a work of fiction. Names, characters, places, and incidents either are products of the author's imagination or are used fictitiously. Any resemblance to actual events or locales or persons, living or dead, is entirely coincidental.

For additional information regarding the author, including future works, please visit meredithkennon.blogspot.com or her Meredith Kennon Facebook page.

ISBN-13: 978-1466257894

ISBN-10: 146625789X

Other works by Meredith Kennon:

Under the Same Umbrella

Tattered Letters

The Greystone Series, consisting of:

Almost Enough

At Willows Edge

Return to Greystone

The Gown Shop on Regent Street, although a stand-alone novel, has many characters first met in the Greystone Series

Also by Meredith Kennon:

A Grandmother's Home Companion

A Nostalgic Treasury of Seasons Past and Simpler Times

Acknowledgements

I want to express my great appreciation for the help I've received in the writing of this book. I thank my dear husband Henry, who assisted me every step of the way, and my daughter Katy, who always helps me with the *big picture*. Without their support, this book would not have come about.

I also thank Katy Williams of Bennington, Nebraska, and Melissa Wiedrich of Coon Rapids, Iowa, for giving freely of their time to help me with this effort.

I want to especially acknowledge Tammy Gray of Ennis, Texas, who has given me invaluable help in marketing, as well as editorial areas. I can't thank her enough. She is T. L. Gray, the successful author of the Winsor Series, Christian Romance.

I thank Henry and Joni Wiedrich of Gretna, Nebraska for their help in legal areas and the building and maintaining of my blog, meredithkennon.blogspot.com and also my Meredith Kennon Facebook page.

I appreciate the enormous help I received from photographer Rae Wiedrich of Roscoe, South Dakota, for her help and advice in the creation of the cover.

I would like to acknowledge the internet website,

BBC WW2 People's War. It is an especially valuable tool for understanding the conditions on Britain's homefront, and I thank the people for sharing their personal stories of the war.

I thank my family, especially my aunt, Phyllis Blake of Sioux Falls, South Dakota, who approved my use of a photograph of my grandmother for the cover. Grandmother Mary was born a few years before Lottie Hill, my fictional heroine, but she grew up in the same era and experienced both of the wars as an American.

I express my continued awe and praise for the British and Scottish people on their homefronts in both of the world wars. Their dogged determination was as key to their victories as the men who fought in the sky, on the land, and on the sea. I, too, believe "There Will Always Be an England," as expressed in the patriotic song by Ross Parker and Hugh Charles, which became popular in 1939, just before the war.

I especially want to thank you, my readers, who have encouraged me to keep writing. Thank you so much for your continued support.

For my children

The Memoirs
of Lottie Hill

by

Meredith Kennon

Prologue

As the airplane lifted off from Eppley Airfield in Omaha, Nebraska, twenty-five-year-old Erica Sinclair felt both excited and nervous to start a new life far from home. Everything that had ever mattered to her had somehow disintegrated in the last few months, and she was desperate for change—desperate enough to do something drastic. She had accepted the job as an Editorial Assistant at *The London View*, a position she'd seen listed on the internet. Knowing only that it was considered a trendy, up-and-coming cosmopolitan magazine with an internet following worldwide, she had applied for the job without saying anything to anyone.

According to her father, it was a hasty move, "an unwise and impetuous one," he'd said, when she told him as a *fait accompli* that she'd been offered the job and had accepted it. He insisted angrily that she could have had—and, with a change of attitude, might still have—a promising future in his own company.

She didn't want a future with her father, whose morals had always been sadly lacking, repeatedly hurting the woman he'd married.

Erica's mother Anne had died of cancer four years before, and Erica had never really recovered emotionally. She'd been to counseling, and although the sessions had helped, she missed her mother so much at times, she could hardly bear it.

As Omaha faded from her view from the airplane window, Erica wished her last conversation with her father could fade as easily. As she had grown accustomed to over the years, he berated her on a number of counts. He delivered his final authoritative pronouncements by dealing two devastating blows simultaneously—remarks calculated to knock her off her feet, to silence and crush her. First, he stated cruelly that if her drastic decision to run off to England was a dramatic ploy to rekindle her ex-boyfriend's affections, she could have achieved the same objective by merely dropping a few pounds. This, of course, made her cringe and actually take a step back in self-defense, but then he dealt his final blow. He was absolutely certain that her deceased mother would have seen Erica's present actions as immature and impulsive and would have been deeply disappointed in her.

Those blows hit with their usual effect, but this time, Erica found her voice, refuting tearfully, "I don't agree with you, and how I wish she were here! I believe she'd want me to follow my own dreams and not sink slowly into the quicksand of Midwest Consulting. I studied to become a journalist, if you recall."

"I remember writing the checks, well enough," he replied caustically. "Vi thinks it's time you started paying back a little for your privileges, which are many."

"And I think you pay way too much attention to the opinions of your latest distraction. And why should I care what Vi thinks, anyway? Besides, I know that Grandpa Bruckner set aside all the money for my education years ago. The tuition checks were to be written from that trust, which—in fact—they were. Mom told me that herself before she died, in case you should try something like this!"

"Something, like what?" he'd countered furiously, embarrassed at being caught in a lie.

"Taking credit for my education and then strong-arming me to do whatever it is you want me to do out of obligation to you. Besides, playing the dutiful daughter as the office underling is not my idea of a future."

"Perhaps your mother could have better spent her time teaching you to respect your elders and show appreciation for all you've been given."

Remembering his falling-out many years ago with his own father, she'd retorted, "As you did, of course, with Grandpa Phil."

Seeing him nearly upset his morning coffee, Erica exited his office, shaking with anger and trying not to show it as she left the building, A blast of piercing cold wind met her as she came around the corner of the high-rise, and dashing to her car, she suddenly felt better, realizing that she'd had the last word, for once.

"Would you like a beverage, miss?" asked the friendly stewardess. Erica was jolted out of her thoughts and graciously accepted a soda and a tiny bag of pretzels. She finally took notice of her fellow passengers, hearing bits of conversations and the urgent cry of an infant at the back of the plane.

The man seated beside her commented on the lovely day and made fun of the bags of pretzels saying, "The packaging costs as much as the pretzels inside it. It's a wonder they bother at all."

Erica agreed amicably and then looked again from the window, as the patchwork quilt of Iowa's farms disappeared beneath a blanket of clouds. Smiling to herself about her blanket-centered thoughts, she realized she was chilled and spread her long oatmeal-colored cardigan over her. She closed her eyes against the whiteness of the enveloping cloud and retreated again into her thoughts.

Her decision to do something entirely new with her life had little to do with her ever-disappointing relationship with her father, but it was galling to her that he had been absolutely right about it having everything to do with her sudden breakup with her boyfriend of two years.

Andrew Wilkins, the son of her father's partner at Midwest Consulting, stoically broke up with her one evening across a restaurant table and bowl of greasy corn chips. It was then that he declared his intentions of accepting the position of marketer for the company's technical expertise internationally. She later learned that her father had known of Andrew's plans a full month before she had, which rankled deeply.

Andrew calmly explained that while he cared about her feelings, he couldn't see himself doing justice to the company while maintaining a long-distance relationship with her.

Erica's hurt reply had been, "If you are so concerned about me or my feelings, shouldn't you have said that the other way around? Since entire relationships are made and maintained on the internet these days, why don't you just be honest and say you want to break up with me?"

To her shock and dismay, he'd answered bluntly, "All right, then. I do feel it's time we broke up. Things have changed between us, and we might as well face that now, before I leave for Japan."

She'd wanted to argue that nothing had changed for her, but suddenly feeling ill, she excused herself to the restroom before having to face the large platters of enchiladas they'd ordered. Moments later, realization dawned that she had her own car in the parking lot, so she did not return to the table at all, but went out the restaurant's side door and drove off. Andrew could deal with getting home, however he might.

If she felt slightly childish for taking that action, she'd never regret it, and even thought of her escape with some relish from time to time. However, she did hope that she'd grown up in the past few weeks and would like to think she'd behave more adult-like in life's future disappointments, which were sure to come.

I'll face them head on, just as Mom always said I

should, thought Erica victoriously. Next stop, New York. Final destination, London!

Chapter One

Fifteen months later, on a crisp June morning, Erica awoke in a languid state of contentment and sleepily reached to silent the humming vibration of the alarm clock on her mobile phone. She pressed the 'snooze' button with a happy sigh, just as she had done every morning since her move into her boyfriend's London flat five months ago. She reminisced happily about the funny way they had been introduced at a New Year's Eve party. Their relationship had moved forward with such speed, she now found herself actually "living with someone" for the first time.

Lying there, Erica's conscience was pricked, as she remembered her mother's counsel on the subject some years ago.

"Cohabitation," her mother called it, a word that to Erica's young mind had a rather sinful ring to it, even before she knew its meaning. During one of their intimate talks late at night, in the early days of her mother's illness, Erica had been sent to fetch the dictionary, and her mother made her read out the definition.

"Cohabitation: To live with someone, having a sexual relationship outside the bounds of marriage. To live as married without religious or legal sanction."

Erica remembered meeting her mother's steady gaze and word-for-word the counsel she had been given. "Considering some of your father's choices over the years, I'm not suggesting you jump into marriage quickly, my dear, just because you suddenly find yourself believing you're in love. I am just suggesting that you don't jump at all–into their bed, or otherwise."

"Mama!" Erica had cried in mortification.

Her mother's response was, even now, locked in Erica's memory. "Sometimes mothers must be blunt, sweetheart, and you aren't a child anymore. I won't always be around to advise you. Doing things in the proper order is important and has value, even if it's not popular today. Marrying too quickly can be a mistake, too, as I am daily reminded, but I was blessed to have you, so I could never ask for more. I just want you to be wiser than I was."

Uncomfortable now with the memory, Erica pushed it to the back of her mind and returned her thoughts to the man lying next to her. She remembered the sweet, unexpected discovery of absolute happiness that had driven her to choose such a life so impulsively, going against all the things her mother had taught her. She justified herself, thinking, times are different now, Mama. Things do change.

Erica never before used the 'snooze' option on her cell phone until living with Dean, but together they found lovely, affectionate ways of waking together to the sounds of the busy city. She loved their quiet morning conversations.

On one such morning, she confided to him that, upon awakening, she much preferred the sound of birdsong to the slamming of apartment doors and the relentless morning traffic. On that occasion, he lovingly told her that he'd long had his sights on an attractive residential area not far from their flat, where the birdsong could be heard from one's own quiet garden. That remark alone, in Erica's mind, was promising of his intentions for a long life together, and she repeated it to herself whenever she longed for his reassurance, which wasn't always forthcoming.

Beneath their cream-colored blanket, Dean lay sleeping, and she stared at him longingly, willing him to wake. She was tempted to ruffle his crop of thick, sandy-colored hair, but caught herself in time, remembering that his once-cheerful and amorous morning personality had changed noticeably in the past two weeks. She'd seen a different side of him recently, and she definitely did not want him snapping at her at this early hour. He had pressures from work, he explained when recently hurting her feelings by shunning her affectionate advances.

Well, she thought indignantly, his own alarm will go off in exactly twenty minutes, and it will be his loss as much as mine. Sighing again, only this time in disappointment, she turned off her alarm altogether and slipped out of bed soundlessly to go shower.

She wanted so badly for this to work out with Dean. Surely, she hadn't mistaken his declarations of love. He had reassured her so many times in the past, but likewise, how many times recently had he diminished her faith in herself and in him by speaking harshly to her? Surely, it must be the stress from his work, she thought. Perhaps, if he got a different job, things would return to the way they were in the beginning.

Now, more than a year after her breakup with Andrew, Erica knew that she had never really loved him and was grateful for what he'd done. If he hadn't had the courage to break up with her, she would have never left Omaha at all, nor would she have met Dean. Her father apparently still hoped she would get back together with Andrew, because in the only phone call she'd received from him since moving to London, he reported that although Andrew had been dangerously close to the tsunami in Japan, he had escaped unharmed.

Erica marveled that she hadn't even thought of Andrew when she'd heard of the disaster, thinking how strange love was, and fleeting, apparently. She didn't want love to be fleeting. She wanted it to last forever and through all kinds of trials, getting stronger every year.

Washing her hair vigorously, she knew—to be completely honest with herself—that she couldn't say whether or not she was truly happy here in London. Nor could she say, at this precise moment, that she was absolutely in love with Dean in his present state of mind.

She certainly wasn't in her element in his unappealing second-floor flat in the thick of London. The elevator was presently out of order, it was very expensive, and as much as she was willing to help with expenses, it was often beyond what she was comfortable paying.

On the bright side, she acknowledged they were but two flights of stairs from street level, and on top of that, her job was finally showing promise. Although *The*

London View had a large online following to which they kept up-to-the-minute information ever-flowing, quarterly they published a popular high-quality hardcopy edition, and it was for this division that Erica worked.

The June edition had hit the stands days ago and was selling well, and today the specific writing assignments would be made for the special edition of the magazine commemorating the tenth anniversary of the attacks of 9/11. Erica's eagerness on the project had been observed, and she had been praised for her work. She had even been told unofficially that she would get a real writing assignment as a reward for her efforts and that her American perspective would be a plus for her. For the first time, she would get to write a real article and make use of her journalism degree.

She was told to come to the preliminary assignments briefing that morning at nine sharp, and even Dean's present lack of interest in her couldn't totally squash her excitement and self-esteem.

After her shower, she wrapped herself in her toweling robe and briskly towel-dried her wet hair. Finding Dean still lying in bed asleep, she glanced at the clock, and seeing that she had plenty of time to finish getting ready for work, decided to slide between the sheets again and take advantage of the extra minutes to curl up in the crook of his arm. She whispered, "Good morning, Dean."

"If you say so," he answered sarcastically, startling her. "How many times have I asked you to let my alarm do its job and not preempt it? You know I've had trouble sleeping!"

At that precise moment, his alarm buzzed, and he reached to silence it.

Fighting off the insecurity she'd worked so hard to overcome in her months of counseling after her mother's death, Erica dismissed her negative thoughts by literally picturing them as trash on the floor and imagining herself sweeping them into the dustpan and into the garbage can. As she had been taught, she visualized putting the lid on tightly, thereby disposing of her unwanted, self-destructive thoughts. "There—done," she whispered to herself, firmly dismissing the thoughts that had so much power to crush her.

Wanting desperately to convince herself that she was indeed in love with Dean, she moved closer to him. She reached to stroke the dark stubble on his handsome chin, saying teasingly, "I do know you've had trouble getting your sleep, and as you see, I didn't preempt anything—only attempted to make your waking a bit more pleasant."

"Don't you have rather a big day?" he asked, stretching lazily away from her and reaching for his robe. "Do you want the shower first?"

"Yes, I do have a big day, and I've already showered, as indicated by my wet head and strawberry-scented body wash," said Erica in a voice of determined cheerfulness. She reached playfully for his robe, inviting him sweetly, "But we have a few minutes to spare."

"Maybe you do," he snapped. Perhaps regretting his hasty reply, he added, "Pay me no mind, Erica. I have a meeting with Marshall this morning, and you know what kind of mood that puts me in. If the company isn't booming, I must be the reason. He overreached this time, against my advice, so I hope he remembers that conversation as it actually happened. I'm not taking responsibility for this one."

Troubled by what that could mean, Erica released her end of his robe and moved back to her side of the bed. Trying not to sound anxious or petulant, she said, "I surely hope you don't then, Dean. Maybe he's waiting for you to stand up to him."

"Or he's waiting for a reason to sack me," he countered angrily. Tears immediately collected in her expressive brown eyes, and he said more gently, "Like I said, pay me no mind. I'll grab a shower. Hey, before you go this morning, could you leave a cheque for the rent? July's is due in a few days, and as it always takes a little longer for your American bank to process the transfer, and as you may be assigned to go somewhere exotic, who knows when you'll be back?"

"I won't be going anywhere for that long. Besides, I thought you were paying it this time. I had to last month, if you remember, what with your car repairs and all," said Erica, somewhat troubled. "Besides, I won't be going anywhere immediately, I'm sure. Oh never mind, I'll do it now while we're thinking about it."

"I'll get the next two months, darling, I promise." Casting a teasing glance at her, he said, "Just make the cheque—that's cheque with a *q-u-e*—out to me, like you did last month. By the way, isn't today your important day?" he asked charmingly, abruptly changing the subject. "Are you going to wear that smart gray suit you bought last week?"

"Yes, but aren't you changing the subject?" teased Erica, relieved to see his mood improve.

Ignoring her question, he stepped into the bathroom, asking sweetly, "Turn on the coffee machine, would you darling?"

She laughed. "Fine. The cheque—with a *q-u-e*—and the coffee. Anything else?"

"Not now," he said provocatively before closing the bathroom door.

After turning on the coffee machine, Erica reluctantly wrote the large check for their flat and put it on the table by the door. She knew she had some savings in an account at home, but she was determined not to live beyond her means. Nor was she willing to ask her father for financial help, no matter what.

The rent check was quite a lot of money for a place that didn't feel like hers. She had only the little bedroom for her things, and looking around at the black leather and chrome furniture, there was little to show that she even lived there. On the other hand, she thought, I haven't been here long enough to influence anything.

The flat was in a choice location, as evidenced by

the high rent, but wasn't somewhere she wanted to live for very long. There was too much coming and going at every hour of the day and night for her to ever feel peaceful. She couldn't read a book inside their flat in silence, let alone anywhere out of doors, as she always loved doing as a girl.

Although she didn't miss her father one bit and was glad she'd left without having to ask anything from him, she did miss her previous life, living on a acreage of property on the outskirts of Omaha. Her father's commute had been easy enough, and spending her summer vacations with the horses and helping her mother with the garden and canning every year was something she'd always loved and probably taken for granted.

Since moving to England, every weekend she'd longed for a drive in the country. Dean had a car she'd yet to see, but he wouldn't give in to her weekly request for a few hours out of the city. If he was going to keep a car and pay to garage it, why not use it, she'd reasoned. She had also argued more than once that if they weren't going to use it to escape the city once in a while, they would be further ahead saving for a better place to live by getting rid of the car altogether. He had been utterly opposed to that.

Erica always vacated their bedroom for Dean's use

in the morning and got dressed, did her hair and applied her makeup in the tiny, adjacent second bedroom. When she moved in, Dean assured her that keeping her things in the other room would be best all the way around. She teased him that his reason for this was, no doubt, the space needed for his many pairs of shoes. Now, it occurred to her, unhappily, that breakups could be more easily accomplished when the parties hadn't merged their things too intimately. Was that the reason he'd insisted? She dismissed that unwelcome thought and concentrated on the upcoming day.

As she finished the straightening of her naturally curly, collar-length brunette hair and took extra care with her makeup, she gave herself a final, critical glance in the mirror, hating her curviness. She saw the time and made for the door, calling, "I'm off. See you tonight, Dean. Hope your day goes well."

He emerged from the bedroom, and Erica noticed how professional he looked in his best suit, dark tie, and crisp laundered shirt. His eyes no longer had that worried, hunted look she'd seen in them minutes before, and it relieved and reassured her. They complimented each other on their appearances, kissed briefly at the door, and she was off to the office to get, at long-last, an actual writing assignment for the magazine.

Erica made eye contact and smiled amiably to strangers on the street, because that was what people did in the Midwest. She wasn't about to give up everything about her past, although if she were to be completely honest, she knew that her unreciprocated smiles and Midwestern accent were about the only things she'd been able to retain since moving in with Dean. He had indoctrinated her in the differences to be found in the languages of the two countries, so as not to "humiliate herself," which were his words, not hers. Andrea, her immediate supervisor at the magazine and closest friend in London, had loaned her the book, *The Diary of an American Au Pair*, which she had devoured twice before returning. Oh, how she could relate!

Crossing the street to the tube entrance with care, she chuckled to herself as she remembered Dean saying, "You know, darling, you could try to drop that cornhusker accent, now that you've been here a year."

⸗

Chapter Two

Arriving at the office in Broadgate, an impressive modern office building viewed easily from the A10, Erica took the elevator to the ninth floor and stopped at her desk before making her way to the meeting.

She had been instrumental in helping identify and set up appointments for the coming week with important people worldwide, whose remarks on the 9/11 attacks would be of interest to their readers. In that way, they were to take a broad look at the world through their special edition of the magazine.

In addition to that, there had been many personal-interest stories of the English—particularly Londoners—that had come to light in the years since that terrible day in 2001. Such stories were always read eagerly, and gathering the information on such personal accounts to present to the panel, so they could then decide which ones to include in the special edition, had been the work that Erica had most recently been engaged in. Most of that was accomplished now, so the interviews for the worldview were what remained to be done.

Erica had thoroughly enjoyed being part of this

work, because as an American, she appreciated any memorial of that event. Although she had been but a young girl in high school, that terrible day had affected her deeply. She vividly remembered the announcement of the attacks that stunned the world and everyone in her English class that morning. She would never forget the sad days of mourning that followed. In recent weeks, she'd found it interesting how many lives in the United Kingdom had been impacted tragically and personally by the multiple attacks on America that terrible day a decade ago.

Upon entering the conference room, she recognized all but one of the faces, a well-dressed young woman of about her own age. Making eye contact, they nodded to one another.

An hour later, trying to keep her emotions in check and her face unreadable, Erica packed her laptop and some desk supplies into the computer carrier. She carefully stowed her itinerary in the side pocket and sat down to read her assignment in full. Glancing at the clock, she could barely take it in that she'd soon be heading home to change her clothes and pack for her long train journey that very afternoon to Stirling, Scotland.

While some of her colleagues were excitedly

readying themselves for important interviews with international celebrities, she, on the other hand, was to begin work on a story that would be published, not in the 9/11 Special Edition, but in December. According to the cover sheet of the dossier detailing her assignment, one of the elderly owners of the company, Mr. Paul Davies, had asked that someone write a feature story on a woman, a former mentor and friend of his wife's, as a personal favor. This woman, Charlotte Hill of Stirling, Scotland, of a once-prominent shipping family out of both Glasgow and Liverpool, would be one hundred years old on Christmas Day. He'd indicated that he wanted the story to be comprehensive of her life—certain that the public would love it. By the tone of the introductory paragraph in the dossier, it sounded as if there were perhaps some in the office who were less enthusiastic about the project, but in response to his request, the woman's life was to be chronicled in the coming months in preparation for its publication in the December issue.

Erica's assignment was to take the next ten days interviewing the woman at her Scottish home on the outskirts of Stirling. It normally wouldn't take that long to gather the material, but she was to have but short periods of time each day to meet with the old woman, and even then, only as her strength allowed. Upon returning to London, Erica would write up the preliminary draft, and at intervals, she may be expected to return to Scotland for a day, as necessary, to complete her assignment to the boss's satisfaction. That done, she would help check the article for accuracy, once the final draft had been written up by someone other than herself, who had more writing experience.

Immediately after the meeting, having first read her assignment synopsis and knowing she'd be unable to hide her disappointment for long, she made for a quick getaway. Unfortunately, she was intercepted by her female department head.

Erica was able to stem the tears that were threatening, but knew she couldn't hold that pose for long and wanted desperately to escape.

Her boss, a tall, severely-dressed woman of an indeterminate age, said discreetly and matter-of-factly, "I know you were hoping for an assignment for the 9/11 Edition, Miss Sinclair, but don't take this too much to heart. We are entrusting you with this interview and the early drafts, and that's important, too. Other more prestigious chances are bound to come your way, and we owe it to our readers to put our best foot forward, particularly in this special edition. Don't you agree?"

Erica found her voice and tried to answer the question as adult and stoically as possible, but instead came off more like a petulant teenager. "I wonder you trust me with any assignment."

The woman gave her a much-practiced smile, no doubt intended to signal understanding, but to Erica signaled only condescension, even pity.

Turning to go, the woman turned and announced nonchalantly and far less discreetly, that once done with her assignment in Scotland, Erica would take up her new position in the customer service department, where much help was needed. "We might have to float you a bit and give you some experience in the advertising group after that," she'd concluded.

Taking in that final blow, Erica made her way back to her desk and glanced at the clock. With pounding heart and shaking hands, she tried to clear her desk as quickly as possible. She was interrupted by her friend and supervisor, Andrea Frey, who had come to sympathize.

Erica asked why she was assigned to interview the

old woman, or to even help write the article on the centenarian, when she was about to be demoted to Customer Service.

Her friend answered firmly, "It isn't a demotion, Erica, not at all. They are bogged down at the moment, but it's temporary. I'll get you back! Replacing you on the 9/11 project was talked about last Friday, but I didn't tell you, because I thought I'd talked them out of it. You'd earned your spot, and I made that case. I found out this morning at an early meeting that they were giving your assignment to the new woman, but by the time our meeting ended, you'd already gone into the conference room, or I would have warned you. I really would have, Erica."

"Then why give me an assignment at all?" asked Erica, now exasperated.

Sheepishly, Andrea answered flatly, "This morning was the first I'd heard of that project, and since no one was vying for the job, and as they did lead you to believe you'd be doing some writing, I suggested sending you. You do want the assignment, don't you?"

Noticing that her co-workers were beginning to take an interest in their conversation, Erica whispered, "Of course, Andrea, and I know you did your best for me."

Acknowledging the meaning of her lowered voice, Andrea led Erica to a more secluded corner. "I thought it was better than nothing. Not only that, but I didn't want you to be sent to Customer Service right away. I believe in saving face, especially where my friends are concerned."

"And I am grateful to you, I am, but Andrea, who was the new writer at the meeting who got what should have been my assignment?" asked Erica, holding back tears of frustration.

"Oh, that's the daughter of an investor, who made the assignment a stipulation of his recent input of cash. I learned that myself minutes ago from Jack. So it all makes sense, at last."

Erica became angry. "So I get demoted, so the investor is appeased, regardless of my previous work?"

"I understand how you feel, but it's not a demotion, and I wish you'd quit saying that! You've done great work here, and you've been appreciated. You understand how business works by now, don't you, Erica?" As Andrea often did, she nervously tucked her long blonde bangs behind her right ear, and as always, they slid out immediately, swooping across her forehead again. "It's not what you know and never has been. It's who you know, and that's for sure. On the bright side, though, since the new girl gets special consideration, she'll be moving up before long, and I'll get you back before you know it."

Erica shrugged at her. "I hope you're right."

"Listen, I'll empty your cubicle for you of anything personal, once the floor clears this afternoon. And look, I understand your frustration, but try to see it this way; you didn't get sacked. Any job in this economy is a good job, right?"

Realizing that Andrea had tried her hardest for her, Erica forced a smile. "Thanks for trying, Andrea. You're a good friend. Like you said, I've still got a job. See you in a couple of weeks, then."

"About that," said Andrea guiltily, "it wasn't until after I'd suggested they send you, that I realized that you'd have to be gone that long. I know Dean won't like it, either, and I feel terrible about it. What will you do with yourself with all that time on your hands in the middle of nowhere?"

Erica sighed. "That's the easy part. I've been dying to get to the country. That's the upside of this whole thing. I'll read, Andrea, and I'll walk and walk."

"All alone?" Andrea seemed genuinely surprised.

"Of course."

"Well, I'll miss you, but I'll picture you walking and walking through cow dung in the rain with your wellies on." Having said all she could to help her friend cope with her disappointment, she added, "Head office just learned of the project days ago, and they are sending you up right away, in case the interviewing process takes longer than expected. At the meeting this morning—when I put your name in for it—Mr. Rutley actually said, 'We don't want the old bird to kick it before her birthday, since we're going to so much trouble and expense to make a fuss over it.' So, it sounds like he, for one, isn't overjoyed by the project. They don't like it when owners and investors have too much input. He always says they should leave it to the professionals. I have to agree that it complicates things for the rest of us."

"I wonder she agreed to it at all," said Erica absently.

"Who?"

"The old bird—I mean—the old woman. What is her name, Charlotte something?" Erica managed to smile, and after giving Andrea a quick hug, headed for the elevator, staying well-clear of the other journalists, who were excitedly sharing their itineraries. She'd take care with her packing and put on some comfortable clothes for her nearly five-hour train ride to Edinburgh, boarding the high-speed electric East Coast Liner at Kings Cross at five o'clock that same afternoon.

Walking from the tube station to their apartment building, Erica remembered she'd written the check for the month's rent, and by the looks of it, thought it somewhat ironic that she wasn't even going to be there. She was beginning to get her head around the assignment, though, reasoning that it was a writing assignment of sorts, and she would enjoy being out of the city for a while. Maybe she really would spend hours reading and walking, which sounded heavenly. On the downside, it did mean being separated from Dean for a while, but who knew? Maybe the distance would be good for their relationship, and perhaps he might consider joining her there for the weekend. A free vacation, compliments of the magazine? It might tempt him. He wasn't in the least outdoorsy, nor was he a history buff, but there must be something to interest him in Stirling—surely.

Erica's itinerary had her billeted at a little Scottish

inn called The Little Scottish Inn. She smiled at the thought, opened the building door and climbed the two flights of stairs to their flat.

A strange and alarming feeling gripped her as she silently inserted the key into the lock and opened the door to the flat. It was quiet enough, as one would expect it to be, but she sensed that someone was there. Shaking now, she closed the door soundlessly and took off her new and uncomfortable high heels. She had no intention of warning the burglar by clomp-clomping around in her heels on the hardwood floor. Silently, she put down her bag from which she'd taken her mobile phone. She grabbed her umbrella from its stand with one hand and was poised to call emergency with the other, when she heard a woman's high-pitched laughter coming from the bedroom at the end of the hall.

Erica approached the noise but then froze when she heard an indistinct male voice. Then he laughed—Dean's laugh. Hoping for any explanation other than the obvious one, she went to the end of the hall and pushed open the bedroom door that was already slightly ajar. She entered the room white-faced, dropping both her phone and umbrella when she saw Dean in the arms of another woman. They were both in a state of some undress, so apparently she'd caught them in the act or perhaps just before the act, to be more precise.

Dean jumped quickly off the bed, as if somehow Erica might forget she'd seen him there. Without saying a word, she picked up her phone and left the room, closing the door with a bang. She was relieved that he didn't try to follow her right away, wishing desperately she had the option of leaving the flat immediately, but she had packing to do. She slipped into the second bedroom to get her things and closed the door.

Moments later, she heard the door of the other bedroom opening, then some quiet conversation that she couldn't make out, and finally footsteps down the hall.

She wasn't surprised, moments later, when Dean knocked on the door saying, "Erica, can we talk?"

Quickly locking the door, she said, "No, Dean, we cannot."

"I just want to explain. It's not as bad as it looked."

"Leave me alone!" she shouted.

It took but a moment for her to realize that, as much as she would like to, she couldn't pack up everything and leave the flat empty of her belongings—not if she was going to make her train on time. Oh, how she wanted to, though. She didn't have a car to move her things, even if she had somewhere to leave them, which she didn't. She calmed herself as much as possible, grateful that she had most of her belongings in one room and decided to first pack the items she'd need for Scotland. Then, she would pack anything else she could stuff into her two large suitcases and one smaller one, taking as much with her as possible. She didn't want to leave Dean with the impression that she'd be back to patch things up with him.

She hurried as quickly as she could and within minutes had all three bags stuffed to capacity and standing in the hall outside the apartment door. Dean followed her down the hall and back, asking repeatedly for a chance to explain. At the door, she said, "I'll be back for the rest of my things in a couple of weeks."

Slipping into her expensive shoes and spotting the check she'd written for the rent, she picked it up and methodically shredded it to bits in front of him. Scattering the tiny pieces about on the floor, she said angrily, "There, Dean, is your cheque with a *q-u-e*!"

As she stepped into the hall, she said, "Don't

follow me!" Slamming the door, she took a deep breath to slow her pounding heart.

As she made two arduous trips down the stairs with her bags, she did not allow her heart to absorb the full impact of what had just happened. She couldn't. Instead, she occupied her mind by comparing her behavior now, of tearing up the check, with that of stranding Andrew at the restaurant many months before. She decided that she wasn't being vindictive this time—simply pragmatic.

By the time she got all her cases to the outside door, she was perspiring and exhausted. Of course, in her haste, she'd not taken the time to change into anything more comfortable, which she knew she'd regret ruefully before the end of the day. Looking at her feet, she thought despondently, "Did I really put these shoes on again? Did I even pack my walking shoes?"

Knowing she had brought far too much to lug to the tube and realizing that finding her walking shoes amongst the stuffed bags on the pavement in front of the apartment building was far too demeaning to contemplate, she suffered a few moments of panic. She knew she was terribly cash-short—a situation she had intended to rectify that day—and, for the first time ever, regretted her lifelong habit of using cash only. Up to that point, first Andrea and then Dean had allowed her to write a check to them, thereby accessing cash through their bank accounts. Her plan had been to meet Dean for lunch somewhere, enabling her to get some cash through him and say goodbye to him, as well.

It wasn't as easy as one would think getting a bank account in England, so she hadn't pursued it. She did have a debit card she'd never used, but it was attached to an American account with no money in it, a precaution against getting one's bag stolen. She was trying to remember who had taught her that principle of caution, so she could curse them, because she was beginning to see a fatal flaw in its implementation.

Her brain frantically traveled at the speed of light with no apparent solution until she spotted a taxi. Simultaneously, she remembered that she had been given the magazine's travel credit card with her itinerary, and raising her arm, hailed the taxi and escaped with her dignity intact. They could fire her if they wanted to, but she was going by taxi to the station.

She wasn't quite sure what happened to her sense of judgment after that first lapse, but within the hour, she'd taken the taxi to a trendy shop for a comfortable, however expensive, jogging outfit, complete with matching running shoes, socks and two coordinating tops in lime green and lemon yellow. Before leaving the shop, she took off her constricting pantyhose and uncomfortable heels and tossed them into the shopping bag, exchanging them for the new socks and shoes, recognizing it was the first thing to go in her favor all day. From there, her same driver, who she had told to leave the meter running while she shopped, took her to the station, where she generously tipped him with the last of her cash.

She had plenty of time, so it occurred to her to stow some of her stuff in a station locker until her return to London, but she knew that she could never sort through it all, any more than she could have found her walking shoes in front of Dean's flat. It simply couldn't be done, so even if she should have to pay a little extra for the excessive luggage, she still had the magical credit card, which was solving one problem after another for her today.

Managing her luggage at the station proved to be a bigger obstacle than she'd envisioned, but somehow she accomplished it with a little help from another traveler who took pity on her. Taking the handle of one of her large bags, the kind young man suggested, "Traveling light is the only way to go by train unless you want to pay dearly for a luggage delivery service."

"I'd better not do that. I've done enough damage already. It's my first time to travel by train. I wished I'd had more time to organize myself," said Erica embarrassed. "I'm early; is there somewhere to leave my bags, so I can walk around and get something to eat?"

"There is, but be sure to collect them early. Listen, I've got time; I'll take you there."

She labeled her bags carefully, and when they were safely stowed, she turned to the young man to thank him and offer to buy him a cup of coffee—as she had no cash to offer him for his trouble. She was too late, for he was already walking quickly away in the direction from which they'd come. He turned and waved, so she waved back, hoping he knew how grateful she was for his help.

Free of the big bags, she stuffed her purse and computer case into her Zoe's Boutique shopping bag, thinking, "I don't suppose someone could have warned me to travel light. Was I somehow supposed to know I couldn't check my bags all the way through?"

She realized she hadn't eaten all day, and although

she knew she was still too upset to eat much, she quickly found a nice little eating place. There, using the company card, she paid far too much for a sandwich, of which she could eat but half. She then found the ladies' room and exchanged her gray business suit for her lemon/lime jogging suit with matching hooded jacket. She stuffed her office suit carelessly into the bulging shopping bag with its coordinating uncomfortable heels. She felt strongly that she'd rather never see the suit or the shoes again, but her Midwestern frugality prohibited her from disposing of them in a hasty act of indignation.

She went back to get her luggage, where she necessarily accepted the help of another kindly traveler, and settled herself to wait for her departure. Suddenly having an attack of guilt, she phoned Andrea and told her what had happened, confessing the use of the company credit card with abandon. She promised to pay it back as soon as she was in London again. Andrea commiserated with her and promised to fix it with management if she could be allowed to use some of the truth, if necessary, for leverage. Erica agreed—not much else she could do.

There were lots of stares from seasoned travelers as, with great difficulty, she managed to get her three bags on the luggage rack at the end of the carriage. She boarded the train, cringing at the thought of dealing with her bags at least three more times before getting to her destination.

She called Andrea again from her window seat just before her train departed to make sure she hadn't been fired.

Andrea said, "It's all been taken care of. I went into the office of the head of accounting—no sense talking to an underling, I thought. Turns out she recently experienced what you did today with her almost-ex. She's getting divorced and said she'd document your expenses as absolutely necessary."

"So I'm not sacked?" asked Erica with relief.

"Not this time," teased Andrea. "She said to use the company card for your needs until you can get some cash. Your expenses have been deemed necessary, which they are."

Which indeed they are, thought Erica as she hung up. Unable any longer to keep her emotions at bay, she found a tissue and, turning her face away from any curious eyes, allowed the tears to spill over and run down her cheeks.

Chapter Three

Pulling herself back from the brink of humiliation, as sobs of self-pity bubbled up inside her, Erica yanked herself up harshly, determined to save her weeping for later. She took her compact from her bag to check her appearance and moaned when she saw her hair, for in her exertions in the London humidity, her straightened hair had frizzed wildly. On top of that, due to the gamut of emotions she'd experienced in the past few hours, her eye makeup had run and smudged comically. Maybe that's why everyone has been so kind, she thought.

She fixed her makeup as best she could and then finding herself somewhat alone, acknowledged the sheer blessing of having a reserved seat—she must remember to thank the lady in Travel—and the boon of the empty seat beside her, which looked to Erica to be the only one in the coach. Smug now that two things had gone right for her— three, if she counted the kindness of the lady in Accounting—Erica made herself comfortable for the journey.

Moments later, she allowed herself to reflect on the events of the day. Only then, did it dawn on her that the woman she'd found with Dean was none other than Mrs. Marshall, his boss's wife. She wanted to phone Andrea with that alarming and newsy tidbit, but decided to give poor Andrea a break. It hadn't been an easy day for her, either, and she was probably at the office that very moment, helping her save face by putting her personal things into a cardboard box while the office was empty.

Glancing down at her newest, most expensive, and also incredibly comfortable gel-cushioned shoes, Erica felt suddenly relieved to be putting the city behind her. She pulled herself abruptly into the present, realizing she was completely ignoring the ongoing announcements. She thought cynically, I'd better listen. Could be important. Non-stop to Newcastle. Already knew that. We won't be stopping where? Why should I care where we aren't stopping? Why announce where we aren't stopping? Did I miss the safety announcements?

It then occurred to her that considering the day she'd had, it only stood to reason, she may be involved in a disastrous derailment, and she laughed out loud. She caught what she thought was a disapproving glance from the elderly woman across the aisle and felt almost hysterical enough to tell the woman she was off to

Scotland to visit a one-hundred-year-old lady and ask her if she, too, was a centenarian. It was tempting, but her innate goodness caught up with her before she could act on the unkind thought, and instead, she smiled warmly at the woman. To her surprise, the woman smiled back at her with kindly blue eyes that, surrounded by wrinkles and lines, confirmed many years of both laughter and worry.

Erica was humbled as she pondered for a moment on the many kindnesses she'd received that day from people, most of them strangers. She thought of them as her newest and dearest, however nameless, friends. Their bestowal of a simple smile or a helping hand had gotten her through the worst day imaginable. Their human kindness and the boon and power of that little plastic credit card had saved the day. And, of course, there was Andrea. What would she have done without her support, she wondered.

Erica pulled out her itinerary, noting her train change in Newcastle and the time of arrival at Edinburgh Waverly Station to be in about five hours. Looking further, she noted that the amount of time she'd have to switch to her Stirling train wasn't very adequate if Waverly was as large as Kings Cross. She worried about finding her way around a strange place and getting her luggage on the next train, but then, realizing that there was absolutely nothing she could do about any of her current dilemmas, she closed her eyes, locking her heart and mind from feeling or thinking about Dean's betrayal or the difficulties that still lay before her. She sighed heavily as she felt the train pull out of the station.

Moments later, her peace was shattered as her phone blared out its obnoxious tune. She hurriedly silenced it, wondering sheepishly if she was supposed to have turned it off, but had missed the announcement. Seeing the name Dean Saint as the caller on the phone screen, she was again nearly driven to hysteria over the irony of his name and covered her mouth to prevent any sound escaping. She couldn't bear to hear what he wanted to say to her, and she didn't intend to. She was sure that his calling had something to do with the destroyed check and nothing to do with her broken heart. Seeing that her battery was dangerously low, she turned off her phone altogether. She laid her head back and closed her eyes against a life that was too miserable to bear thinking about.

Andrea was finally organizing herself to go home

from work. She was the last one out of the office, and she was emotionally drained. Her friend Steven Black had called her that morning offering to make reservations for them to eat somewhere nice, and the prospect of that dinner had kept her going all day. Now, if she didn't hurry, she'd keep him waiting on the curb by her flat.

She pondered on the crazy day she'd had and how badly she felt for her American friend. "I wonder why she didn't answer her telephone," she said aloud as she went down in the lift alone.

She was so weary of worrying about Erica, she was almost irritated with her, saying even more loudly, "It's not like we have to shut off our phones for train travel, Erica! Surely you know that much!"

Minutes before, while packing the remains of Erica's personal things into a box and noting the time, Andrea reminded herself to pick up the pace, so as not to keep Steven waiting. She stowed the box in an unused locker, put the key in her desk, and was making for the lift, when her intercom buzzed. Her first impulse was to ignore it, because if it were either Erica or Steven, they'd no doubt ring her mobile phone rather than go through the switchboard, and she really didn't want to speak to anyone else. But, things as they were, with Erica in the state she was in, Andrea knew she'd better answer it—just in case.

"Hello, Andrea here," she said tiredly.

"Hi, Andrea. This is Margie at the switchboard. I was just about to turn on the telephone answering system and leave for home, when this call came in. It's some guy from Scotland. He sounds pretty irate, but the gist of it is that he wants to know why the privacy of his elderly, frail grandmother is being violated and who in the hell (those were his words) authorized anyone to write anything about her. Do you want to take the call? I overheard Miss Leed talking about Erica's assignment earlier, and I figured you would know about it. Besides, you're the only other one here."

"Blast it! What next?" exclaimed Andrea, setting down her bags and collapsing into her chair. "Okay, put him on." She nervously tucked her bangs behind her ear, and they immediately slipped back over her forehead.

Andrea waited for the beep, indicating they were connected. "This is Andrea Frey. How may I help you?"

"I thought I'd been cut off," was the man's curt reply.

"No sir, I was being asked to take the call, since

I'm the only one still here. Am I to understand that the family didn't make the arrangements for the interview?"

"Am I to understand that you journalists actually care about ethics?" he retorted.

"Sir, if we have a problem to solve, let's solve it. If you could be a bit civil, I'm sure we can sort this out," said Andrea with feigned patience.

"What's there to sort?" he snapped. "I'm ringing to cancel the interview."

"Well, for instance, the request for this story came from one of our owners, via his wife, who is a friend of your grandmother's, I understand. That must be where the misunderstanding originated, if there is one." She wanted to add, "Maybe you don't know everything," but refrained.

"I don't care where this started. It ends here. Nobody is going to interrogate my grandmother for a stupid magazine."

Thinking of poor Erica already on her way to Scotland, Andrea took a deep breath. "Sir, our journalist happens to be en route there now. The plan was for the interviews to take just a few minutes a day, so as not to tire your grandmother unduly."

"When I got wind of your plans, I dashed up here,

only to learn that she didn't know that anyone was coming, nor did her nurse. Does that sound like we were in on the plan? You journalists will do anything to get what you want," he said, seething.

"It's not like she is the Queen of England and we're the paparazzi! How is it you even found out about the interview, then?" asked Andrea suspiciously.

"My cousin saw the letter from Dorothea Davies, saying the plan had been put in motion. She, my cousin, put me onto it as soon as she found out. I'll admit I know who instigated this, but he does nothing in the interest of my grandmother. How could you pursue this without following up?"

"For one thing, this project came from the top. I don't make a habit of fact-checking my boss's requests. Do you?"

"I don't really have a boss."

"How nice for you," she shot back.

When there was no answer from the other end, Andrea said, "Listen, I will ring our journalist now. She can get off at her next stop, wherever that is, and turn around. We are terribly sorry for this upsetting inconvenience. I'm sure you will hear from Mr. Davies to express his apologies."

"Is that so?" he asked caustically. "So professional, aren't you? Can you possibly imagine how upsetting this would be to a woman in as frail a state as my grandmother?"

"Well, no one would ever accuse you of acting professional." Andrea could feel herself losing patience. "Tell me, was it you, then, who told her about it, upsetting her so badly?"

"Of course not!" he barked. "Only her nurse knows of it, now."

"Well, I suppose your grandmother is not unduly upset then, is she? Would you mind giving me your name and a number where we can reach you?"

A silence ensued as he debated whether to keep sparring with this incorrigible woman or admit defeat. He finally gave her his information politely, and she thanked him with equal politeness. After all, she felt like the victor, so she could afford to be generous.

Before hanging up, she said, "Wherever the mix-up occurred, Mr. Hill, I'm sure we'll get to the bottom of it. Let me assure you that you will not be bothered any further. Goodbye."

She hung up, held her head in her hands for a few seconds to reset her emotions and then reached for the telephone again. She punched in Erica's number and, to her dismay, was taken directly to voicemail. She threw the phone down, grabbed her bag, and pulled her mobile phone from its pocket. She tried ringing her again, thinking that maybe Erica had blocked calls from the office after her rough day. Routed immediately to voicemail again, she cursed her phone before putting it back in her bag and heading for the lift.

On the train, Erica awoke to discover there was heavy cloud cover, and it seemed much darker than it ought to be.

Her elderly neighbor across the aisle noticed her looking out the window. "Looks like we're in for it."

"I never thought to check the weather before leaving," admitted Erica. Remembering she'd left her umbrella on the bedroom floor, she could only shake her head.

"Oh, it's supposed to rain buckets! Are you getting off at Newcastle, dear?" asked the woman in her high, child-like voice.

"I change trains and go on to Edinburgh, then Stirling, yet tonight. I wonder what time it is." She reached into her bag for her cell phone and remembering its waning battery, put it back. "Would you happen to have the time?"

"Sure thing." Erica's new friend proceeded to turn her bag inside out, looking for her own mobile phone. Apologetically, she said, "I used to always wear a wristwatch, but my niece decided I should get with the times. Now I rely on a little telephone that I can't find unless it's ringing, and sometimes, not even then. Now that I'm with the times, I can't get the time." She laughed heartily at her little joke until Erica was forced to laugh with her.

Newcastle was announced, and everyone began gathering up anything they had strewn about. Erica was ready quickly and felt guilty as she watched the little white-haired lady trying to get everything back into her bag.

Feeling her stomach rumble, Erica realized she'd eaten but once all day and would need something besides the bottle of water she always carried in her bag. She wished she'd been thinking more clearly when she'd tossed the unwanted half of her sandwich earlier, because it would be just the thing, now. Surely, she could grab something in Newcastle, she thought. Remembering she had no cash, she hoped the credit card would continue to work its magic.

Andrea found Steven waiting outside her door, just as she had feared. "I am so sorry. I've had a hellish day, and I don't think it's over yet."

From his great height, he smiled down on her. "We'll still make it in time for our reservation, and you can tell me all about your hellish day. I've got the car just around the corner."

"I didn't have time to freshen up or anything," lamented Andrea, wishing she'd at least checked her appearance before leaving the office.

"No matter; you are beautiful! You can take my word for it!" he assured her sweetly.

Andrea watched as his face reddened. That was the first time he'd said anything remotely romantic, and she could see that he was embarrassed by it. As they took off down the pavement, she put her arm through his offered one and wondered why she never seemed to fall in love with the good guys. Steven was definitely a good guy and good-looking, too, but she knew there was little hope for them romantically. She had a terrible predilection for bad boys and had pretty much written off marriage altogether, considering it the epitome of folly. Putting those thoughts aside, she wondered again what had become of Erica.

Although she didn't have lots of time, the station at Newcastle was easily navigated with the help of her elderly companion, who had stuck to her like glue. She pulled one of the larger bags for Erica, perching her own small bag on top.

Finding her platform nearby, Erica looked around for a vendor and something to eat. Seeing nothing at hand, she was a bit dismayed, but was glad she'd not lost time looking, for her train was soon boarding.

As if reading her mind, her friend pulled a tuna sandwich from her carryall and gave it to her. Tears threatened as Erica accepted the sandwich with gratitude. "You've been a lifesaver, and I don't even know your name. Holding out her hand, she said, "Mine's Erica Sinclair."

"I'm Millicent Wells. Call me Millie. You know,

you looked a little distraught, even pale, when you first got on the train. I made up my mind to look out for you, so I saved my sandwich for you. My niece always packs one for me, because, in my opinion, anything that might be available on the train is either terrible or outrageously expensive."

"There was something available on the train?" asked Erica incredulously.

"Not worth mentioning, I assure you," said Millie.

"But this is too kind of you. What will you eat?"

"Oh, I'm home. Last stop for me. I was just helping you find your way around. My Henry will have something fixed for me. I make a run to London once a month to visit my sister in the nursing home. He knows the drill." Putting a piece of paper in Erica's hand, she said, "This is my address and telephone number. If you ever find yourself in need of me, please ring me up. I don't make new friends often, but I do make them for life. You're American, aren't you?"

"It's that obvious? I try not to broadcast it, because I tire of hearing what people dislike about my country. I don't walk around telling them what I disapprove of here."

"That's just talk. They don't know," said Millie.

"I'm old enough to have a great appreciation for your country. I was quite young, but I vividly remember the war that took so many of my loved ones. Without the help of America, the outcome would have been far different."

Millie helped Erica load her bags unto the rack and the intercom muffled any other attempts to talk, so they grasped each other's hands, parting as lifelong friends, and Erica followed the crowd onto the train.

Leaving the station, Millie's forecast proved true, and the rain began to come down heavily. It rained so hard that little could be seen from the window. Erica felt a bit bereft without her friend and hoped fervently that the rest of the trip would go smoothly.

She opened her sandwich and ate it facing the window, so as not to offend the person seated next to her. He was a suited gentleman, whose rigid countenance communicated he'd never consider eating anything on the street or in a public conveyance. She realized the smell of the tuna was probably arousing the taste buds or offending the noses of everyone in her car, but it couldn't be helped. She was hungry to the point of weakness. She ate as quickly as possible and had a satisfying drink of warm water from the bottle in her purse. She was still hungry, but never had anything tasted so good. Millie was truly a lifesaver.

Finally, Edinburgh was announced, and although she couldn't see anything from her window, due to the unrelenting rain, Erica was nervous and excited to find her way to her connecting train and make the final leg of her journey. A little more comfortable with train travel, she alit to the platform, looking for the signs that would direct her to her next one and dreading the burden of her mountain of luggage. She managed to stack it ingeniously, she thought, and slowly made her way to the next platform. Around her, people were exclaiming about the heavy rain, and Erica again lamented leaving her umbrella in Dean's bedroom.

Seeing her reflection in some glass, she tried to remember her polished appearance when she'd left for work that morning. How much had happened in the last fifteen hours! She could no longer identify herself with the person she'd seen in the mirror that morning. In fact, she was no longer that person. She was forever altered, but she took heart in the thought that at least she'd hit bottom and there was nowhere to go, but up.

At that moment, her luggage toppled around her, so

she stacked it again, this time with the help of a little girl, whose mother was telling her to hurry or they'd miss their train. Barely able to hold back the sobs of despair that were building inside her, Erica made it to the coach with only moments to spare and collapsed into her seat, exhausted. The young man sitting beside her said something slightly sympathetic, which was all it took. The dam broke inside her, and although she kept her sobs contained, tears poured down her cheeks like spring streams. The young man gave her a clean handkerchief, telling her she could keep it, and she mopped herself with it all the way into Stirling.

Relieved somewhat by the release of emotion, Erica was able to calm herself enough to think ahead about taking care of her personal needs, collecting and managing her bags, yet again, and finding transport to The Little Scottish Inn. Disembarking like a seasoned traveler now, she collected her bags and looked hopefully for a taxi queue. Help came this time from an elderly man, who waited with her bags while she visited the restroom and then patiently guided her to the taxi queue.

She longed to get something to eat from a vending machine but couldn't bring herself to inconvenience her elderly escort further by stopping, yet again. There would be something at the inn, even at this hour, she reasoned, so she waited in line for her taxi. She watched gratefully, even emotionally, as the driver took full responsibility for her luggage, accepting no help from her. With tears still dangerously close to the surface, she whispered, "It wasn't easy, but it is over."

At Cairnview that morning, Graham Hill faced his grandmother, which he always did upon his arrival. It was required of him and only perfunctory good manners on her part, he knew, but manners were compulsory for her. He'd lost her trust two years before when he'd taken direction from his older cousin, misinterpreting his greed as real concern for their grandmother. Consequently, he was caught looking for financial information in her library. Rather than installing an expensive security system, as her solicitor had recommended, she'd locked everything of value in her desk and secured it only with a simple alarm linked to her room. Graham was caught red-handed and summoned to his grandmother's room immediately the following morning.

He was still allowed to visit, reporting to her on his

arrival and departure, but knew he was on probation, of sorts. Upon being caught and found guilty, Graham had tried in vain to make her understand that he'd been manipulated by his cousin John, believing he was doing that errand in her best interest, but she had been immovable.

Since then, her health had deteriorated, and he daren't upset her if he wished to see her at all, so any attempts to explain away his past crime had never been allowed. She was still civil to him on his infrequent visits and allowed him the use of the house and stables, but their relationship had been damaged permanently. He knew that she merely tolerated his visits and had since kept the library locked whenever he was there.

He'd fully mourned their relationship, almost like someone would a death, and although he wasn't over it, he'd come to grips with it and was willing to have what little remained. One thing he did know was that he wasn't going to be responsible for her death, which could be the end result if he pressed her to listen to his side of the story. He'd been taken in by his cousin, and this was his penance. There was no way to fix it anymore.

Chapter Four

"Where to, love?" asked her driver cheerfully.

"The Little Scottish Inn," she said, "Off Polmaise Road?"

"Aye, not more than two miles from here. Takes just a few minutes normally, but in this rain, it could be a wee longer," he answered in his heavy local accent.

They drove out of the station in the wind-driven rain, the driver fully concentrating on his job. Finally he said, "Do they know you're coming? That's a dirt road that takes you the last bit to the inn."

"A dirt road? Really?" she asked in dismay.

"Well, it's a muddy road, tonight, love, but aye, it's a quaint little place; been there forever." he replied, as if that explained it.

"Well, they are expecting me, but I didn't make the arrangements myself."

"In this weather, only a four-wheel drive can take your luggage down the muddy road, though, love. If you've got a mobile, go ahead and ring them now. We'll wait for them, so not to worry. I won't put you out in this." He leaned forward over the steering wheel and tried to see the road in the downpour.

"I just tried turning on my telephone. It's dead," said Erica dismayed.

He reached for his radio. "Let me see if dispatch can rouse them at the inn." After a couple attempts, he said apologetically, "Radio's down. The storm must be interfering."

"It's all right, really. There might be someone there waiting for me, anyway." She wondered if she could at least get herself up the driveway, if not her bags. "If no one is waiting and the rain lets up, do you think I could make a dash for it without my luggage?"

"Got your umbrella and anorak at hand?"

"Neither. No overshoes, either. I came unprepared for this, but if it's not too far."

"I suppose you could walk it. Folks do it all the time, but not in this. Best thing would be to go back to the station and find somewhere else to stay."

"Oh, I couldn't. It's been paid for and everything," said Erica desperately.

The driver made another unsuccessful attempt to contact dispatch. "We're almost at the edge of Haggs Wood now, love. Time to decide. I can take you no further. If you want to hoof it in, then I'll loan you an anorak and torch and take your bags back to the station. They can fetch them for you tomorrow."

"I'll run for it. I'll tie my hood over my head. You better keep your anorak yourself. The night isn't over, and you're still out in it. Thanks for all your help, really."

"Well, here's my torch. That, I insist you take if I can't convince you to go back to the station. You will ruin your shoes for sure, but if the rain lets up, you'll get there, all right. It's not far."

At that very moment, the rain eased off dramatically, so Erica listened to his quickly given directions, which seemed straightforward enough to her in spite of his heavy accent. She assured him that her bags were all labeled, and when she went to pay with the credit card, he said he had an arrangement with the inn.

"Get along now, lass, before it gets worse again."

Erica threw her new office suit coat over her hooded head and opened the door.

Leaning out the window, he yelled, "Stay to the edge of the woods, so you don't get lost, and stay on the grass, so you don't slip. The trees will block the inn's lights, though, so you won't see them until you turn the corner of the wood. Cross the foot bridge at the little burn, right there. Shine your torch around and reflectors will show you where it is."

"Got it," she yelled, "And thanks!" Walking backwards and waving and then turning and bravely facing a rising wind head on, Erica hurried towards the edge of the wood, which she could barely see, but trusted would be there.

In the Smith's tiny cottage, a full quarter mile from the inn, the old couple lived on their meager, but satisfying retirement, Mrs. Smith made coffee, porridge, eggs, and toast for their morning meal. When she and her husband had finished theirs, she put the remaining eggs on a platter for their guest, who had yet to join them, and set it on the warming shelf. To her husband Ian, she said, "Americans like their toast warm, did you know that? They want the butter to melt into it. I'll make some up fresh for her, now that she's moving about."

"I hope she got a few hours of rest," said Mr. Smith in his soft Scottish accent. "She was all done in last night. Your porridge will be just the thing for her. Looking out the window towards Haggs Woods, he said, "That was some gandiegow!"

"Our guest wouldn't call it that, poor little thing. I wonder what she's doing so far from home. Last night she was so weak, she hardly said a thing. She shivered so, her teeth rattled. She just kept saying that she couldn't see the lights. With nothing but a wee beam from her torch, she couldn't see a foot in front of her. It must have been awful frightening. She was that terrified. I thought I'd never get her warm."

"Lights went out about half past twelve, I think. Still not on—not that it bothers us much," said the old man proudly. He stood and stretched, nearly touching the ceiling.

"I can appreciate the wood stove today, but I prefer my little electric for cooking any day of the week." She cheerily checked the progress of the toast in the oven.

"Well, the fire will dry us out a bit, too. Your little electric cooker isn't much use for that," said Mr. Smith in his soft, kindly voice.

"It certainly feels good enough this morning," agreed his wife. "Electric heaters will do the job, too, you know, my dear, if you can bring yourself to turn them on. Sometimes it's all right to run with the times."

"People depend too much on electricity, and if you're going to go on about a telephone again, I'll be heading out. I'll do some cleanup here and then go on over to the inn. Having a telephone within a five-minute walk is plenty close enough for me. Mark my words, Arlene, one day they'll find that all that ringing and jangling of the nerves isn't good for a body," he asserted in his gentle voice.

"A hundred years, it's been now, dear," said his wife. "I think we'd know that by now, if it were so."

"Five minutes to a telephone is close enough for anybody," repeated her husband tenderly, putting on his work shoes and tying the laces. "I'm going to clean up any mess the storm made and maybe straighten my wood pile at the inn. Too wet to do anything else. I won't forget to tell them about their guest and have them fetch her bags from the station. Tell her I'll walk her over to the inn after I come back for lunch.

Before heading out the door, he turned back as he had done for fifty years, and placed a gentle kiss on her lips. "Thank 'e for the breakfast."

Mrs. Smith watched fondly from the window as he made his way around the standing water and onto the turf, where it wasn't so slippery.

That's where she was standing when Erica appeared, wrapped in their son's old robe and carrying only her toothbrush. She had carefully made her way down the narrow winding steps from the tiny room above. Peeking into the kitchen and sitting room part of the cottage, Erica saw the little woman who had looked after her so kindly the night before. "Good morning. Can you point me the bathroom?"

"Just behind the washing machine in the lean-to, dear. My Ian made us wait to marry until he had the bathroom all finished. We were the first cottage around here to have all the modern conveniences." Mrs. Smith proudly indicated the room with the low slanted ceiling behind the kitchen. "The water won't be warm enough for a bath, I'm sorry to say, my dear."

"That's fine." Erica smiled tiredly. "I'll just wash up a bit." She moved past the warm stove and into the lean-to, making her way around the drying rack. There, her jogging suit hung low, having been washed—she didn't know when. She looked around for her shoes, but didn't see them. She smiled when she saw that the short privacy wall for the commode wasn't a wall at all, but the washer itself. Glad that old Mr. Smith didn't seem to be around anywhere, she still felt slightly vulnerable in a bathroom with no walls.

The bathtub had pride of place in the midst of it all, and a tiny sink was tucked into the lowest corner of the lean-to. Carefully ducking her head, she brushed her teeth and washed her face in cold water. The little mirror over the old washing machine was mottled and discolored, but Erica didn't really care what she looked like at the moment. After last night's terror, she was just thankful to be alive.

Back in the kitchen, little Mrs. Smith showed her to the gate-legged table and presented her with food she accepted with gratitude. Her hostess brought her a cup of hot coffee and then quietly puttered around the kitchen, adding more wood to the firebox. The silence was easy and appreciated.

Erica found it difficult to eat her breakfast, in spite of the fact that she'd eaten so little the day before. Her throat was raw from calling out again and again for help just hours before.

She looked around noting her shoes, clean and looking almost new, drying on a wooden box by the stove.

She took in the furnishings of the quaint little house, which had been her safe haven in the howling storm. In spite of its smallness, the cottage wasn't at all cluttered, but seemed to have everything necessary. The idea of an uncluttered life appealed to Erica, and she found herself quite envious of the kindly couple. "I like your cozy home. It feels warm and safe like a blanket."

"Cozy for sure. Can you think what it was like around here when we were raising our two boys?" she asked proudly.

"Don't think I can, but I prefer its coziness to the big, sprawling house we had northeast of Omaha." Seeing that Arlene didn't know where that was, she added, "It's in Nebraska—kind of in the middle."

Arlene nodded and said, "I have heard of Nebraska. I wouldn't know what to do with so much space, would I? Clean it, I suppose. Anyway, I would like to have a few words with the driver who allowed you to walk from the main road."

"He didn't want to," Erica defended him hastily. "I had had such a long day, I just couldn't imagine going back to the station and trying to work out new accommodations. The rain let up, so I decided to make a dash for it. I soon realized that 'not far' is a relative term." She shook her head at the memory, before continuing, "He made me take his flashlight, though, and of course, he had no way of knowing that the electricity would go out."

"No, of course he didn't, but you poor girl. How far did you travel yesterday?"

"I took the fast train from London. I'm on an assignment for a magazine."

"I was afraid you were going to say New York!" exclaimed Mrs. Smith, laughing in her reticent way.

"I brought so many problems upon myself yesterday from failing to do two things. I didn't pack properly and I forgot to charge my telephone, but that's a long story."

"I've got time to listen, if you want to tell me. Last night you said your name was Erica Sinclair. My husband is Ian Wells. Why don't you call me Arlene?" She smiled encouragingly.

"All right," said Erica timidly. "Well, I got up yesterday morning, having high hopes of a writing assignment for the special edition for the magazine I work for. That was the first thing to go wrong, but thinking back now, it was probably the least of my worries. If only I'd known how the rest of the day was going to go." She looked up, and seeing a clock, exclaimed, "Is that the time?"

"Aye, my dear, you had a very late night."

"But I'm supposed to be at Cairnview in two hours!" cried Erica in dismay.

"You're going to Cairnview? Well, I never. That explains why you were put up at the inn, then. Cairnview is just a quarter mile from our cottage, a wee more than that from the inn."

"A quarter mile?" What might not have seemed any distance to walk yesterday, sounded insurmountable today.

"You'll be fit for it, tomorrow, dear, but perhaps you could telephone Cairnview to let them know you won't be there today as planned."

"But I have to go. It's been scheduled. Oh my gosh! I don't even have my clothes!"

"Your clothes will find you, love. Perhaps, you could go later in the day. There is a telephone at the inn. You could fix a time for this afternoon. I'm sure they would understand. They are such fine people."

"I have a mobile phone, but the battery is dead. I

forgot to charge it again last night," said Erica bleakly.

"Wouldn't that have required electricity?" asked the woman innocently.

"Oh I forgot! Is it still out?" lamented Erica.

"Aye, but it should be back on before long. You can make your way to the inn and start fresh tomorrow. Ian said he'd take you there himself after his lunch break. To be helpful, she added, "My mother always said there's only twenty-four hours in a day and tomorrows were for getting the rest of it done."

"Oh, but they will be expecting me. I just can't cancel on them at this point. I'll see if I can get my skirt and jacket in some state of acceptability. I can always carry my heels in a bag and change them out."

"My dear, you had nothing with you but your little handbag and a weak torch."

"But I'm sure I had my suit jacket!" cried Erica. "I must have lost it in the storm."

"You came in with only the little bag hooked on your arm, love. More the reason to settle at the inn and wait until tomorrow. They have no electricity at Cairnview, either, I'm sure."

As if on cue, the electricity came on, and the small

refrigerator began to hum. Erica said, "I can't cancel on them with so little notice! I have to get there. Maybe I'll just wear the clothes you were so kind to wash for me and go casual. I hope they won't think less of me."

"They would surely think you a dunderhead if you crossed the boggy turf in your Sunday best, lass. This isn't London. They'd think you had no sense at all if you went all gussied up across country. I'll loan you some wellies, so your shoes don't get muddy again. They were clarty, and no mistake!"

"I look awful. I don't suppose you have a flat iron?" asked Erica sheepishly. "For straightening hair?" she clarified.

"No, dear," answered Arlene regretfully.

Embarrassed, Erica said, "You probably think I'm terribly silly. You know, so many strangers have been kind to me since I left the apartment yesterday. I am truly overwhelmed by it." Her eyes filled with tears. "I'm not sure what I'd have done if I hadn't run into your house. In fact, I nearly did run into it. Thank you so much for helping me."

"My dear, it was nothing at all," said Arlene genuinely. "Nothing at all," she repeated melodiously.

At Broadgate in London, Andrea got to work early to look at Erica's itinerary. She needed to call the inn and warn her off going to Cairnview. On her way there, she bumped into the department head, Miss Leed, who had let Erica down so brusquely the day before. Andrea was happy to see her, however, because time was getting short, and she could get things done more quickly with her help.

"Miss Leed, I'm so glad I bumped into you. We have a big problem with the Scottish centenarian story!"

"Did she die?" asked the woman, cackling irreverently.

"No," said Andrea sharply. "No," she said more gently, "it's something else."

"Good heavens! My humor is misplaced entirely, isn't it?" apologized Miss Leed sincerely. "What is the matter?"

"No one at the house agreed to the interview, and I have been trying to reach Erica's mobile since yesterday afternoon to call her off. The old lady's grandson, Graham Hill, rang the office just before I left yesterday. I was the only one here, so I took the call for Margie. She was getting an earful from the guy. We've got to reach Erica before she shows up for the interview at eleven. He'll eat her up!"

"All right," said her boss, "It's still early. We'll save her that embarrassment. Come along with me. I have her itinerary. She might prefer hearing the bad news from you, though. Hearing my voice won't do her any good at the moment."

Andrea was surprised at her admission.

Miss Leed lead the way down the broad hallway to her office in the corner. "When you finish speaking to her, patch her over to Travel, so they can get her a ticket home. Not a good way to start the day, is it?"

"For us or for her?" asked Andrea, without thinking.

"Point taken, Miss Frey. I really do feel badly about the way things have turned out for her."

Moments later, they learned that Erica had never arrived at the inn the night before. There had been a terrific storm blow through around midnight. No one at the inn had heard from her, but they'd assumed she'd stayed elsewhere.

The woman at the inn said, "Can you hold on a sec? Someone here seems to know something about her."

Andrea waited nervously, hearing muffled voices on the other end. Finally, the innkeeper came back on. "I can tell you this much. A taxi driver arranged for us to get her bags from the station this morning and some things she'd left in his backseat. It takes a four-wheel drive to get from the main road in wet weather. We pick up our guests on Polmaise Road at any hour, but we have to wait to be telephoned making arrangements, you understand, or we could wait there all night."

"Right, so she took a taxi to a different accommodation because of the weather and left her bags at the station, anyway? Why would she do that? And why leave her belongings in the backseat of the taxi?" Andrea raised her voice in her exasperation.

"I'm afraid I can't answer those questions for you, lass," said the distressed innkeeper.

"No, I suppose not, Do this for me, would you, please? If you see her this morning, tell her to call her office. There has been an important change of plan that she must be made aware of as soon as possible."

She quickly gave them the office number and requested politely that they call if they heard anything more.

Chapter Five

Erica had gone over the directions to Cairnview with Arlene three times to make sure she had them right. All she was carrying was her handbag and a borrowed string bag for her shoes, so she could change out of the borrowed wellies before entering the house. When she'd realized that she'd left her computer, as well as her shopping bag of clothes in the backseat of the taxi, she momentarily panicked, but consoled herself that the driver would make sure she got them back. Yet one more problem to straighten out, she thought discouragingly.

Grateful she had a small tablet and pen with her, she felt a little less unprepared, but wondered what Mrs. Hill would think of her frizzy-haired London journalist with an American accent arriving on foot without so much as a folder. Oh yes, and wearing a trendy jogging suit tucked into borrowed rain boots. Erica was in such a low, but determined mood, she barely noticed the sun trying to peek out from beneath the gray clouds.

Directions in hand and no time to spare, she headed out southeasterly in the direction of Cairnview, rather than northeasterly in the direction of the inn. Time didn't allow for any other way to go about it. Everything had gone wrong so far, but nothing was going to stop her from trying to keep her appointment. She'd come here to prove she was a journalist, and she owed it to herself to try.

Andrea's office intercom buzzed. It was Miss Leed. She went directly to the point. "I'm glad you gave the inn our number. They called back, saying that their handyman had come in to work and reported that Erica had gotten lost trying to make it to the inn on foot from the main road last night. The storm took the lights out, so without the lights from the inn to guide her, she had no way of finding the inn and lost her way. By lucky chance, she managed to find the handyman's cottage, and that's where she stayed the night. And, they don't have a telephone at the cottage. It explains a few things, and at least we know she's safe."

"Right, until Graham Hill gets hold of her!" exclaimed Andrea. Forgetting herself in her distress, she said, "Miss Leed, just so you know, besides being disappointed with her assignment yesterday morning, having put so much energy into the 9/11 edition, and getting demoted to make room for someone less qualified…" Andrea stopped only long enough to draw a deep breath. "And having a long and exhausting train ride, and getting lost on foot in a storm in a country foreign to her, Erica was caught off-guard before ever leaving yesterday, when she found her boyfriend cheating on her when she went back to their flat to pack."

There was an awkward moment of silence, before Andrea said contritely, "And I had no right to speak to you in such a way, not to mention not having Erica's permission to tell you anything about it. I shouldn't have blurted that out. It's not like it's your fault. You have every right to sack me."

"No, Miss Frey. I think perhaps you are just reacting to the relief of finding her after worrying for so many hours. Let's see if we can help her now. Where are we at the moment? She must still believe she has an appointment in an hour, then. If she doesn't show up at the inn soon, we can assume she is still trying to make the interview. I think it's time I get the grandson on the telephone."

"After a difficult conversation with him yesterday, I assured him he could expect an apology soon and would not be bothered further."

"Well, I can deliver an apology as well as the next person," said Miss Leed. "There must be a way to spare poor Miss Sinclair further troubles."

"Well, I wish there were. I already tried phoning him a few minutes ago. He gave me his number yesterday. He's not answering, of course. How is it that almost everyone has a telephone on their person, and we still can't get hold of anybody when we need to?"

"Did you try texting? Don't ask me why, but that often gets results when telephoning doesn't."

"I did. I wrote, 'Still unable to reach journalist. She may still show up there. Be kind.'"

"Can't we get the number to the house telephone?" asked Miss Leed.

Andrea said anxiously, "And let the cat out of the bag? Mrs. Hill doesn't know of any of this and must not learn of it. Her grandson seems to think she'll go all apoplectic and have a stroke or something. We can't possibly risk ringing the house!"

"All right, calm down. We'll think of something. We'll have to. I think I need to speak to Mr. Rutley, who will speak to Mr. Davies."

"Who will talk to his wife, who won't know what

to do," finished Andrea despondently.

On the morning after the storm, Graham slept later than usual and upon waking and seeing the sun trying to peek through the overcast sky, he felt invigorated and glad he'd come, even though the reason for his visit had been disconcerting. In addition to the heavy rain and wind, his sleep had been disrupted by rerunning his conversation with the woman at the magazine. He knew his anger should have been directed elsewhere. He had studied Shakespeare's *Henry IV*, and remembered his teacher's lesson on the line, "Don't shoot the messenger," but how dare they send someone up here without discussing it with the family or her nurse or both? It rankled still, but he knew where the real blame lay, and he wasn't up to pursuing that yet.

As always, just being at Cairnview seemed to renew him, in spite of his painful regrets of the past. His thoughts went to his ex-girlfriend, Jenny, who couldn't understand his obsession of going to Scotland, when he always suffered such guilt in doing so. She had actually suggested, although only once, that she thought it slightly masochistic behavior and proposed that he not go back. He now knew that argument was the beginning of the end. Too bad we dragged it out for months afterwards, he thought.

Entering his en suite bathroom of gray marble that had been put in for his parents many years ago, he flipped the switch and groaned when he realized that the electricity was still out. He'd have to wash up in cold water, he thought, and then he was going to pack. All he'd have to do later in the day was grab his bag and go.

Graham hurriedly dressed to go out and check the grounds for downed limbs. He would take the day cleaning up if need be, before catching an evening train for Newcastle, where he worked as a full partner in the same accounting firm his father had for so many years. If there wasn't too much to do on the grounds, he thought he'd fill the remainder of the day working in the stables and talking to the horses.

Six years ago, his grandmother replaced their retiring stable hand with a young neighbor, Kyle Johnson. He fed and exercised her two gelding hunters and an aging bay mare that had earned her retirement by producing many a prized colt. Kyle was a bright young man who was pursuing his law degree from the University of Stirling.

Graham had known him for many years and trusted that he had put the horses safely in the stables before the storm.

Today, Graham thought he'd help Kyle do the morning chores and let the horses out into the paddock long enough for his grandmother to have her morning viewing from her bedroom window. Later, he would let them out to graze in the pasture behind the stables. He longed for a ride, but knew that after such a storm, the terrain would be slick and boggy in places. Kyle would not encourage it, either, knowing the old lady's passion for her horses. Graham had to laugh at the irony that he'd rather break his own leg than that of one of his grandmother's horses, considering his precarious standing in her affections. Although he knew she still loved him, she no longer trusted him. Losing that trust had been a tragic consequence of his actions and a powerful lesson that he knew he'd carry with him the rest of his life. If only he could explain.

If his parents hadn't been killed in a car crash four years ago, none of this would have happened. Even if he'd been a little older and more mature, he would have seen through his cousin's feigned concern for their grandmother. Graham's own dad had always been his mother's obvious favorite, so his cousin wouldn't have had any opportunity to stick his nose in her business at all if his parents had lived. Like Graham, his father had been an accountant, and she'd trusted him implicitly with all of her affairs. After his death, such trust would have eventually come to him, if he'd not allowed himself to be manipulated. Her solicitor, Mr. Adamson, handled all her affairs now. If not for the obligatory cheques he received from her at Christmas, which were signed by her solicitor, he wouldn't even know the name of her bank.

Packing carelessly, he tried to dismiss the invading thoughts to no avail. Being in his parents' room brought to mind everything he'd once cherished. When it was decided that his grandmother couldn't live alone anymore, his mother moved up to Cairnview permanently, and his father worked in Newcastle during the week, coming to Cairnview on the weekends. Graham had traveled up with his father many times.

When he was younger, he spent wonderful summers here. His pet name for his grandmother was *Grams*. She'd always called him *Gram*, instead of *Graham*, so the rest of the family was always in a state of confusion, trying to get them to call each other something else. She continued to call him *Gram*, even as he grew into an adult, until he'd lost her trust so completely.

Oh, what I'd give to hear her call me *Gram* again, he thought, tempting the tears that were always lurking dangerously near the surface whenever he came to Cairnview.

Shaking such painful reminiscing from his mind, he pulled up his old jeans and slipped on a warm hoody. He knew his grandmother would be awake and waiting eagerly for the appearance of the horses already, for that was the only reason she kept them at all. They were her last connection to her young life, and even though she'd never ride again, she enjoyed watching them from her window on the upper floor.

Graham had tried to convince her to move to the main level when she became wheelchair ridden four years ago, soon after her son's violent death, but she couldn't bear to give up her view. Graham had gone so far as to talk to his older cousin about the feasibility of putting in a lift for her, but his idea had been shot down quickly.

I should have known then, he rebuked himself silently.

John had been adamant. "Until we know where she

stands financially, I wouldn't dream of mentioning the idea of a lift to her! Do you want to pick up all the outstanding bills when she dies?"

"My father always said she was well enough off," Graham had argued. "Why shouldn't she be? There has never been any talk to the contrary."

John had replied cruelly, "Your father was an accountant, not an investment advisor. He may have known the state of her chequebook, but we really don't have any idea about the health of her other investments. Until she dies, we won't know what we're up against. Not only that, who's to say her solicitor is doing right by her? And a private nurse—she has a private nurse! That must cost the earth, too. Think how much better off she'd be in a nice nursing home, fully staffed."

"You can't be serious! How could you even think of such a thing? She's your grandmother as much as she is mine."

"It's her welfare that I'm thinking about. The best thing that could happen for her and her estate is for her to turn over power-of-attorney to me now."

Graham had tried to fight back. "That's unfair. Grandmother hasn't lost her wits, and she's always been extremely careful with money. If she can afford it, a lift in the house would give her that much more quality of life. She could enjoy something of her house besides just her bedroom and the view of the horses that she loves so much."

"Those stupid horses! She'd mortgage the place to keep those useless animals, if she hasn't already," his cousin had ranted.

Before dropping the idea completely, Graham had retorted, "So what if she did mortgage the house to keep her horses? Would that be so bad? You have no intention of doing anything but selling the place, from what I can see, and the mortgage could easily be paid off from the sale."

Knowing he'd lost the battle, Graham had dropped the idea without mentioning it to his grandmother. Now, just four years later, she was no longer interested in any of his suggestions, due to his one lapse of judgment.

Finding the kitchen empty, he flipped the light switch and cursed that the electricity was still out, but even more so, his inability to remember, as it was the third switch he'd tried in as many minutes. He had intended starting the coffee machine he'd brought here a few months back, but he'd have to wait.

His grandmother's cook, Fran, would arrive in an hour and make breakfast for everyone, and he looked forward to it. If there was still no electricity, she'd fire up the old cooker, proud to be doing things the old way.

Cook was getting on in years, too, but she still came for three or four hours each morning to get the meals in order for the nurse to heat up later in the day. When Graham made his visits, he tried to ignore the disapproving stares from his grandmother's nurse, but he actually drew strength from Fran, for she knew little about the estrangement and treated him as she always had in the many years he'd known her. She even stayed a little longer to bake some of his favorites whenever he was around. He was glad for Nurse Martin's professionalism, though, for she would have certainly had innumerable opportunities to tell Fran about the whole affair, poisoning her towards him, too, and apparently she had not. He respected her for that.

As always, Graham knew that in spite of the painful memories, he was always able to center himself after being at Cairnview, if only for a few hours. He thought of the old estate as home and knew his cousin would sell everything the second their grandmother died. Every time he came, he feared it might be his last visit.

Jenny had often accused him that his obsession of stealing another visit at Cairnview was driving a wedge between them, but he didn't see why it should. He'd spent so many wonderful summers there while growing up, why shouldn't it be important to him? Everything had changed after his parents died in that awful car crash. In the fog of his grief, Graham had let John take advantage of his love for his grandmother and for Cairnview. He'd been naïve and stupid to allow himself to be so manipulated, and it galled that it would never be possible to make things right with her.

Stepping out the kitchen door to the covered step, Graham said aloud, "No more. Time to enjoy being here. I'm home." He saw Kyle, in his easily-recognizable, loose-limbed stride, walking towards the modern stables. He waved at him and hastened there himself, leaving his other chores until later. He was anxious to allow himself the pleasures of his visit, now that he'd suffered the requisite pain in full.

In spite of her late start, and surprisingly weary,

both mentally and physically, Erica believed now that she would indeed make it to her appointment on time. The timepiece she relied on was the dead cell phone in her bag, so she had no way of knowing the actual time, but Arlene's directions had proven to be very good. She could see Cairnview through the trees. It was a lovely vine-covered white-brick house, and Erica immediately liked its size and boxy, Georgian shape. "How perfect," she whispered to herself. She took in the picturesque landscape around her, and her heart raced a little at the excitement of finally getting there.

Having a need to catch her breath, she leaned against a nearby tree and used the time to get in the right frame of mind. Looking about her, she noted that the grounds weren't immaculate. The storm had torn some leaves off trees and even a few branches littered the lawn, but overall, the grounds were well-kept and welcoming, with just enough trees and vegetation to draw one's eyes to the house itself. There was plenty of open space around the house, too, and Erica suddenly realized that open pastures and rolling hills were what she had missed so much from their acreage in Nebraska. Seeing the rise of the Highlands to the north of her, she marveled that so much beauty could be packed into one place.

At home, the bluffs from the river gave interest to the view from their house, but a view of any kind was what she had longed for—wide-open space in which to breathe. How did city people live contentedly, she wondered, enclosed as they were on every side with buildings and people and noise?

Standing there, waiting for her racing heart to slow, she knew that there was something else she'd missed recently, and if she'd been in a proper state of mind when looking through the train window yesterday, she might have recognized it then. The last few minutes' walk had made her realize that it was her need for 'green' that had made her suffer so in London. And, no, she would correct those who might mock her—tiny gardens and parks packed with humanity didn't do it for her.

Waiting patiently for her breathing and heart rate to return to normal, Erica determined to pay attention to the details of the charming estate and remember them. When finished with her assignment, she wanted be able to describe her experiences, all the things she had seen and the fine people who had helped her along the way.

Perfect strangers had dragged her bags to help her

get from place to place. On the train, she'd met Millie, who had been so kind as to save her sandwich for her and help her get around the station at Newcastle. There had been the driver here, who had been so concerned for her welfare. In the end, his advice of going back to the station would have been the smart decision, but then she'd have missed out on meeting Mr. and Mrs. Smith. She would have never slept in the attic of their quaint cottage or seen their *modern* bathroom tucked into the lean-to, of which they were so proud. She would always remember Arlene's motherly concern and kindly deeds.

Yes, she'd be eager to share her experiences, but with whom? She felt a sharp pain in her heart, and she knew Dean had indeed broken it. She rubbed her chest with her free hand as she turned into the driveway and neared the house. She'd put the pain away until settled at the inn. Then, she would feel. Her mom always said that feeling was necessary in overcoming trials and pain.

This is a trial and I am in pain, she thought, but right now I have a job to do. She marched up to the house, and looking down at her muddy boots, made for the north side, where Arlene said she'd find the kitchen entrance and a warm welcome from the cook, who was a friend of hers.

Chapter Six

Climbing the three steps to the kitchen door, Erica noticed two men near a well-kept barn to the northeast of her. The shorter of the two waved upon seeing her, so she returned one to him. She was about to knock on the door, when it opened suddenly.

"I saw you coming with your arms full and knew you'd want to take your boots off out here," the lady said welcomingly. "So you're the lucky lass, today," she said, taking Erica's handbag and shoe bag from her.

Erica nodded hesitantly.

"It's a chilly one this morning, isn't it? My Ben said he had a mind to drive me up here, but I told him to save that thought for January, when it really mattered." She laughed merrily. "When you get your boots off, just leave them here on the step and come on in and have a cup, and we'll see what needs doing today."

Confused, and trying to understand the woman's accent, Erica changed out of her muddy boots, setting them out on the stoop, and put on her new shoes that were handed to her.

The woman led her into the kitchen, which was

spacious and mostly white. A wall to the right had a row of old brass hooks. The woman handed her the bags. "You can hang your things there, dear."

Hanging the string bag, but keeping her handbag, Erica took in the large kitchen. White tile, white appliances, white curtains. Almost dizzyingly white, thought Erica. It was warm, though, maybe too warm. She sat down where indicated, and took a deep breath, which caused her another sharp pain like the one she'd felt a few minutes before, when thinking of Dean.

Bringing two cups of coffee to the table, the plump, silver-haired little cook said, "The electricity came on just in time, so their breakfast is ready and waiting. Nurse Martin will ring for it any minute. Mrs. Hill doesn't have breakfast until eleven, so I don't have to come in so early anymore. You're here early, though. You can call me Fran. What's your name?"

"Erica Sinclair." She swallowed cautiously, aware of her sore throat. "I was told you were expecting me."

"Well, we knew they'd send someone up from Cambusbarron. I'd say by the sound of you that you're an American."

Erica nodded.

"We get lots of different girls, but I'll say this for your bosses, they train their girls very well. Just the one time were we unhappy with one of them. She couldn't seem to do anything right, that one, but it's a good group overall."

"Who's a good group?" Erica halted the progress of her coffee cup halfway to her mouth.

"Deb's Daily Services?" Fran looked confused. "No one told me we'd changed companies."

Hands shaking, Erica said, "I'm terribly embarrassed for not explaining myself better when I arrived, but I assumed I was expected in a different capacity."

"Oh?"

Feeling short of breath, Erica waited a moment to continue. She forced a smile and said, "I know I'm not dressed for the part, but thanks to the storm, my clothes haven't caught up with me, yet." Still seeing no spark of recognition on the woman's face, she went on, "I'm Erica Sinclair with *The London View*, here to interview Mrs. Hill for the magazine article?"

"Well, I never." Fran was red-faced and flustered. "Here I am blathering on, and you have an appointment with Mrs. Hill. Let me take her breakfast up and find her nurse. It won't take her long to eat this little bit. She feels her best at this time of day. You go ahead and finish your coffee, love."

Erica sat staring straight ahead, trying to pull herself together. Yet another glitch?

A door on the far side of the kitchen opened, and the taller of the men she'd seen with the horses came in. He had wavy brown hair and dark gray eyes, and she couldn't help but notice his lean, muscular build. He must have removed his muddy boots, she thought, seeing him step into the kitchen, wearing a worn pair of leather house shoes. He smiled mechanically. "Fran's here, I assume. I smell breakfast, and I'm starved."

"She just went to tell the nurse that I'm here," said Erica with as much confidence as she could muster. "Do you work here, too?"

"No, I visit my grandmother occasionally." He grabbed the hand soap and washed his hands at the kitchen sink.

"I see." She actually did not see anything and was at a complete loss as to what else to say to this disarmingly attractive man.

He dried his hands and took his platter carefully from the warm oven. He helped himself to a cup of coffee. "Thank goodness the electricity is back on. Fran's coffee is the best." He eyed the painfully shy, yet very attractive girl. "My machine can't come close."

"It is very good," she agreed. "Our—or rather, my—coffee machine can't compete, either."

Erica felt the sharp pain again, thinking, I'll need to start making a list of my things to remove from Dean's flat.

"I assume you've eaten?" he asked, interrupting her thoughts.

"Of course," said Erica warily.

Graham plopped himself down across the kitchen table from her and over-salted his eggs. "You don't sound like someone from around here."

"I am an American." Her guarded voice exposed her vulnerability on the subject.

"Is that so?" he asked tersely, digging into his breakfast with enthusiasm.

"I certainly hope you don't have a problem with that." She was in no mood to defend her country this morning, but certainly would if need be.

"I don't have a problem with you being an American," he said, eyeing her suspiciously, "but I am confused as to why you've come earlier than the usual time and why you require an audience with Nurse."

"I was told to be here at eleven—to see Mrs. Hill?" His intense gray eyes disarmed her so completely, she had to look away. She held tightly the handle of her handbag with both hands, hoping somehow it would stop the room from darkening and whirling around and around.

Graham methodically spread his toast with butter, and as he was about to ask the girl her purpose in coming—although he had an uneasy feeling that he already knew the answer—he heard a thump, as she collapsed to the floor in front of him.

Before Graham could push back from the table and get to his feet, the nurse and cook rushed in and were at the girl's side. They looked to him for some explanation.

He pushed his brown wavy hair back from his forehead, as he did when distressed. "I was getting around to asking her what she was doing here, when she fainted."

"Look how flushed she is. I think she may be feverish," said Nurse Martin.

"Surely, I'm not responsible for that," said Graham

defensively.

"Don't talk rubbish," said Fran sharply, wondering why the lad couldn't get along with amiable Nurse Martin, who was now checking the girl's head for lumps from her fall.

Together, the women arranged the girl in a more comfortable position and looking up at Graham, who was standing over them and not knowing how to be useful, Nurse asked, "What room shall we put her in?"

Shocked by the request, he cried, "None!" Seeing Fran's sudden disapproval, he asked more calmly, "I mean, shouldn't we call an ambulance or something?"

The nurse said, "I'm expecting the doctor any minute and feel it would be best to make her comfortable here until he sees her and determines what is best. There may be no need to send her to a hospital."

"Shouldn't her family be contacted right away?" asked Graham, desperate to unload the girl on someone else.

"Lot of help they'd be," said Fran, being in the know and proud of it. "Her family is in America and her home is in London."

"We'll keep her here for the time being," said

Nurse with authority. "I'd like to keep her well-separated from Mrs. Hill, in case she's contagious. Why don't you clear your room out, Mr. Hill, and we'll put her in there. And Fran could you fetch a blanket?"

When Fran left the room, Nurse spoke softly to her patient, trying to get a response. Erica moved her head and opened her eyes briefly, but was soon unconscious again. Looking up at Graham again, the nurse said, "I understand, Mr. Hill, that this young lady that has come to do the article about your grandmother."

"Once I learned you weren't informed of it, I did everything I could to prevent it. And for the same reason I didn't want her to come here in the first place, I don't think we should keep her here, now."

"As yet, we don't know how your grandmother will feel about it, but even so, no matter how it came to be or how she may react to it, I am certain that if your grandmother knew of the girl's presence here, she'd want to do the right thing."

Fran marched in with a blanket. "I agree. Someone from this family invited the lass here, and until we have a better plan, we are obliged to look after her."

"I'm so glad that you two are in command of the

situation," said Graham sarcastically. "If she could be dangerous for my grandmother's health, I insist she go elsewhere. It is her employer's fault that she's here at all, and I'm going to ring them right now." He bolted from the room, taking the uncarpeted oak stairs two at a time. In his room, he found his telephone where he'd left it charging. Seeing he had some text messages, he opened it and read, **Still unable to reach journalist en route. She may still show up there. Be kind.**

He saw two more texts from his office, which he shot off answers quickly, seeing as they were urgent, and he then listened to one voicemail about a social event he'd already declined.

Rather than ringing or texting the lady from the magazine on her mobile, he scrolled down his calls until he found the office number he'd used the first time he'd telephoned there, hoping to reach someone higher up in the office hierarchy than Andrea Frey. Poised to push the *Call* option, he heard the others coming up the stairs.

Frustrated and angry that they were bringing her up, he moved to confront the women until he heard a male voice giving instructions. He knew the doctor must have arrived and agreed with the women that the girl needed to be kept at Cairnview. He threw his phone down in anger and quickly set about clearing his bed for her, wondering why Nurse couldn't give up her room, or some other room couldn't be cleared for the unwanted guest.

Nurse barged in with sheets for the bed, and before he could ask her those pertinent questions, she ordered, "Pull those sheets off, please."

There was nothing to be done but obey the multiple commands that came from the doctor, Nurse Martin, and even Fran, so Graham begrudgingly did as he was told, wondering why this girl's health had suddenly become so much more important than his grandmother's. He was told to leave the room while they tended to her, so he left as ordered, forgetting his telephone and belongings in the process. Halfway down the stairs, he remembered them and swore under his breath. He paced around the main floor, waiting for a chance to retrieve his stuff. He finally went back up again, and still unable to get back into his room, stood in the hall, leaning against the wall, for the lack of anything better to do.

Down the hall in the opposite direction of the stairway, he heard his grandmother's voice, and by process of elimination, tried to figure out who she could be talking to. Moving closer to her room, he recognized Kyle's companionable laughter and then his grandmother's tinkling laughter joining in.

Kyle always used the back kitchen stairs. Two years ago, his grandmother had determined that the no-longer-used, but once-beautiful and spacious garden room to the rear of the house was to be divided in half and the northern half converted for use as a tack room. Graham had eagerly helped in the conversion, knowing it would make her happy to have the tack room closer, giving her more opportunity to talk to Kyle about the horses. But hearing them together and enjoying each other's company, he felt a wave of jealously wring his heart. Fighting the tears that were his constant companions whenever he came to Cairnview, he moved towards her room.

Dr. Benson's voice boomed down the hall. "Stay away from your grandmother's room, Mr. Hill. You'll have to wash your hands thoroughly before you can go in there."

"Kyle's in there, and I washed my hands when I came in from the horses, as I always do." He was tired to the bursting point of being ordered around.

"For heaven's sake, I'm talking about protecting

your grandmother from anything the girl might expose her to. Kyle came in the back way, having had no contact with the girl."

"If that's even a remote concern, why bring her up here at all? The hospital is obviously the place for her," Graham retorted.

"I don't think so, besides, if we take precautions, there is no danger. That's why we chose that room for her. They will be quite safely separate, and Fran is going to keep company with your grandmother, while Nurse Martin sees to the young woman."

"But," began Graham.

"All of your grandmother's nursing needs have already been met today. We'll contact the girl's relations and find out what they want us to do. She's seems to be suffering from pleurisy, which is a condition of the lungs, but mostly, I suspect she needs rest. She appears to both Nurse Martin and me to be suffering from exhaustion. The hospital, under those circumstances, would hardly be the place for her; I think you would agree."

Graham grumbled, "A lot of difference it would make if I didn't. I found out about her coming here to do an interview with my grandmother, and when I learned from Nurse that my grandmother knew nothing of it, I tried to put a stop to it. It was my cousin's doing, of course, but I was hoping to spare her."

"We'll sort it out, but not right now," said the doctor with finality.

"I need to get my telephone and bag," said Graham, resigned.

"Nurse just put your things in the hall. Be sure to wash your hands thoroughly before entering your grandmother's room, and we'll take the precaution of having you not touch her, for now."

"I didn't touch the sick girl, Doctor," he said, walking back to his room. Under his breath, he added, "Besides, my grandmother and I haven't touched each other in two years."

He grabbed his things, took them downstairs and put them by the kitchen door. Remembering he'd left some books lying around the sitting room that belonged in the tack room, he gathered them up and made his way to the tack room by way of the garden room entrance off the back hall. He passed a strange girl on the way and asked rudely, "What are you doing here?"

The redheaded college student replied sharply, "I

happen to be cleaning my way through school, if you don't mind. I work for Deb's Daily Services. B-T-W, someone's mobile is going off by the kitchen door."

"B-T-W?"

"By-the-way!" she snapped. "What planet have you been on?"

"What's it to you?"

"Is that your mobile?" She enunciated very slowly, as one might to a person who spoke no English—or perhaps an alien from another planet.

"Don't worry about it," he retorted.

"I'm not in the least worried about it. Who are you, anyway?"

Feeling foolish, he mumbled, "None of your business," and hurriedly entered the welcome atmosphere of the tack room. He breathed in the calming smells of leather, linseed oil, and something else that never failed to comfort him—the distinct scent of horse. There, he put the horse books back on the shelf, wondering what else he should do before leaving.

Kyle came down from Mrs. Hill's room by the back way, and passing through the tack room, waved as he left, saying, "I picked up a few downed branches, so that's done, mate. I'll be back later to put the horses in, unless you are staying and want to do it."

"I was planning on going back tonight, but we have a surprise guest, so I'm not sure of anything right now."

Kyle smiled with understanding and said, "I'll check back later, then. Enjoy your company."

Graham groaned and waving him off, turned to his father's favorite saddle. He applied saddle soap with care and then conditioned the old, cracked leather with linseed oil, treating the saddle like a trusted friend from another life.

After two meetings, Andrea went into her office and closed the door. She looked at her telephone and briefly wondered if it was possible that it was *her* mobile that wasn't working. That would account for her not being able to reach either Erica or Mr. Hill, or perhaps they simply had no signal.

She picked up the office phone, instead, and rang the inn number again, only to have it ring and ring and then give her the option of leaving a voice message. She said, "Yes, this is Andrea calling again from *The London View*. You were to ring us here when our employee finally arrived, and we are anxious for her wellbeing. Please let us know what is going on."

Next, she double checked the number and called Graham again. It rang and rang and finally invited her to leave a message. She said contritely, "Mr. Hill, we have lost our journalist and believe she may be with you. We apologize for all the trouble we've given you. If she is there with you, please, please have her call her office. Thank you."

Miss Leed stuck her head in. "Any luck, yet?"

"No, I just left voice messages at both the inn and Mr. Hill's mobile. It's like she dropped off the earth!" exclaimed Andrea.

"Well, nearly. She is in Scotland, after all." Miss Leed smiled, hoping to insert a little comic relief.

Andrea smiled obligingly, but felt no better. "I was just now wondering if having no mobile signal up there has been the whole problem, but somehow, I just don't think so. It worked just fine the first time he rang here, unless that was a house phone. Oh, I'm so worried, I don't make sense anymore. I simply don't know what to do at this point."

"We do know that she made it as far as the

cottage."

"Yes, she's safe enough that way. She must be at Cairnview by now, poor thing, and I can't imagine she's getting much of a reception."

As if on cue, the telephone rang, and Andrea reached for it immediately. "Andrea Frey, here."

"This is Margie. Miss Leed is out of her office. There's a telephone call from Stirling. Will you take it?"

"Yes, thanks." She waited for the click. "Andrea Frey, *The London View*."

"Sorry you caught me in the loo," said the male desk clerk apologetically. "Everyone else is at lunch. Our handyman has gone home and come back again since we last spoke to you. He said that his wife said that Mrs. Johnson said that her son, the stable hand at Cairnview, was aware that an unexpected guest had arrived. Should I keep her room that you are paying for or let it go?"

"Why shouldn't you keep her room for her?" asked Andrea. "Let me know when she shows."

Miss Leed took the telephone. "Hello, this is Miss Leed. Please do keep the room for her, if you would be so kind. We are convinced she will show up sooner or later. Thank you, sir, and we are sorry for our abruptness. We have been very concerned for our employee."

She hung up the telephone and sighed. "Miss Frey, may I take you for a cup of coffee somewhere nice? I'll tell switchboard we are going out and to ring our mobiles if any news of Miss Sinclair comes in. I'm thinking something high in carbs and calories might do us some good right now."

Chapter Seven

Three days passed before Erica was truly awake. She'd been semi-alert several times and had been assisted to the bathroom and given sips of water and a concoction of Nurse Martin's, which was full of calories and nutrients. She'd even given automatic responses of gratitude for such services, but then went back to sleep again immediately, often sleeping for ten hours at a time.

She awoke to the sight of Millie, sitting in a chair by the window. "Mama, is that you?" she asked in childlike wonder.

"Oh no, my dear girl. It's me, Millie. Don't you remember me?" She rushed to Erica's bedside. "I came to Cairnview two days ago, when they called for me. They put me in a precious little bedroom next to yours."

"Oh, Millie, of course I remember you. How did they know to call you?"

"Joann, the good nurse here, went through your bag when you got ill. She was trying to contact someone in your family, but your telephone was dead and she couldn't find any telephone numbers until she came upon the piece of paper I'd given you at the station. I came the next morning. Of course, there's been lots of contact with your office. They were frantic for news of you."

"My cell phone needed charging," remembered Erica vaguely. "There was a storm, and I got lost."

"I know, dear," said Millie affectionately. "You've been through a very rough patch, but you are going to be all right, now."

"I should call someone at the office."

"Your friend Andrea has rung every day, at least twice. They had no idea what had become of you for a few stressful hours, She'll want to talk to you soon. Your friends there sent their best wishes."

"Friends, as in plural?" Erica was puzzled, but was becoming more alert. "What day is it?"

"It's Friday, love. You traveled on Monday, and that's when we met on the train."

"On the train," repeated Erica. "You gave me a sandwich. I slept in the sweetest little cottage," remembered Erica. "I was afraid of missing my appointment."

"You collapsed in the kitchen here at Cairnview. Oh, you caused quite a stir here at the house and beyond," said Millie in her high-pitched voice. "The people at the inn were trying to find you, too. It was finally Mrs. Smith, who had all the answers, but she had no telephone—only her husband coming and going from the inn, so it took some time for the information to travel."

"Oh, Mrs. Smith—Arlene, she said I should call her—was so kind to me."

"She has come every day to check on you, so we have become friends. Mr. Hill, the grandson, has been pacing the house, wanting to return to Newcastle, but his grandmother requested he stay on until you were sorted out."

"Oh, I remember him. He didn't seem to want me here."

"Well, I might as well tell you," said Millie, sighing. "He found out through a cousin about the article on his grandmother, so he rushed up here to prevent it, after learning from Joann that no one here was aware of your coming. He went back and forth with Andrea on the telephone while you were traveling, but because she couldn't reach you, of course, you came as planned."

"They didn't want me to come?"

"I only know all this, because Joann and Andrea have told me all about it," explained Millie innocently.

"Oh, this is too awful! I've got so much to do. I've got to get out from under their feet and get back to London. I have to get the rest of my stuff out of Dean's flat, and I have to find a place to live!"

She went silent, the blood drained from her face, and she crumpled in tears. "Dean doesn't love me, Millie. I don't think he ever did. I've got nowhere to go. Mama warned me about men like him! I need to find a flat in London. Do you know how hard that is?"

Millie took her in her arms and soothed her. "All in good time, dear. You are to stay here until you are well. I'm not your mama, but I won't desert you."

"I'm so glad you're here, Millie." Mopping her face with the tissue Millie gave her, Erica cried, "I can't stay here, though. I cannot bear to see any of them. It's all too embarrassing! I would be terrified! I remember being in the kitchen. Her grandson didn't want me here, and I didn't know what to do. I just wanted to escape."

"And escape, you did," said Millie smiling. She reached to touch Erica's forehead. "Joann will be glad to hear that your temperature is normal. You can bear to see Joann and Fran, dear. They've been looking after you all this time. Aren't you hungry, love? You've had almost nothing in days!"

"I'm starved!" exclaimed Erica with a weak smile.

"First things first, then. I'll be right back."

Erica was presented a full Scottish breakfast, in spite of it being the wrong time of day. Fran had determined that she should have the proper foods to wake up to, after which, Millie stayed nearby while she showered. Erica was weak, but her strength increased with every hour. So much so, she was frustrated when the nurse insisted she sit in a chair by the window after she was dressed. When the nurse left the room, she complained to Millie, "I can't bear to just sit here and think. I don't want to think about Dean or my job. I just can't! I have to keep moving."

"I think that's what got you into this pickle, love," counseled Millie. "If you'll sit here like a good girl, I'll give you your telephone."

"It's dead," bemoaned Erica dramatically.

"It is not," declared Millie proudly. She reached into the bureau drawer and pulled it out. "I couldn't find your charger when I went through your things, so I had Kyle pick up a new one. Here it is, all charged and ready to go."

"Oh, Millie, you are a guardian angel!" Erica eagerly reached for the phone.

Holding it just out of her reach, Millie said, "Under condition that you don't call that Dean fellow! He's bad for you. I had a nice long chat with Andrea, once I'd charged your mobile. You may ring her. She seems a good sort."

Erica shook her head. "You seem to know everyone. By the way, who is Kyle?"

"Oh, he's a good boy. He takes care of Mrs. Hill's horses and goes to law school. There are such good folks here. Joann is an excellent nurse, and Fran is absolutely top drawer. She's the cook, you know."

"I remember her now."

"Listen, before you go and ring up your friend, let me warn you that there is a possibility that you may still be expected to write the story, after all. It's not so terrifying of a thought, is it? Mrs. Hill—who has asked that I call her Lottie—has taken to the idea, which has her grandson in a state. To tell you the truth, I think she's decided to talk to you, mostly to aggravate him. But not until you are well, of course. Dr. Benson has been here repeatedly, and he will have something to say about your activities for the next few days, and it will be his decision when you are well enough to meet Mrs. Hill."

"Do I have to meet her? I mean, if she's just seeing me to get under her grandson's skin."

"It will work out," soothed Millie. "Just a little motherly advice, but thanking your hostess seems only right and proper."

"Of course, I know that. How stupid of me. It's just that…" Catching her reflection in the dressing table mirror, she cried, "I have to find my make-up and flat iron. Look at me! And I have to get my stuff sorted out. I just threw things in my suitcases."

"You certainly did!" exclaimed Millie.

Erica looked at her expectantly.

"Well, I didn't have anything to do, so I hope you don't mind that I went through your cases. I washed and pressed your clothes and hung them in the cupboard," said Millie sheepishly. "At first, I couldn't see why you'd brought so much, but then I talked to Andrea. I had to win her confidence, before she told me anything about your breakup with your boyfriend, of course, but then I understood the reason for bringing as much as you could. I got you sorted out."

"I was living with him, Millie! I thought he loved me. I feel so stupid."

"There, there, everything will work out in the end. You'll see." Millie made Erica's bed and tidied the room. Looking sheepish, she said, "I admit I did a little mending, too. And you left some things in the backseat of a taxi, most importantly, your computer, which have been returned to you since you became ill."

"Oh Millie," cried Erica. "I haven't been mothered in years! My mother died five years ago."

Millie's heart went out to the girl. She perched on the footstool by Erica's chair and tenderly smoothed her hair. "I'm so sorry to hear it. How awful for you, my dear!"

"I don't know how to thank you. I can't believe you really came. How is your husband getting along without you?"

"He is always happy for me to gallivant, because he's an avid golfer. Millie laughed. "I'll be heading home soon, once I know you'll be all right."

"I'll never understand it, Millie. Why did you befriend me so?"

"I felt very strongly that I should, so I did. I

suppose I should explain that Henry and I were never blessed with children, but rather than bemoan it and feel sorry for ourselves, we found that if we kept our eyes open, there were plenty of opportunities to make a difference in people's lives. You were one of those opportunities. Henry will want to meet you."

"Then, I'll make sure he does," promised Erica.

Millie got up to leave the room. "Now, make that telephone call, and I'll leave you in peace."

"Erica!" Andrea popped up and closed her office door for privacy. "It was like you dropped off the earth! I tried and tried to reach you to tell you to turn around before you got to the house."

"I know. What started out as a rough day, only got worse. It's called piling on in football, back home—fifteen yard penalty."

"What? Are you sure you're all right?"

"Not really, but I've been looked after, and I am getting better by the minute."

"Judy and I were absolutely frantic about you!"

"Judy?"

"Miss Leed," explained Andrea. "We came to be

on a first-name basis because of you."

"Seems like lots of people are on a first-name basis on account of me."

"And that horrible Graham Hill. Have you met him yet?"

Erica cringed at the thought. "Barely. I collapsed in front of him."

"He's a brute, so keep your distance. Listen, I'm sorry, but in a flash of stupidity, I told Judy about Dean," admitted Andrea. "I'm so sorry, I shouldn't have. But, since I'd already told the woman in accounting and had no other way of explaining the state you were in, I told her. Turns out she's a pretty good egg, once you get to know her."

"And you told Millie everything, too," scolded Erica.

"Oh, I know, but we were all so worried about you. How are you feeling about the whole Dean thing? Are you all right?"

"I'm trying not to think about him. I can't stop crying if I do. Too much else to work out, right now. I'm not going back to him, if that's what you are wondering. I've got to find a place to live, for one."

"Listen," said Andrea in a hurry, "I'm terribly sorry, but I've got to run to a meeting, but we'll talk soon, all right?"

Erica stared at the telephone, and feeling utterly bereft, sank into the glorious misery of self-pity, and while yet alone, cried her eyes out.

Erica was in control of her emotions, but terribly self-conscious when she and Millie went down to dinner that evening. They went straight to the kitchen to see what needed to be done in order for Fran's crock-pot meal to be served up, and to their surprise, found Fran there.

"What's this?" asked Millie. "I thought you were going home earlier today and letting us help ourselves."

"Mr. Graham said that I should, too, but when he's here, I sometimes like to stick around to do more baking than usual. He usually gives me a ride home when I'm here late. What with all the excitement about the girl…" Suddenly seeing Erica, she stopped mid-sentence. "Well, look at you! I almost didn't recognize you!" Fran looked her up and down in approval.

"Hello," said Erica shyly. She knew she looked different with her hair straightened and wearing a neatly pressed white shirt and her skinny jeans, which were now a little baggy. It was the first time she'd been dressed properly, since pulling off her expensive suit in the train terminal that awful day.

"You look so much better! Thin, of course, but that can be fixed." Fran smiled at Erica reassuringly and returned to the task at hand. "All right, then, let's put this food out. You are eating in the dining room tonight."

"Then I'll do the washing up," said Millie, "and Mr. Hill will drive you home to your husband."

"My Ben will be glad to hear that our girl is up and about."

"You're quite a celebrity around here," whispered Millie to Erica, as they carried platters of beef roast, potatoes, and carrots to the dining room. Fran followed them with freshly-sliced homemade bread and a plate of butter.

They found Graham there, setting the table. As she left the room, Fran said, "I'll let you drive me home tonight after you eat, Mr. Graham."

"Of course, Fran," he replied cordially.

He stared at Erica for a moment, as if trying to place her. She found her nerve, and setting the food down, went around the head of the table to shake his hand. She determined to hide her nervousness with formality and boldness. "Hello, I'm Erica Sinclair. It wasn't my fault that I was sent here, but I do feel inclined to apologize for overstaying my welcome."

"Well," said Graham haltingly. "Yes, Miss Sinclair. I am Graham Hill."

"I know," said Erica, meeting him eye to eye.

"Now that everyone knows each other, I'll fetch the nurse for dinner." Millie nervously left the room.

"I'm sincere, Mr. Hill. I am sorry I passed out on your kitchen floor. I'm sorry for being a nuisance. I'm sorry for imposing myself and my friend upon your hospitality. I'm sorry we postponed your travel back to London."

"Newcastle," he corrected her abruptly, his gray eyes never leaving hers.

"Yes, Newcastle. My mistake." Erica refused to look away in retreat. "Anyway, we will both be leaving as soon as possible and will no longer disrupt your lives."

"I would have thought that your friendly Miss Wells might have told you that my grandmother wants to meet you Monday morning to explore your ideas about the article. To be on the safe side, that is the earliest the doctor will let you two be together. She is going to see you, because I made the mistake of suggesting she *not* do so."

"My friend's name is *Mrs.* Wells, and I'm sorry you are so against it, Mr. Hill. It was my original intent to visit her only briefly each day, so as not to tire her. I was booked to stay at the inn just long enough to get enough material to do justice to the story on her life."

"I could argue that was the intent, based on the mountain of luggage you brought with you."

"You are not in possession of all the facts, Mr. Hill, and some of them are simply none of your business. Why are you so against the article, anyway?"

"I'm against it—not that it's any of your business—because I know whose idea it was in the first place, and he never does anything without an ulterior motive."

"I don't understand," said Erica, regretting it immediately. She wished she'd quelled her curiosity and maintained her immovable, disinterested pose.

"I don't either, entirely," he replied, relaxing a little, "but he would like nothing more than for my grandmother to die, so he can get his inheritance, or more correctly put, sell his inheritance. I think he wants you to upset her or find out what she's worth, or, oh, I don't know, but he's up to no good."

"I thought the idea came through Mrs. Davies."

"She was manipulated, I'm sure." Graham felt uneasy in Erica's presence and didn't know why. He stepped back and folded his arms in front of him.

Erica noticed his prideful stance and tried to ignore his disarming good looks. Assuming her own prideful stance again, she declared, "I will get out of your hair as quickly as I am allowed. You can count on it. It's not comfortable being an unwelcome guest, and I was hoping to go home tomorrow, but if your grandmother wants to meet me, I suppose I can stay on at the inn through the weekend. I understand that the doctor has ordered more rest for me, anyway."

"Which you can do at the inn," he prompted.

"Yes, didn't I just say that? Well, I won't know until Monday whether your grandmother is in favor of the article or not, but perhaps, when I meet her, I will thank her for her kindness to me and insist that I have to get back to London. Would that make you feel better?"

He was surprised by the offer and raised his chin

proudly. "Well, yes, as a matter of fact, it would."

"All nicely swept away—never to think of again." Erica couldn't help being provocative. "Don't you just love a happy ending?"

Graham looked at her sharply, but before he could say more, the other women entered the room and he seated them. Having to have the last word, as he went around Erica's chair to his own place at the head of the table, he whispered, "You must be a friend of Andrea Frey's."

She opened her mouth and shut it again. She could hardly know what he meant by that and didn't feel well enough to banter with him anymore.

Erica faced the weekend with some foreboding. She learned she was under doctor's orders to rest at Cairnview, not the inn, making it easy for him to check on her while making his regular visits to Mrs. Hill. He also wanted her to eat small meals frequently, and there were plenty of people around to make sure she did it.

She longed to escape Graham's unwelcoming stares and dreaded the meeting with his grandmother, but Millie was staying on, too, which made it all a little more tolerable. Besides, the only way she was going to get out of there was to do it on her own, and she shrunk from it just thinking of the mountain of clothes she'd brought with her, all of which needed to be repacked. The very thought of dragging them all back to London was enough to squash any ideas she had about leaving on her own. Besides, her leaving would only make it easier for Mr. Stuck-up Hill, and why would she do that?

Millie was staying on with the intent of seeing her as far as Newcastle, so Erica owed it to her to stick it out, in spite of Graham's hostility. His glares stung her fragile self-esteem, though, reminding her of Dean's betrayal and her gullibility to his attentions. For some reason that she couldn't understand, even seeing Graham from a distance unsettled her, and more than once, tears had threatened without warning.

She took a book outside to sit in the sun on Saturday afternoon, but didn't open it. She looked around her, appreciating the view. She saw what must have, at some point, been a well-kept rose garden Though no longer tidy, she appreciated the wildness of it and the courageous roses blooming in the bramble.

She saw Graham and another dark-haired man— probably Kyle, she thought—ride out on some handsome horses and felt a twinge of envy. She loved the freedom of riding a horse, and it had been a very long time since she'd had the opportunity.

Seeing a sweet old horse looking on longingly as the riders loped away, Erica walked over to the paddock, and the mare came to her expectantly. "I don't have a thing for you, old girl," she said. "Maybe later, Fran will let me bring something to you." Noting that the riders were no longer in view, she said, "You don't get to go with them, either, do you? We're in the same boat, you and me—stuck here with nothing to do."

Graham fueled his fire of discontent by fussing that the troublesome journalist had been given his room and never vacated it, even though she was obviously much improved. His mood was felt by anyone in his presence, and when he went riding with Kyle, the only conversation they had was short-lived.

Kyle said, "I heard that the girl that's staying with you is really pretty. I also heard that she's a journalist."

"Who'd you hear that from?" snapped Graham, wondering if his grandmother shared everything with the stable hand.

Kyle smiled knowingly. "I heard it from my mum, who heard it from Arlene Smith. Arlene is always in the know and without a telephone, at that."

"Well, good for her," said Graham with sarcasm.

"Mum's heard that she's lost lots of weight. Said that's one of the reasons the doc didn't let her go to the inn to recuperate. Thought she'd do better eating Fran's cooking."

"She's a scarecrow," said Graham. "Never trust a skinny woman."

"Thanks for the advice," said Kyle patronizingly, before taking off at a gallop.

Chapter Eight

Upon waking Sunday morning, Erica thought the weekend would never end, but she perked up when she remembered Fran saying that Arlene Smith had arranged to visit that afternoon.

Fran rarely came to Cairnview on Sundays, but she showed up that afternoon, still dressed for church, to prepare the tea and serve her famous lemon sponge cake. She had made the delicious treat the day before and had hidden it well from any midnight nibblers.

Kyle and Graham had just come back from riding, and when Graham saw her go in by the kitchen door wearing her Sunday best, he was concerned that something may be amiss. By the time he made it to the kitchen to wash, she already had her best white pinny tied over her navy-blue dress and was slicing the sponge with care.

"Lemon sponge!" he exclaimed. "You're an angel, Fran. I haven't any in ages. I think you hid it from me."

"Yes, I did. I'll cut some off for you." Fran fetched the dessert plates. "We're having a tea party on the lawn. You can help me set it up. Our guests are leaving in a couple of days, and Arlene Smith is coming to call. Kyle's mum may come along with her. Joann is off today visiting family, so she won't be one of the party."

"Joann?"

"Nurse Martin. Our recent crisis seems to have put everyone on a first-name basis."

Graham's grandmother couldn't come down the stairs, and he knew she didn't like being carried. "Whose idea was this?"

"It was your grandmother's idea, lad. I will watch for her distress signal, if she should need anything while she's alone. It's all worked out. She can watch from her window, and the visitors will pay their respects before they leave."

She saw his glee transform into anger, and misunderstanding it, she said, "There's enough for everyone, lad. You can't eat a whole cake, anyways."

Graham had a definite grouch on that even his grandmother could observe from the upper floor, but always obedient to Fran's requests, he set up the table, drug out the chairs, and placed the cushions and tablecloths as directed. He couldn't say 'no' to Fran, because he'd thought many times that, since the death of his mother, she filled the void with her unconditional love. He recognized that his visits north were to see her as much as for any other reason. Although he did as he was told, he made sure everyone knew he disapproved of the party.

Still dressed in her Sunday best and bringing Kyle's mother, Louise, with her, Arlene showed up at Cairnview at the appointed time. When the party gathered in the warm afternoon sun, it would have appeared to the uninformed to be a reunion of sorts. Arlene fussed over the weight Erica had lost since she'd last seen her, and Millie, Louise, and Fran exchanged stories and recipes, laughing gaily.

In the course of the conversation, Erica was mortified to learn that she had been staying in Graham's room all this time. She thought about seeking him out to apologize, but the only time they were in the same room was at dinnertime, and the opportunity did not present itself. He was definitely avoiding her.

In the evening, after Lottie was asleep, Nurse, Millie, and Erica played three-handed euchre in the sitting room. Graham sulked at dinner and went out that night. If not for the arctic wind that blew in every time he entered a room, the camaraderie at the house made one want to linger. To Erica, it felt like summer vacation at home in Nebraska, and likewise, she knew it had to end. Part of her wanted it to end, and soon, and yet, coming here had allowed her to temporarily forget all her problems still waiting for her in London. Millie kept reassuring her that she would be able to face it all, once her strength returned.

It had been less than a week since her arrival, and yet it felt like so much longer. She had five new friends, who she hated to part with. Fran, Millie, Joann, Arlene, and even Louise treated her like she had always belonged to them, and their caring was like a warm blanket, even a kind of maternal nurturing that she had long missed and dreaded parting with. "It's Cairnview," she whispered. "It's put a spell on me."

Graham thought his grandmother enjoyed his discomfort, when on Monday morning, she asked him to bring in the girl and make the introductions. When he voiced his reluctance, based on the possibility that Erica was still contagious, he thought he was pressing his point quite convincingly, until her piercing glare stopped him— quite literally—in mid-sentence.

"Graham, I want you to do this for me. The doctor

wouldn't have permitted it if there was the slightest chance of me getting ill. Once you've done that, you can go back to Newcastle and get on with your work. You must be getting behind."

Graham tried to speak, but she raised her hand to stop him.

"Before you go, please arrange for the internet to be hooked up. I understand that out here in the country there are fewer options, but I'd like that done right away, whatever the cost. I believe the girl will need to be 'online.' Isn't that what they say?"

"Of course, but that's a bit premature, seeing as she's not agreed to stay, yet. Besides, I've asked you about it several times to enable me to work and communicate with the office from here, and you've refused."

"You sound like a bad-tempered little boy, Graham," she scolded, shaming him. "Get the internet hooked up, anyway. If she doesn't stay, it will be here for your use, won't it?"

He looked at the ceiling, checking his emotions that always ran so high in her presence. With forced dignity, he said, "Consider it done, then."

"That's better. Thank you."

Soon after, Graham tapped lightly on her door again and entered with Erica in tow. "Grandmother, this is Miss Erica Sinclair from *The London View*, and Miss Sinclair, may I present my grandmother, Mrs. Charlotte Hill."

"How do you do?" said Erica meekly, taking in the feminine setting and the delicate scent of lavender. The room was decorated in pale pink and soft gray, and it was beautifully furnished with fine antiques, from the handsome bed and elaborate dressing table, to the old-fashioned radio. It was like walking back in time, and there was nothing visible to destroy the allusion, except for the modern en suite bathroom, much like the one in her own room, which could be partially seen through the door left slightly ajar.

"Very well," said Lottie. "Come in and have a chair. Let's have a little talk." She dismissed her grandson brusquely. "You are excused to go, Graham. Don't forget about the internet and have a safe trip home."

"I won't forget," he replied stiffly, "and I'll be as safe as anyone else on the train."

She looked at him stoically. "Very clever. "Goodbye, then."

Erica moved to the small upholstered chair by the east-facing window, wishing she could check out the view to the northeast to see if Stirling Castle was part of it, but she was too nervous to take even that much liberty.

Once Graham was gone, Lottie directed her attention to Erica.

"You are probably wondering if I can see Stirling Castle over the trees from here. Yes, I can, but not today, because of the mist."

Erica's jaw almost dropped in her surprise. "Did you read my mind, Mrs. Hill?"

"No, but it's what everyone does when they come up here. They want to make sure I have a view, and I do. Graham thinks I stay up here for the view of my horses, but it's also my need to see into the distance, which is as important to me as air."

"I have that same need," admitted Erica. "I realized it upon arriving here at Cairnview the other day. It was almost like coming up for air, like you said."

"I've seen you from my window. You like horses and enjoy reading under a tree. How you could live in London, even a month, is hard for me to fathom."

"It is difficult," Erica shook her head. If you only

knew the half of it, she thought.

Lottie got down to business. "Let's come to an agreement. I'm thinking I'll keep you around for a while if you are open to the idea. I talked to Paul Davies, and he has agreed to loan you to me to write my memoirs if we get along all right. If you agree to the idea, he will proceed to get a temporary release from your London job until we've finished. I will pay them for your services, and you will continue to get paid by them."

Overwhelmed by the woman's personality, Erica could only nod.

"Now, these are my terms. We will meet after breakfast for our longest session, and again briefly in the late afternoon, if I'm feeling up to it. We'll cover everything that's worthwhile, the good and the bad, but I only will decide what gets printed, both in any article or my memoirs. You will be in my confidence, which is a sacred trust."

Erica nodded again, mesmerized by the dominating presence of a being so little and frail. Her long gray hair was tied with a ribbon and draped over her right shoulder. Her deep blue eyes were bright and knowing—her demeanor and manner, the picture of elegance and grace.

She wore an old-fashioned, pale-blue bed-jacket of quilted satin—something that Erica had seen only in old movies.

Lottie continued, "I haven't yet made up my mind about how much of my life to share, but everyone that would mind my sharing is no longer alive, so we shall see."

Erica finally found her voice. "Yes, ma'am," she said.

"That sounds so American, dear. I'll never get used to it. I think, just this once, we should break with tradition and address each other by our first names. I will call you Erica, and you will call me Lottie."

"Oh, I couldn't, not yet, Mrs. Hill," exclaimed Erica anxiously.

"Well, why not? I'm not 'Her Ladyship,' you know. Your desire to be respectful to your elders is commendable and shows that you've been well-taught, but I'd rather forget that when we're working on this project. We need to be equals. I've been thinking about how to proceed, ever since Dr. Benson told me about your being here and the circumstances under which you came. I want to go about it like this. I will try to remember the events as exactly as possible, and to do so, I must imagine myself to be at the age I was at the time of the happening. That's why you must address me as Lottie, or I'll lose my train of thought."

"It will feel very odd," said Erica with reluctance, "but I wouldn't want to be responsible for you losing your train." She noticed the old woman's feminine manners and dignified bearing, and thought she looked very regal, indeed. In fact, she thought 'Her Ladyship' seemed very fitting and would have been much easier to say than 'Lottie.'

Lottie chuckled, her frail shoulders shaking. "Oh, my train goes off the rails completely sometimes, with no distractions from anyone, so not to worry. Sometimes, it's more like a 'stream of consciousness.' Did you ever read *To the Lighthouse*?"

"Required in high school. Can't say that I appreciated the so-called classic at the time."

"Well, that's how I think and often how I talk. 'Stream of consciousness,' is such a nice phrase, but speaking that way is nothing new for me. Now, after we gather the facts, if I'm still alive," she said, chuckling again, "I'll give my perspective of the events from my vast age, but not until later. So you understand, if you address me formally, you'll take me out of time, which may confuse me. I'll admit I do get confused occasionally, but don't write that down. I have a couple of grandsons—well, one in particular—who would like to think I'm completely dotty."

"Graham?" Realizing her error, Erica apologized quickly. "He didn't say I could call him that, by the way. Sorry."

"Don't apologize all the time, either. If we are going to do this, we have to make the best use of our time," scolded Lottie. "No, not Graham. He's easily influenced, but it is his cousin John, who is so blatantly interfering. Now, I am going to rest a spell and then have my brunch, which I eat at eleven. Can we meet after that?" Lottie beamed with childlike expectancy.

"Of course," said Erica. "May I just say that on behalf of our magazine that we are sorry for the way this came about."

Lottie waved her away. "No more apologizing. That's a terrible habit, really, Erica. You must try to stop doing it all the time. Apologizing is absolutely required to gain forgiveness for something grievous, but to apologize all the time just to make yourself feel better is, well, it's.."

"Shallow?" asked Erica timidly. "And selfish, even?"

"Exactly," said Lottie pleased. "See? Look at us! I had the thought, and you found the word! I think we'll get on swimmingly, to use one of my favorite words. How about that royal wedding? Did you watch it?" she asked, changing the subject abruptly.

Taking a moment to keep up, Erica replied, "When in Rome, as the saying goes. Our magazine covered it, so I pretty much had to watch it."

"Indeed," said Lottie. "I didn't watch it, but I saw all the pictures. Joann got me the magazines. Don't think I got yours, though. What is it again?"

"*The London View*."

"Oh yes, *The London View*. How nice. A royal wedding is so romantic," said Lottie wistfully.

It wasn't until she'd been dismissed that Erica remembered her promise to Graham to decline his grandmother's offer. She felt uneasy, but who could refuse a personality like hers? He'd soon be gone, anyway, and the sooner the better for her.

Just then, hearing tires crunching on gravel, she walked along the upstairs hall to the window that overlooked the front door. She saw Graham throw his bag in the trunk—the 'boot'—she corrected herself quickly, as Dean would have done.

Graham got in the passenger's seat, which, of course, to her was on the wrong side of the car. She recognized the driver as the other man she'd seen from a distance, but had yet to meet. Graham felt her gaze and looked up. Neither waved, and she turned away from the window, embarrassed at being seen.

He probably knows I'm staying, then, she thought.

"Good," she said aloud.

Chapter Nine

Shortly before noon, armed with a notebook, her high-tech voice recorder and laptop, Erica made it back to Lottie's room and entered with the light tap she'd seen Graham do before entering.

"Set yourself up, Erica from America, and we'll have a go at this," was Lottie's eager greeting.

Opening her laptop, Erica smiled at her hostess's rare brand of humor and told herself to buck up and quit being a mealy mouse if she wanted to keep this job. "Um, Mrs. Hill—I mean, Lottie—I would like to have your permission to do some recording, in case I miss something and want to retrieve it. I realize that this requires trust, which I haven't earned, yet. How do you feel about it?"

"For now, yes." Lottie nodded regally. "What are your thoughts about how to begin?"

Shyly, Erica said, "On the train, still believing I was expected by you, in which case I was sadly mistaken, of course, I had the notion that you could just talk as randomly as your thoughts took you. Should you get stuck, I could shoot a question at you from some that I'd prepared ahead of time." She paused to think and then added, "Having met you, I really can't imagine you getting stuck, though."

Lottie smiled warmly. "Oh, it's a strong possibility."

Erica liked her and wondered why she had been so terrified of her.

"Sometimes I can't see very well in the afternoon with so little light from the east window, so when I ask you a yes or no question, as a matter of efficiency, please don't just nod or shake your head. Speak up, because I don't hear that well, either." Lottie laughed her young, tinkling laughter, making Erica smile. "There, I made you smile. That didn't hurt much, did it?"

Remembering to speak up, Erica said loudly, "Not too much," again wondering why she had been so terrified of her.

She is a human bulldozer, thought Erica. Not in a bad way, she clarified to herself, but there is nothing to be done but to do as told and otherwise stay out of the way. Maybe she is a little terrifying, after all.

Lottie's voice brought Erica suddenly out of her thoughts. "Very well, as much as I like doing things orderly, I won't start at the beginning. I have certain parts I want to tell, and should I die, well, we may as well start with priorities." She thought for a moment, and said, "My grandsons could benefit from this project if they valued my experiences, but that is neither here nor there. I actually began toying with the idea of getting my story on paper a few weeks ago, when I sent Kyle—do you know Kyle?"

"I think I've seen him around, but we haven't been introduced."

"He is a fine boy. Well, I sent him upstairs one morning, because I had a vivid dream in which I saw my mother tucking some papers into a cubby hole between the rafters in the attic. I awoke realizing that it was more than a dream—it was a childhood memory. I remember startling my mother, and she turned and scolded me for sneaking up on her. How is it that I had to be a hundred years old to remember that moment and realize its importance?"

Rhetorical question, thought Erica, keeping quiet.

Lottie went on, "So, Kyle went up and found a treasure trove behind a board nailed between two rafters in a dark corner of the attic. They were too dusty for me to go through. I tried and went into fits of coughing. If you are

151

willing, I would like to have your services as a personal secretary, as much as a scribe, and as we go along, it would be helpful if you could either trigger or validate my memories with the letters and papers that may apply. I don't anticipate too many surprises, because I always knew my parents didn't get along, so her stash makes sense in many ways. All of it must be catalogued and dated, though, if possible, which will fill your time when I am resting. Does that sound too daunting, dear?"

"Not at all. It sounds terribly interesting!"

"Then, let's begin," said Lottie eagerly.

Erica turned on the voice recorder and poised her fingers over her keyboard.

"In about my seventeenth year," began Lottie, "I began to notice things that younger children do not, and what I became aware of was that my father had a problem—or rather, we had a problem because of him. He ran roughshod all over my mother, but of course, it wasn't her only. He had always done so to the servants, and Mum had to find replacements often, but when I reached that age, I began to take real notice of the way he treated her. He wasn't pleasant to any of us, except maybe Robert, but he was particularly cold and rude to my mother. They had terrible fights at night when they thought everyone was sleeping, so she must have fought back when she thought she could. I couldn't make out what they were arguing about, although once I actually listened outside their bedroom door. They argued in angry whispers. It still sends a shiver down my back when I think of it. Our house servants came during the day only, but my governess lived in."

Lottie looked at Erica suddenly, who had stopped tapping the keys on her laptop. "What is it, child?" she asked with concern.

"Oh, just that my parents fought all the time, too. No servants, so no need to whisper, ever. Lots of shouting—mostly my dad's. I heard every word."

"I am sorry. We have a bit in common, don't we?" Lottie was beginning to like this girl.

"We do," said Erica, smiling sadly.

"I used to have dark hair like yours, too. A bit darker than yours and not straight—more wavy, and very thick. My mother used to fuss about it being too much to deal with. I always rather liked it, though.

"I have to iron my hair every day. It's naturally very curly," said Erica, rolling her eyes.

153

"Now, why would a person do that? When I was younger, girls my age would pay for a permanent wave. I didn't need one, I'm glad to say." Lottie looked Erica over from head to toe. "Are you comfortable, dressed as you are so professionally?"

Erica looked down at her office attire. "As comfortable as I ever am when I work."

"Well, our meetings will be short, so dress casually from now on. It makes no sense to change your clothes all the time. You are in the country, now." She looked blankly at Erica.

"Did you ever talk to your mother about the fighting?" asked Erica, getting them back to the subject.

"I did one day when we were out by the paddock. I loved the horses, and my mother liked getting out of the house on a nice day. She seemed more relaxed and approachable. I ventured to ask her why she let my father treat her the way he did. She looked at me sharply and asked, 'How would I make him stop with servants, ever-listening? I have to keep playing my part. Can't you see that?'"

Lottie seemed to drift off to sleep for a few moments, but Erica determined she was merely time-traveling, which proved true, when she suddenly went on as if she hadn't stopped.

"Now, the reason they were playing their parts so well, was because my mother—her name was Lily—was a Maitland from Liverpool, once great shipping giants there and in Glasgow. Appearances were everything to my father and probably her father, although not at all to my mum. Not exactly sure when she discarded the whole idea of playacting to impress people, because she had been raised in a family of 'new money' and that is what they did. In a nutshell, 'new money' people often escaped their pasts, whenever possible, and vied for the attention and acceptance of the 'old money' people, hence playing the part. Must have been very tiring. That's it," she said victoriously, "I think my mother simply got tired of it."

"There really weren't many opportunities to make acquaintances here with the moneyed people, so my father invited Glasgow people for large dinner parties, even house parties from time to time, housing some of the guests at the inn. Those parties wore my mother out completely, partly because those people weren't her friends. She didn't seem to have friends at that point, although she did later. My father died in the war in 1941, and we didn't grieve him. Too much going on, which I'll get into later."

Erica took notes copiously and glanced at her recorder, making sure it was still doing its job.

Lottie continued, "When my parents married, I think my mother was actually coerced by her family to marry him. Once married, my father was very keen to move up here and become important in the Glasgow shipping industry. My father, whose name was Gordon Jackson, by the way, expanded the Maitland empire, becoming partners with my mother's father, whose name was Charles Maitland. I don't think the men got along very well, from the little I remember, but they certainly appreciated each other's fortunes, well enough. My father had just inherited his, when his grandfather left him everything, having disowned his son for reasons unknown to me. Those grandparents were never mentioned because of that, I suppose."

"Would you like to know more about them, because at the magazine, we have tools to do things like that," offered Erica, eager to please.

"I don't think I care, dear. I should, shouldn't I?"

Rhetorical, thought Erica, keeping silent.

"My father wanted the Maitland name to help him win prestigious contracts, I should think. My grandfather, no doubt, needed an influx of cash, so the deal was made, and my mum was the pawn. She told me once that she considered herself plain and was afraid of becoming a spinster, so had gone along with the scheme, although she was only twenty-four years old. There are picture albums downstairs, and I'll have Fran tell Kyle to take them along with the boxes of my mother's papers and put them in the library, where I assume you'll want to work. I want very much for you to correlate and validate my own memories with the photos, letters, and papers. Memories can be deceiving sometimes, did you know that?"

Erica nodded.

"Don't nod. Speak up, child. Anyway, I don't fear death, but I want to leave something behind of myself. Quite self-aggrandizing, don't you think?"

Having just been told to speak up, she did so clearly. "Quite a natural inclination, I should think."

"Very diplomatic answer," said Lottie, playfully. "You'll have to be brutally honest at times, dear. I don't bite."

That's a relief, thought Erica, smiling.

"Because you already know that I'll be brutally honest with you," added Lottie matter-of-factly.

Too true, thought Erica. Realizing that Lottie was waiting for a response, she said aloud, "I'll work on it."

"I have a gift, Erica, in that I am able to discern people's motives and character. It is serendipitous that you have come right now, and I have a great hope we will get along. You are just the kind of person I need."

"Not to interrupt, but I see myself as a bit of a train-wreck right now, but I would love a shot at this, I really would." Erica was eager but had some reservations. "Are you sure you want to entrust this to a stranger? It's all so terribly personal."

"Right now, I have reason to distrust certain members of my family. A stranger suits my purposes. Besides, your train-wreck status means that you're at loose ends and might be willing to stay until it's completed. That's all for today, I think. I'm suddenly very tired."

Fran showed Erica to the library after lunch, where shoe boxes of letters and papers were sitting on two card tables pushed together. They had been set up beside the desk for sorting the papers, and an old tablecloth was laid out on one of the tables. Fran informed her that she could use that to catch the dust from the papers and smiled proudly when Erica told her it seemed that she had thought of everything.

The library was about the size of Lottie's bedroom, which was directly overhead. The large window in the library faced south, rather than eastward—as Lottie's window did upstairs—because adjacent to it eastward was the one-story garden room.

Erica had found the garden room and the tack room areas by mistake two days before, when she'd opened the door at the end of the hall, thinking it opened onto the backyard. Upon seeing it, she could imagine the many-windowed room in its glory, years before, and the wonderful parties that must have been held there. She could picture many vases of flowers and lovely ladies in flowing dresses. Now, the garden part was just a place to store outdoor furniture and unused flower pots.

How sad, thought Erica.

In the library there were two walls of bookcases on opposite walls, which were filled with fine books all the way to the high ceiling. The large window, which faced the double-doors, was dressed in heavy, tapestry-looking draperies. When pulled shut, the light of the afternoon sun was cut off, giving the room a cozy, cocooned ambiance. Fine paneling surrounded the window and doors, adding to the snug atmosphere.

The enormous mahogany desk had been cleared for her use, on which there was nothing but a ream of plain paper, an expensive pen and pencil set, and a stack of three old picture albums.

Before Erica could begin to work, Millie appeared at the door and said apologetically, "Dr. Benson insists you rest after your sessions with Lottie for a few days. Even if you can't sleep, dear, the rest is important."

Knowing it was futile to resist, Erica made her way to her room, closed the curtains, and lay down on her bed.

After three hours, Millie came in briskly, letting in the light. "You'd better wake up, love, or you'll never be able to sleep tonight."

Upon hearing it was after three, Erica forced herself out of her unconscious safe haven. As always, upon awakening, she was engulfed in sadness. She knew she was grieving the loss of something that had been an allusion, but she missed it all the same. She had checked her phone constantly for messages from Dean, and as much as she was glad there were none, she was as equally disappointed.

After a cup of tea and a tempting piece of chocolate cake, Erica went back to the library, where she began the process of unfolding each piece of paper and brushing off the dust and spider webs. She noticed that there were few envelopes, which might make dating items more difficult.

She decided to sort them, not chronologically, because that was impossible at this point, but by category. She separated them into four piles: letters, photos, financial papers, and personal notes written by Lily herself, to which Erica included anything that didn't fit into the first three categories. The largest pile was the financial one, more paper than all the other categories combined. Those would be the easiest to sort chronologically—dated nicely—but the most difficult for her to understand. She didn't want to bother Lottie with too many questions about the undated papers, because that is why she had been hired. She thought letters and photos could be readily dated, at least approximately, with a little research, beginning with the wealth of information to be derived from the photo albums. The handwritten notes would be the most difficult to date, she thought.

Having made a good start, Erica went in search of Millie to spend some time with her before dinner. They sat together in the rarely-used sitting room and talked and talked. They had become best friends.

As Millie was going home in the morning, Fran had made a lovely soup and homemade bread for them to dish up for themselves. Nurse had taken the afternoon off, once she was sure that Millie could meet her patient's needs for a few hours. She had her mobile phone on her, in any case, so she had gone off happily into Stirling in her own little car to shop and have dinner with a friend. She was wisely getting in as many outings as she could, while extra people were there to cover for her.

Millie took up Lottie's meal and visited with her while she ate. When she came downstairs with the tray, she found Erica laying the kitchen table for them. They sat across it from each other and ate together companionably.

Erica said, "I'm glad grumpy Graham is gone. I'm so relieved I didn't have to face him after breaking my promise about leaving."

"According to his grandmother, his high-speed train didn't leave from Edinburgh until tonight, but that he was, no doubt, drowning his sorrows in a few pints of Scottish ale while waiting."

"Fine by me," said Erica, with feigned indifference.

Millie smiled at her affectionately. "His attitude towards you was unkind, to say the least, and I don't disregard your feelings at all. I felt the same, but there seems to have been an estrangement of sorts with his grandmother some time ago," said Millie, "and I think he's jealous of anyone in her good graces. He's not such a bad fellow—more a tortured soul, I should say."

"The absence of his hostile, unwelcoming personality may help me to think more tolerably of him, Millie. But feel sorry for him? I don't think so. I'll leave that for you to do."

The subject of Graham was dropped and they giggled together like school friends when they agreed that manners could be dispensed with entirely and proceeded to mop up the bottom of their soup bowls with their buttered bread.

Before they retired, Erica embraced her friend. "I am going to miss you so much! I can't bear to think about it."

"You'll do fine. I will telephone you, and I'll get Henry to come up here with me to see you before you go home. We'll stay at the inn, and I'll find him somewhere expensive to golf."

"That would be wonderful!" Erica's face beamed with delight.

"Promise me you'll eat and take care of yourself. And in a weak moment, don't call Dean Saint. What a name for such a scoundrel! Aren't you grateful you found out about him when you did?"

"Yes, but I can't turn the feelings off like a water tap, can I?"

Millie answered firmly, "You will, my dear, on the very morning you wake up and realize you are more angry than hurt."

Chapter Ten

When Erica awoke the next morning, she was sadly aware that Millie would be going home to her husband in a couple of hours. She knew she would miss her terribly. Her appearance at Cairnview had made all the difference and had been the catalyst that brought about the camaraderie that had prevailed there.

Once she'd dealt with her daily waking anguish of Dean's rejection and accompanying shame, Erica became painfully aware that she had some unfinished business in London that could not be ignored.

As she put on her make-up, she derided the person in the mirror for having fallen into Dean's snare. She paid more rent than she should have, and it struck her now—although it hadn't at the time—that Dean's insistence that her mail go to the office was another obvious indicator. "An indicator to women a whole lot smarter than me," she bemoaned aloud. Staring at her reflection, she realized that he'd had no intention of their relationship being anything more than a short-term affair—an affair.

As she straightened her hair she mulled over the problem of getting her things out of Dean's flat. She suddenly thought of a solution to that problem and also to her continued lack of cash, not that she'd needed any since her arrival, but knew she soon would.

She hurriedly donned her favorite jeans and t-shirt and went down to the library. She got online for the needed telephone numbers and then breakfasted with Millie, after which she and Kyle drove her to the station in Lottie's car.

When Erica met with Mrs. Hill late in the morning, she entered shyly and set up for the interview. Expecting to get right to it with her down-to-business centenarian, she was surprised when Lottie said, "Tell me how things are coming together for you."

"Me?" asked Erica, immediately regretting it.

"I wasn't aware of anyone else in the room," said Lottie with a sly smile.

Erica felt embarrassed. "Yes, well, I went along to take Millie to the station this morning."

"And was that difficult for you?"

"It really was, Lottie. We met only a week ago, which seems impossible to me."

"I hope it's all right that she told me how you met.

Yesterday, when she brought my dinner, I interrogated her," admitted Lottie shamelessly.

"About me?"

"I had her fill me in on a few of the details of your 'train-wreck.' Don't blame her. I winkled it out of her," said Lottie. "Do you read Jane Austen?"

Erica smiled. "Mrs. Jennings in *Sense and Sensibility*."

"Oh, I can see that we will get along very well together. My nurse loved the movie so much she took me into her sitting room and made me watch it with her. I can't remember if the word 'winkle' was in the book or just added for the movie. I think it must have been in the book, too." Lottie looked blankly at Erica momentarily before saying, "No matter. Have you made all your arrangements for being here?"

"Mostly yes, but I must move out of your grandson's bedroom and into another before he returns. I was in there for days before I knew it was his."

"It isn't his room. It belongs to me, at present. As for your moving out of it, I don't think so. I'm trying to teach him to be flexible, you see. Besides, I like knowing that you are in the nicest room with the en suite. You may think I'm hard on him, but I'm going to die soon, and he has to learn some important lessons before I go. His parents died a few years ago, tragically. My son, Gregory and his wife, Jane."

Erica saw Lottie's face pale. "I didn't know," she said sympathetically. "I'm very sorry for both of you. My mother died not long ago."

"Millie told me."

"It helps knowing that about your grandson. It explains a few things."

"It may be my fault for pitting him against you, but like I said, there are some things he simply must learn. Now, as for your settling in, is there anything you need help with?"

"Kyle took me to the post office after we took Millie to the station, and with his help, I finally got some cash. I get paid electronically to my bank back home, so I've not had access to cash. I fixed that this morning and have it set up so I can now transfer funds electronically into my debit card account."

"Very good," praised Lottie. "So you met Kyle, then."

"Yes. He drove me. I also mailed my apartment

key to a moving company in London and sent a text to my ex to have everything of mine put into one room, so there'd be no confusion. My things will be stored until I get back." Erica's sense of accomplishment was overlaid with loss.

"What you just said, 'sent a text to my ex,' would make great lyrics for a song, don't you think?" asked Lottie, teasingly.

"I missed my calling, apparently," said Erica flatly.

"I'm just trying to cheer you up, child," said Lottie with concern.

Erica nodded, and then remembering her directive to speak up, said clearly, "I know."

"I used to collect ditties, as a child, when the first war came. Do you know what a ditty is?"

Erica smiled genuinely. "Not really."

Lottie beamed with the pleasure of seeing Erica smile. "Perhaps we should check the dictionary and see if it's a real word."

Erica realized that her mood affected Lottie's and determined to be more fun. "I thought it might be one of those language things I'm finding it hard to pick up here—like, 'Before leaving on 'holiday' be sure to 'post' your letters, and put your 'kit' in the 'boot' of the car, which is in need of 'petrol.'"

Lottie laughed heartily, sending her into a coughing fit. "I'm fine. I'm fine," she said, waving her handkerchief, as she laughed and coughed.

Erica watched the door, half-expecting Nurse to appear and show her out by her ear. She handed Lottie a glass of water and then quickly got online. When the coughing subsided and Lottie had recovered, Erica said, "I looked up 'ditty' in the online dictionary. It means a short, simple song or a poem intended to be sung."

"We're on the internet?" asked Lottie excitedly.

"High speed broadband. Got it this morning."

"Oh, that was quick. Graham can get things done. I'll say that for him."

"He seems unhappy. Well, he was certainly unhappy about my coming."

"I'm trying to teach him to stop interfering. His cousin John is an expert at it, but I don't buy into any of it."

"I think he's protective of you." Erica was defending Graham and wondered why.

"I don't need his protection," declared Lottie.

"No," said Erica, "I can see that for myself."

"Are you a fighter, Erica, or a runner?"

"Oh, a runner, definitely," she answered without hesitation.

"I'm a fighter. I don't recommend it to everyone. It has its downside."

"I should think," agreed Erica.

"How are you getting on with the paper sorting?"

"I've begun organizing them by categories as I was getting the dust and spider webs off. I will have more time now that Millie isn't here to put me to bed all the time," she said, smiling.

Lottie smiled back at her affectionately. "The doctor told me that you are to rest, so you will be on your honor to do so until he says differently. Have you found anything interesting, yet?"

"It's all fascinating and incredibly tempting, but I'm trying to be methodical, so I haven't read anything yet."

"Well then, ditties," said Lottie, switching tracks abruptly. "I was just a child when the Great War came. It was the war to end all wars, or so we thought. I was just a tot when it started. My family had lived here at Cairnview, but a few years. My father had the house built. I found out later that my grandfather wanted us to live in Glasgow, so my father could be on hand at all times for the business, but my father was determined to build here. I can't imagine being anywhere else, now, but I think my mother was lonely here.

"When I got much older, my mother told me that my father had wanted to commute to the city, which took much longer then, so as to have a prestigious address in the country. Not sure how prestigious it ever was. My father couldn't get anyone to sell him a piece of land in the wealthiest area, so he had to settle for this spot, which was lucky for my mum."

Erica didn't looked up, making many notes for future reference.

Lottie cleared her throat and paused momentarily before continuing. "She didn't want all that competition. He bought this land off what was originally part of the inn's acreage. His whole intent on living here was to impress his Glasgow associates, I've realized. He probably wanted the freedom of living on his own in town, too, as much as anything. Hard to say whether he was faithful to my mother." She looked blankly at Erica.

"Ditties," prompted Erica with a smile.

"Oh yes, that's where we were. The ditties are all I really remember about the first war, except that the house felt strangely happier. We housed some officers here towards the end of the war, because—I learned later— some trench warfare training was conducted in Stirling."

"By the time it ended, I was almost seven. My brothers were, I suppose, about nine and eleven. Robert was the eldest and Edward was younger. My father was hard on both of them, but particularly Edward, because he was rather frail and didn't like the rough and tumble, like Robert did. It was Robert who taught me all the ditties. I remember him going on about wishing he was old enough to join the army."

Lottie cleared her throat again and took another drink of water. "My mother's oldest sister's husband was killed at the very end of that war. I remember Aunt Isobel coming to us and bringing along her two children. She was inconsolable at the injustice of his surviving so much of the war, only to be killed in the final days. My mother didn't know what to do for her.

"My father stayed in Glasgow for days at a time to avoid it all. He was in a reserved occupation, because shipping was essential. My auntie hated him for that, and they had a terrible row one night. He said the most awful things to her. I remember that quite vividly. She left in a hurry the next morning, and Mum never saw her again. I did happen to see her once more, but no matter. That's for later. So many memories."

Erica sat silently, watching the emotions play over Lottie's face.

Without warning, Lottie began to sing,

"Au revoir, but not Good-Bye, Soldier Boy.

Brush that tear drop from your eye, Soldier Boy.

When you're on the deep blue sea,

Will you sometimes think of me?

I'll be waiting anxiously, Soldier Boy."

Tears were rolling down hers cheeks, so Erica reached for a tissue and handed it to her. Lottie looked up, staring at Erica as if she didn't know her.

She's somewhere else, thought Erica, another place and time. She kept silent, so as not to jolt her back too harshly.

Lottie wept, dabbing the tears from her face now and then, and then smiled sadly at Erica. "That was a ditty."

Erica felt sad, but it wasn't for herself. Rather, she felt Lottie's deep sadness, inspired by the mournful song. "Yes. Did you lose someone close to you in that war?"

"No, not that one. I think I'll rest, Erica. We won't try to meet again this afternoon, as I had previously hoped. Remembering is tiring business."

"I know," said Erica compassionately.

"I know you do, dear."

Erica spent the rest of the day in the library, trying to put the papers in some kind of chronological order, but it wasn't going to be as easy as she'd hoped. There were many letters, only some of which were dated. It didn't take Erica long to recognize Lily's handwriting, for she was the author of some of the cryptic personal notes scattered throughout. One little piece of paper was particularly crumpled and drew Erica's attention. She opened it gently, so as not to tear the aged paper. It read simply, "I'll never be happy again!"

She took the picture albums to bed with her that night, so she could memorize the faces of the family. Soon, she could identify each of the Maitland's faces with ease. In the oldest album, there were pictures of Lily as a child, the youngest of the three sisters—not plain, but ordinary, and noticeably shy. Isobel was the oldest and very pretty, Erica thought. Anna was second oldest—tall and nice-looking.

One page in the album held the wedding portraits of the three Maitland brides. The eldest two were radiant. Lily was lovely in her beautiful satin gown, but she looked melancholy, Erica thought.

In another album, there were lots of baby pictures of Lily's children. There were several pages of photos of Lily with her small children on outings, but few with her husband. Maybe he was the photographer, thought Erica.

There were pictures taken by the castle and at the local fair. Lily looked her prettiest in a photograph taken at a picnic with a spaniel puppy on her lap. Erica couldn't stop looking at it. She found it interesting that sometimes the plainest children grow up to be, if not beautiful, certainly striking. Lily was striking with her high cheek bones and large eyes.

The pictures of Lottie, especially, interested Erica. She had a head of dark hair as a baby. She seemed a normal, happy child in the pictures, as did her brothers.

The family was noticeably well-to-do, thought

Erica. She remembered a school friend in Omaha, who lived in the poorer north side. Erica's family lived outside the city, but she attended school with the north Omaha children. Her mother was careful to dress her simply and avoid any semblance of wealth. The girl's name was Kimberly, and she believed that rich people had no excuse to complain about anything. Erica remembered that conversation and had given it some deep thought over the years. She'd concluded that everyone has problems—just different problems.

She could tell by the family pictures and estate pictures in the albums that everything they had screamed of wealth, from the car to the elegant clothing to the fine furnishings. Of course, money couldn't buy companionship, and Lily was lonely, thought Erica. Who did she have to share things with?

Erica wondered what the rest of Lily's life had been like and paged through the last album. The last picture taken of her was labeled 'summer of '69, age 88.' To Erica's surprise, although she appeared to be very frail, Lily smiled prettily at the camera—not just her mouth, either. Her eyes were smiling, too. She looked peaceful, thought Erica, and content—even happy.

Before dropping off to sleep, she texted Andrea, **R u dating some new bad boy? Haven't heard from u.**

When she went up to Lottie's room the next morning after their late breakfast, she was distressed to learn that Lottie wasn't feeling well. Nurse met her at the door and said that she'd had a bad night.

"All these memories," whispered Erica. "Are they a good idea, then?"

The nurse stepped out into the hall. "Good memories work like medicine, and the bad ones, well, we have to take the bad with the good. She wants this time with you, so who am I to tell her otherwise? I care for her, but I'm not in charge of her. Do you see the difference?"

"I think so," said Erica.

"Everyone lives their life and takes their chances every single day. Whether it be getting into a vehicle or an airplane, riding a horse or just doing what makes life worthwhile. I try to make sure that she is still allowed to do that. She wants very little these days, so I think we should give her what she asks for."

"Her grandson will kill me if anything happens to her."

178

"He has no room to talk. He's upset her plenty. I better keep my mouth shut on that count, though."

"And you don't recommend I spare her anything unpleasant as we go through her mother's papers?"

"Absolutely not!" said Nurse. "She is in charge of her own life, and she always will be, as long as I'm around. Do you know why many old folks get shut up in institutions?"

Erica shook her head.

"The younger generation doesn't want to worry about them. It's concern for themselves, not their elderly parents, that drives it. Not every time, but often."

"Do you have children, Nurse?"

"Yes, three, all grown. I think you better call me Joann. Run along, I need to check on my patient. Wait until tomorrow then, all right?"

"Sure, but can I sit with her so that you can get some rest? If she had a bad night, I suppose you did, too."

"Maybe later, but probably not. I can rest when she does. Thank you, anyway. You should get out."

Erica went downstairs to the library with the picture of Lily and her handwritten note that she had intended to share with Lottie that morning. She went from

179

there to the kitchen to see if Fran was still around. She was gone, but Erica found some little cakes in the refrigerator and put them on a plate. She filled a glass with milk and was about to indulge when Kyle came through the kitchen door.

"Hi," he said cheerfully. "Want to share those?"

"Sure, I'm just eating out of boredom. I'll get you a glass of milk." She started to get up.

"Stay where you are. I know my way around." Seeing that she was waiting for him, he said teasingly, "Well, eat up. Graham thinks you're too skinny!"

"Graham never looked at me," argued Erica. "He merely scowled in my direction every time we were in the same room. He hates me."

"I wouldn't be so sure." Kyle sat down across from her. He put a whole cake in his mouth at once and washed it down with milk.

Erica watched the process in amazement. "I'd like to get out for a bit. Mrs. Hill isn't up to talking today, so I have lots of time, but I'm too out of shape to do any long hikes, yet. Can you recommend something less challenging?"

"How'd you like to take a drive around and see a

little of the countryside from my battered little car this afternoon?" Kyle grinned at her. "You folks have a late breakfast, so I could buy you a late lunch in Stirling. You've seen a little of Cambusbarron, already."

"Oh, I'd love it, simply love it!"

"Do you want to get to some museums or mainly monuments and scenery this time?"

"Scenery, please."

"Do you ride?"

Erica looked up hopefully, taking a little bite of cake. "You mean, like horses?"

"Yes, horses," said Kyle, teasing her with his eyes, as he swallowed another cake whole and finished his milk.

Erica laughed, enjoying his easy manner. "I grew up with horses. I'm a good rider. I know how to take care of them, as well."

Kyle grinned. "Don't tell Mrs. Hill that, or I could lose my job."

"I won't be here long enough for you to worry about it," assured Erica. "Do you think I could ride, sometime?"

"Let me talk to Mrs. Hill. They are her horses."

"Of course."

Chapter Eleven

Although neither the doctor nor the nurse thought the situation dire enough to call in the grandchildren, Lottie had not asked for Erica to come to work on the memoirs and had agreed without argument when it was suggested that she have complete rest for a few days.

Erica toyed with the idea of making a quick trip to London to sort herself out, but in truth, the arrangements she'd already made were, by far, the wisest course for her to take. As for finding somewhere else to live, that could be put off until this assignment was finished. Just thinking about the trip tired her, reminding her that her body could still use a few more days of rest, so she did as the doctor recommended and stayed put. Joann told her that Lottie, too, had hoped she would take it easy, so together they could proceed with the project well-rested in a few days.

She got a text from Andrea. **Seeing someone nice for a change. Dean has put me off bad boys. LOL**

It was a full five days before Lottie was well enough to meet with Erica. She used the time to good advantage and spent hours in the library, sorting through papers, even cataloguing them electronically, once she'd scanned each with the little desk scanner she'd brought with her from London. It was a time-consuming exercise. She may not have been so thorough about it if Lottie had been well enough to interview, but since she was not, it filled her time.

The financial papers meant little to her, although they were put in chronological order with ease. She knew she'd have to trouble Lottie for more direction when it came to them, but the others categories were arranged chronologically in very general time periods including any information about Lily as a child, then as a young mother, and finally as an older woman.

Erica worried that her approach was almost juvenile, but it was the best she could do until she could meet with Lottie again. So far, she had only allowed herself to read enough from each document to enable her to put it in one of the time periods. She didn't know why, but reading the messages contained in the letters made her feel slightly ashamed, as if she were an eavesdropper, so she read only as much as necessary.

With so much time on her hands, Erica caught up with news from home online. She was aware of the terrible flooding of the Missouri River, which was affecting neighbors to the east of where she'd grown up. She was amazed that even the interstate highway had flooded, forcing its closure. She thought about calling her dad, but decided not to.

She also read novels from the library outside under the trees, talked to Andrea on the telephone, and tended to the horses with Kyle. She didn't ride, because Kyle had yet to get permission from Mrs. Hill, but she enjoyed just being around them. When Kyle saw that she knew her way around a stable, he let her take the mare out of the paddock on a lead. He laughed at her when she said that the poor mare was jealous of the other horses, but humored her by telling her to feel free to take the mare out for walks whenever she thought she was depressed.

Kyle's time for recreation was scarce with his law classes and related studies, but he did take her on a second drive into the village to buy a few necessities.

By Sunday night, Erica had survived another long weekend, but Joann had told her that afternoon that Lottie would be ready to meet with her the following morning.

Erica had finished the first phase of her project,

and with everything tidy now and retrievable, she decided to tackle the handful of photos that she had found, not in the family albums, but in Lily's private stash. She thought lots could be learned by a photo if one paid close attention to details. One in particular drew her attention, so Erica decided to take it to show Lottie in the morning, along with the other items she'd intended to show her earlier. With nervous excitement, she went to bed with the photo albums and turned their pages until she was finally able to sleep.

She awoke to the sound of a lawn mower and got ready for her day. She was halfway through her breakfast when she realized she hadn't thought of Dean. She'd gotten a text from him the night before consisting of one word—'done.' Assuming that meant he had her belongings gathered, she'd texted the moving company to move forward. Then, she'd forgotten him—breakthrough, she thought victoriously.

Erica sought out Joann's reassurance that Lottie was back in good form and questioned her again about keeping anything from her. She was kindly told to do the job as described and to leave the nursing to the professionals. With a smile of encouragement, Joann pushed her through the door, where she found Lottie sitting up in a chair by the window.

"How are you, Mrs. Hill? You look very well."

"Thank you. I'm well-rested. Call me 'Lottie.' How about you?"

"I read three books," answered Erica sheepishly.

"Good for you. I've decided to get up and about before our sessions, instead of afterwards, or sometimes not at all." She laughed, her eyes shining brightly. "I can see my horses from my bed, too, but I always feel it's a bit of an accomplishment to get up and dressed like ordinary people."

"Do you ever get out at all anymore?"

"No, I haven't felt inclined for a long time. My rose garden was once my passion, but when my son and daughter-in-law were killed, I took to my bed and have pretty much stayed here."

Erica nodded. "I understand. I really do. I felt the same for a long time after my mother passed away."

"An advantage for the elderly," said Lottie, "I was allowed to stay there, and you were not."

"True," said Erica, impressed by her insightfulness.

"Kyle has been up to see me and says he'd like to

take you riding. I've seen he's already trusted you with my old mare, Fancy. She just loves getting outside of the fence, doesn't she? I suppose it's her equivalent of my getting up and dressed. We are a couple of old ladies, Fancy and me. Anyway, it looks like you have a way with horses and obviously some experience, so I've given my permission for you to ride, but you must promise me you'll follow Kyle's directions and lead."

"Of course! I'd rather die than hurt one of your horses!" exclaimed Erica.

"Let's not get over-dramatic, child. I still have excellent perspective," admonished Lottie.

"I was in dire need of perspective when I first came here," confided Erica, "but I think I've made progress."

"You're gaining a little more each day. Distance from one's problems is the only way sometimes. If you are too close, you can't see the solutions. A little distance from high emotion is always a good idea, too. Spending some time with the horses won't hurt you, either. They can help more than people realize. I think they have the capacity to empathize with us, but don't write that down. It sounds a little dotty, even to me," said Lottie with a wink.

"Hearing about your experiences and Lily's

struggles, and even your Aunt Isobel's ordeal in the Great War has definitely given me some perspective. My troubles have diminished in size and importance, and I thank you for that."

"I do believe you are smiling more," said Lottie provokingly. "Do your outings with Kyle have anything to do with it?"

"No," said Erica embarrassed, leaning over her computer to hide her face. "Well, yes, getting out was wonderful, but it's only been a couple of times. He is too busy with school to waste too much time taking me sightseeing. You don't miss much, do you?"

"No, I don't," said Lottie. "You could drive my car anytime you wish. I should have told you that before."

"Oh no, I'm not a driver in this part of the world. I'm sure I wouldn't remember what side of the road to drive on if any quick-thinking was required. No, but thanks," said Erica.

"Do you have anything for me from the treasure trove?" asked Lottie eagerly.

Erica pulled the items from the folder. "I do. I'm sure these two photographs are of your mother. The one of the picnic was in one of the albums, so not really new to you, but the other fell loose from a pile of letters from the stash. I apologize for that. It would have been very helpful to know which letter it came out of, but I'll do my best to figure that out."

Taking the photos, Lottie teased, "You aren't going to start apologizing again, are you, Erica?"

"I think I've been doing it all my life. Hard habit to break," said Erica.

"Well, you are safe here, and I hope you will relax and enjoy your assignment as much as I hope to do. While feeling poorly, I was working on my memoirs, all the same. Memories came to me in dreams and during my waking hours, as well."

"What kinds of memories?" Erica turned on her recorder, excited to hear more stories.

"Sad ones, mostly," said Lottie wistfully. "This sounds terrible, I know, but I've buried so many loved ones, I've truly lost count. I always pushed on, trying not to let the grief catch up with me. I should have faced it head-on, I realize now, but things were always so pressing. At the time of my first memory, we were at war with Germany. That's when I learned the ditties we talked of before. It was such a terrible war! To you that may sound silly, because of course, all wars are terrible, but the Great War was trench warfare, and the conditions in those trenches defied description. I've read much about it since, and I have often wondered why there weren't more desertions. Of course, deserters were shot, which would be deterrent enough for most people, but beyond that, our culture dictated that we buck up and bear whatever was our lot—the stiff upper lip thing. Not to make light of your troubles, dear, but having our heart broken was low on the scale of legitimate complaints in times of war. We were taught to buck up, so I did."

"Was your heart ever broken, Lottie?" asked Erica.

"Hasn't everyone's?" Lottie reached for her reading glasses and raised the photos up into the light. She gasped with delight. "This is my mother, all right, but I don't remember her this way. She was quite beautiful, wasn't she?"

"I think so. She looks very happy sitting on the rock in the sunshine. She was obviously hiking, or that's how it appears to me."

"Yes," agreed Lottie. "Her boots are laced up over her trousers and her checked man's shirt is blowing in the breeze. She isn't fussing that her hair is being blown to bits, either, which is most out of character. And the most telling thing of all is that she hid the picture from my father. How interesting."

"Perhaps she'd found she loved hiking and feared your father would squelch it, thinking hiking wasn't an acceptable activity for his wife, since he was so determined to present a certain image," suggested Erica.

"That's a possibility, I suppose. I like the picture of her with the spaniel. I remember it vaguely. The dog belonged to my mother and was the first she'd ever had that she could call hers only. She always had a dog after that, though. What a lovely surprise for me today. Well, done."

Putting the photos back into the folder, Erica was pleased to have given the woman joy. She was wholeheartedly happy that the project was proceeding so slowly. Its snail-like pace was suiting her, and she determined she was going to do some hiking of her own, just as soon as she had all her strength back. She kept back the note that Lily had written, determined to show it to Lottie the next time. No sense killing the mood, she thought.

Lottie surprised them both by talking far longer

than in any session so far. She told several funny tales she remembered of her childhood—about their nanny, in particular. She laughed heartily reciting the pranks they pulled on her. She talked about each of her brothers in detail, remembering their unique personalities and how she had always wanted to protect Edward, even though he was her older brother. Her reminiscing saddened when she relayed the details of their nanny's death, and at that point, Erica suggested they stop.

Nurse Joann had the same idea and opened the door. She asked, "Are you ready for a rest, Mrs. Hill? You don't want to overdue on your first day back at work."

"Tomorrow, then," said Lottie, and Erica excused herself, making for the kitchen, and later, the stables to talk to the horses.

The household fell into a comfortable routine. Lottie and Erica had their sessions, sometimes surprisingly long. Erica took more photos up to show her, and Lottie reminisced about whatever came to mind. Erica shared Lily's sad note, and Lottie remarked that the note was more in keeping with her memory of her mother than the happy photos had been.

Together, they looked at the picture album of Lottie's youth. Lottie talked more about her nanny, who she loved, and her governess, who she did not love, or even like. One morning, Lottie shared bits of her education, and proceeded to talk fluently in French, amazing Erica, and having a good time doing it.

Erica came to believe herself an asset to the project, for Lottie reminded her often that writing down a memory wouldn't be nearly as entertaining as telling one to an interested listener. Erica had replied, "I think it's all fascinating."

As they were finishing up one day, Lottie said, "Now, I want to hear what you've discovered from the letters."

Erica was eager to please her. "There are a few old letters from your grandmother from Liverpool, concerning money, and then quite a large number of short letters from someone who always signed with just a 'W.' They've all been scanned and catalogued electronically."

"But have you read them?" asked Lottie firmly.

"I admit, as much as my curiosity encourages me, it seems hard to do. I could bring them up for you to go through slowly. The dust and spider webs are gone, so they shouldn't send you into a coughing fit."

"I think we will stop for today. We've covered many lovely anecdotal moments, which I am happy to leave for my posterity, but I want those letters read by you, starting tonight," she ordered with mock severity.

"I will. I promise. Sorry to have procrastinated doing it.".

"Get to it, then," commanded Lottie, smiling. "Haven't seen you riding, yet, either."

"Just waiting for the chance." Erica grinned at her intuitive mentor. "I'm not procrastinating that, I promise."

Erica watched hopefully for Kyle to come back that day, but he must have had classes, because he came much later to put the horses into their stalls for the night. She looked forward to riding, but felt she shouldn't appear too eager. She was supposed to be working—not on vacation.

Erica knew, of course, that she had been charged with reading all the material, in addition to sorting it, however intrusive it felt to her. Somehow, though, she felt the letters might be worrying, and it had pleased her that so many of Lottie's recent memories had been happy ones, most appropriate for a memoir.

Putting it off no longer, she read through a few of the letters from 'W' that revealed little. They, 'W' and his companion—probably his wife—had been to the seaside, had traveled to America, and had seen the Great Pyramids. She would tell Lottie of those, however meaningless they seemed at the moment.

Then, Erica found something interesting. The long letter began, "Dear Lottie," grabbing her attention. It had been dated, so she'd had no reason to read any of it up to this point, but the date alone should have sparked her interest during the sorting phase, she noted guiltily. It was the only item she'd found dated after 1941, which was when Lottie's father had died, after which there was no need to hide anything. She was puzzled that it should have been hidden, but quickly realized that Lily could never have given the letter to her daughter, but had hidden it away, instead. Having convinced herself that she was only doing as she had been hired, even commanded to do, she read it eagerly.

August 28, 1948
My Dear Lottie,

I was never very good at sharing my feelings with anyone. For the first half of my life, it never occurred to me that anyone cared how I felt, except for Nanny, of course. Our father was very worldly, and I'm sure my arrival, as the third baby girl, was a huge disappointment to him. He married me off to your father, like any other bargaining chip in a business deal. I was never in love with your father, nor he with me. Of course, I knew that when I married him, so there was no dreadful letdown later on. Does all this shock you? It shouldn't. I remember you asking me why I let him talk to me the way he did. I told you it was the lack of opportunity what with servants mulling around, and that was quite literally true. But, we were never in love, and I think you sensed it, even as a little child. Divorce was ruled out early on. He promised to make a scandal if I tried to divorce him, and it would have been awful for my parents.

It should come as no surprise that your father's death was a great relief to me. I hope that doesn't distress you. It made things so much easier. Strange as it may sound, it even made the war easier.

Just months earlier, the shock of losing my family all at once cannot be described. You were there, of course, so I'm not telling you anything new. And as grateful as I am that you handled all the funeral affairs and insisted I stay in safety here, I am forever changed by it. Your father was as sympathetic as he was capable of, I suppose.

Of course, I had lost Isobel's affections after the first war, and then the second war wiped out the rest of my family. Thinking back on that event, exactly eight years ago tonight, I remember how numbing it all was. I worried that there was something wrong with me, because the normal signs of grief simply didn't present themselves. I didn't feel anything, which was terrifying. I remembered hearing of my Nanny's death soon after I'd married, and I had grieved for months. I have often wondered if it was the immensity of the disaster in Liverpool that not only protected me from being crushed under the weight of it at the time, but also kept me from ever dealing with it in a normal way. Your father's death came next, and I didn't grieve at all. I'm sure the village minister was quite concerned.

Of course, later in the war, when I learned of your brother's deaths, I was devastated and was able to grieve, and in a way, it was a relief to be normal again, but it still saddens me that I wasn't able to feel what I should have felt when my family all died so horribly. Perhaps, grieving so many in such a tragic situation was more than I could take, so I didn't. The war was like that. It killed millions and forever changed the rest of us.

The real point of my writing is to tell you that after a life full of experiences, I am not the same mother who raised you. You see, I know that Gregory isn't George's child. Don't fuss, I won't breathe a word of it to anyone, ever. I happened to dig through your sewing box one day in search of a certain type of button. I came across the picture you have hidden there. No mistaking the resemblance. Reading Elliot 'Gregory' of Inverness on the back of his military picture only confirmed what I already knew. I'm the only person in the world who would ever guess, and your secret is safe with me. For some time, I thought your early baby explained why you and George married so quickly, but I assumed it was his child until I came upon the picture. I just wanted you to know that you could trust me, should you ever want to talk about it. I would understand much better than you would think.

I have often wondered since the Liverpool Blitz, why you weren't killed with the others, and now I picture you and Elliot huddled in a shelter somewhere, not too distant from the house.

If and when I give you this letter, be sure to destroy it. It is the only way your secret will ever get out, unless someone else finds the picture. I would recommend hiding it a little better, though, to be on the safe side. I know I should be able to talk to you directly; after all, you are my daughter and all I have left. George has been a good husband to you, and I am so glad. You seem very happy most of the time, but I see a lost look in your eyes occasionally.

I have come to love Dede. She has been a blessing to us, but I think her presence in our lives has kept us from having intimate conversations. She will be going back to school in a few days, so talk to me if you can.

Your loving mother

Erica put the letter down slowly, realizing the impact it would have on Lottie and how hard it would be to share it with her.

This is just the thing I have been trying to avoid, she thought. She may not want to include it in her memoirs, for obvious reasons, so why even show it to her?

The answer came as if in Lottie's own voice, "I

will not be treated like a child. Don't talk down to me and don't hold anything back!"

"How well I know you, Lottie," said Erica aloud.

She wondered hopefully if Lottie's mother might have been mistaken? But, just having her mother suspect it, even if it wasn't so, would be upsetting to her, thought Erica.

The letter was just plain upsetting, no matter how one looked at it. Erica didn't sleep well that night.

Chapter Twelve

Their session began as usual the next morning. Erica had thumbed through all of the financial pages, simply to have something else to talk about, so she began with that. "There are many financial papers, as I've said before, and at first glance, it's hard to see the significance, but as they were hidden away, Lily must have felt a need to keep them from your father."

"I knew that at different periods, the fighting became more intense, and my father exhibited hostility towards her, even in front of us—my brothers and me. The fights were often about money, but by that time, I was trying *not* to hear their fights—no longer listening outside their bedroom door. The papers have dates on them, I assume?"

"Yes, They are between 1917 and 1940. Of course, after March, 1941, there was no need to hide anything, because your father had died by then. I've scanned them and put them in order, but haven't delved into their meaning, yet."

"I think they may be important," said Lottie absently, as if trying to remember something just out of her reach.

Erica knew it was time to present the letter. "Lottie?"

Lottie looked up and to Erica seemed so worn out already, she hated to continue, but remembering Joann's counsel, pressed on. "I found a letter from your mother to you. She wrote it to you on the eighth anniversary of the August bombing in Liverpool. How terrible that must have been!"

Lottie nodded. "Yes, it was. Very. I wonder why she didn't give me the letter. She didn't destroy it, either. I don't understand."

"You will understand better, once you've read it. I should have spotted it sooner, because of the date, but didn't until last night. From it, I learned that besides the loss of your father in the war, which I'd already known, that in the August, 1940 bombing of Liverpool, your mother lost some of her family. In the letter, I also learned that both your brothers were killed later in the war, and I wanted to say how terribly sorry I was to learn it."

"Yes, we will cover all of that in days to come. I'm sure it was good for my mum to have written it all down. Those were very sad times."

Erica wasn't certain how to proceed. "Would you like to read the letter by yourself? I can come back in a few minutes. It's very personal, and I feel like an intruder. If that sounds dramatic, then I'm sorry."

"Stop pussy-footing around and read the letter. You've already read it and know what it contains—as I have asked you to do—so get on with it."

Erica read the letter slowly and clearly, watching Lottie closely, in case she wanted something repeated. When she finished reading, she looked out of the window at the amazing view and waited.

Finally, Lottie cleared her throat to get Erica's attention. "So she knew. My mother knew it all that time and never said anything. How incredible! The picture is still in my sewing box. I can't remember the last time I looked at it. There was no comfort in looking at it anymore, and it wasn't fair to George. Would you mind getting it? The sewing box is in the sitting room by the upholstered chair in the corner."

As Erica went down the stairs, the hall telephone began ringing. She was glad to see Fran appear to answer it, so she didn't have to. She went directly to the sitting room, where she found the sewing box with ease. She dug clear to the bottom of the box, finding nothing, and then to be extra sure, she dumped the contents out on the floor. No picture. She was putting everything back into the box, when she heard footsteps approaching.

Fran appeared. "There you are. I thought I saw you come through. Could you run upstairs for me and get Mrs. Hill on the telephone? I've got meringues in the oven."

"Of course, I was just going back up now." Erica put the box back in its place and dashed upstairs. She moved the telephone table closer to Lottie's chair, where she was still sitting by the window. "Telephone call for you, Lottie. The photo wasn't there. I dumped out everything to be sure."

Erica watched on worriedly as Lottie went pale and reached shakily for the telephone. There was nothing more that Erica could do, so she went out quietly and closed the door. She wondered if Lottie had forgotten that she'd moved the picture to a better hiding spot, realizing it could be too readily found in the sewing box. Concerned for her, she tapped on Joann's door.

When Joann opened the door to her, she said, "Mrs. Hill is taking a phone call right now, but a few minutes ago, she sent me to find something important to her. I wasn't able to find it, and it's given her quite a shock. I wanted you to know."

"Thank you," said Joann, "Run along, then. I'll let you know when she's ready to see you again. It's all right. Don't fret."

Erica found Fran in the kitchen, where she was very pleased with the outcome of her meringues. "How did I know Mr. Graham was coming today? Sometimes I think I've got psychic powers."

"That was him calling? When is he coming?" asked Erica with dread.

"In time for tea, he said. Departing now."

"Should I get my stuff out of his room? His grandmother says not to, but you know how I feel."

"Aye, I do, but she won't move on it. I've asked her about it more than once, and she's that sure of herself."

"Why?" bemoaned Erica. "It's just another reason for him to hate me."

"Here's another one who's got psychic powers," said Fran, seeing Kyle come through the door from the tack room.

He winked at Erica and then looked at the kitchen clock. "You told me to come in exactly now, Fran. Are you getting dotty?"

Laughing merrily, Fran said, "Sit down and quit sassing, or you won't get anything."

Addressing Erica, Kyle said, "How about a ride this afternoon? The weather is fine, I got Mrs. Hill's permission a few days ago, and it's been too long since they've had a good, long run. I've had lots of exams this week, or I'd have invited you sooner."

"I'd love to, but when? I'm not done with Mrs. Hill, yet."

"Well, let's say I stick around until you are done. How's that?"

"Sounds great. Mrs. Hill is on the telephone at the moment."

To Kyle, Fran said, "Graham called from the train. He'll be here for tea." Turning to Erica, she said, "She's probably off the telephone already now, lass. They never speak long. You can go back up, but first have some meringue."

Kyle said mischievously, "You don't want to be skinny."

"Actually, I have always wanted to be, and I rather like it, but I'm sure it won't last," said Erica eyeing the meringue greedily.

"Not if I have anything to say about it," insisted Fran, as she placed a generous portion in front of her.

Back in Lottie's room, Erica asked, "How are you doing? Do you have another place I could look for the photograph?"

"I can't imagine where it could be, and it gave me a shock to hear it wasn't where it ought to be. It's not so distressing that it is lost, although that is upsetting in itself, but the questions have to be asked, 'Who found it and who moved it?' It's very upsetting, but no, I don't have another place in mind for you to look."

"Two shocks at once," said Erica. "First, the letter, and second, the missing photo. Since your mother didn't think your hiding place a very good one, I will look through the photos in her stash again."

"That's a good idea, dear. Yes, that would be the place to look. Can't think of anywhere else; I really can't."

"Do you want to continue today?"

"I think we'll talk a bit longer. I so hoped I'd learn more of my mother from her papers. The tables have turned, it seems."

"You don't have to tell me about it, Mrs. Hill."

"I'm Lottie to you, my trusted memoir writer, remember?" She smiled sadly.

Erica's heart went out to her, so she changed the subject. "May I ask who Lily was speaking of when she said her family had been killed?"

"Yes, best to leave the other until I'm more composed." Lottie took a deep breath. "She was speaking of her parents, her sisters Isobel and Anna and several of their grandchildren, all of whom were killed by a single bomb that missed its target in Liverpool on August 28, 1940."

"Oh how awful! I should have realized! Why didn't I grasp that?" cried Erica. "I'm sorry. I shouldn't carry on, but I've begun to think I knew these people. I'm sorry, really."

"Now, now, it's all over now, dear. Today has turned out to be a day of shocks for both of us, it seems."

"She said her whole family, I should have been able to realize it, but I couldn't take it in."

"I think sometimes the mind only absorbs what it can handle. It's a safety valve," said Lottie kindly.

Erica slowly got over the shock and watched on as

Lottie shifted time and place to remember. She began, "The family and servants had all packed themselves tightly into the Anderson shelter, half-buried in the back garden. It was covered with sandbags, but it was virtually a direct hit. I won't go into the details. It would be too much for you. Let's just say that I dealt with the funerals, making my mum stay here where it was safer for her, in more ways than one. I was barely able to cope with it myself. There simply aren't words that are adequate. After the war, we referred to it as the first Liverpool Blitz. Poor Liverpool took such a beating. Most people think of London when they hear the word 'Blitz.'"

"That's true." Erica was still shaken. "So much gets forgotten, doesn't it? The magazine is doing a special 9/11 edition to remember the fallen that day. I can't bear it being forgotten."

"I feel the same, my dear. Maybe that's why I want it all put down in writing." She stopped speaking, and by the faraway look in her eye, which Erica knew indicated that she was deep in thought—not a moment of dementia, as some might think—she knew to be still and wait.

Lottie said slowly, "My Aunts Isobel and Anna were stopping for the night on their way to friends of theirs in Northumberland. They had felt it was insanity to keep the children in London under the circumstances. All things considered, they were right enough to get out of London, as the London Blitz began days later, but so tragic to be killed on their way to safety. I saw them right before they died. I could have easily died with them, and would have, but for my decision to disobey, which saved my life."

Lottie stopped talking and was breathing heavily, as if she'd been running. Erica asked, "Are you all right, Lottie?"

"Mostly, yes. So much death. It was all around us. I'll never forget it. The mothers of those poor children came down from London for the funerals. When they returned to London, the Blitz there was already underway. My mother wondered if she'd ever hear from them, but she never did."

Hearing one tragedy after another, Erica was overwhelmed. Tears threatened again, and when Lottie didn't offer anything else, she ventured, "Would you like to tell me who Dede is before we stop today? Your mother mentioned her in the letter."

"Yes, what a good idea," said Lottie. "You know, we are like a couple of steeds in a lather after a hard run, aren't we? Might be best if we slow the pace before we quit altogether."

Erica had great admiration for the woman's wisdom and strength. "I think that would be very wise."

Lottie took herself back in time and began again. "In the months leading up to the war, I was more than ready to leave home. When I was younger, as the only girl, my father insisted on having a governess for me, so I had no school friends. I had no local friends of any kind. Our father made sure his self-conceived status kept us removed from others. My brothers were my friends during their holidays, but the rest of the time, I was alone. I'm sure I would have done much better living in Glasgow, but as it was, I simply had no one.

"When the war started, my brothers were working in our father's company. Both in their thirties and still single, they were each looking for a way out of their present plight. We'd thought Robert would marry a couple of times, but it never worked out. Edward had graduated from the University of Glasgow—very prestigious—with a science degree, but he, too, was working for our father. He kept up his studies on his own, still hoping to get an advanced degree one day, but he'd become impatient waiting for an out. Both of them had.

"My mother had taken ill about the time I would have left home to start a career or go to university. I stayed at home to nurse her for several years. I know now that she had been suffering from depression to the point of being ill and bedridden most of the time. By the time she got better, I found I was rather stuck, not knowing what to do next. In the summer of 1938, I was twenty-six years old. I think that I saw the war as a way out, as did my brothers.

"You enlisted?" asked Erica, in surprise.

"Not exactly, but one day I found a notice in the newspaper, seeking an assistant to the matron of the Childress School for Girls in Shrewsbury. I suddenly wanted that job more than anything I had ever wanted before, so I decided to use my father's influence to get it. My parents were against it at first, but I won them around. The fact that the school was in Shrewsbury, swung their decision in my favor, because Liverpool, where my grandparents lived, was relatively near. Keep in mind that I was almost twenty-seven years old, and yet too afraid to make a decision for myself.

"You can't imagine my excitement when I reported for work. The matron was a wonderful woman by the name of Emma Stout. She became my mentor and helped shape who I was going to be. Up until then I had definitely been a *runner*, rather than a *fighter*."

Lottie looked at Erica meaningfully and smiled. "I suppose you're still waiting for me to talk about Dede."

Erica smiled back playfully. "It's your story, Lottie."

"Indeed," said Lottie. "In 1938, war was already looking unavoidable, although no one really wanted to admit it. Those who had endured the first war couldn't fathom going to war against Germany again. My father wondered only how it would affect his business, since that was the only thing that mattered to him.

"At Childress, though, I had a different perspective. I was called into Miss Stout's office and that was where I first really grasped the plight of the Jewish people in Europe. One by one, Hitler was taking control of the countries of Europe, and although many disregarded the incoming information, many knew that the Jews there were in danger of being wiped out. A delegation met with Prime Minister Neville Chamberlain, asking that some fifteen thousand children be admitted to the country unaccompanied by their parents. The government agreed to waive some immigration requirements to meet the emergency, and that's where we came in. Miss Stout wanted my help determining how many we could handle. We decided on twenty-five, which ultimately became thirty, because the situation was so dire."

"Tell me more," encouraged Erica. She handed Lottie her glass of water and said, "Aren't I the bossy one, now?"

"You are," said Lottie affectionately. She took a drink and continued, "The mission was called Kindertransport, and through one woman's determination, it all began. I won't go into that, but it was quite a miracle that she got the Germans to allow them to take the children out. They were put on trains to Amsterdam, were then loaded onto ferries and brought to Harwich, in Essex. From there, they went into hostels, or foster homes, schools like ours, and even farms. We were very lucky with our girls. Except for one, they were brave, well-behaved, and tried hard to be helpful. Dierdre Bernstein was the exception. She had crying spells during the day and screaming terrors in the night, so I moved her into my room. I held her sometimes all night long. She attached herself to me, so when I finally came home for good, I brought her with me. My father was still alive, but my mother overrode any excuse he had for not allowing her to come with me.

"Miss Stout suggested that Dierdre, although quite young, change her name to Dorothea Burns, not to forget her heritage, but to enable her to cope with the tragedy and get past its hold on her. Dede eventually married a man named Paul.."

"Davies?" asked Erica with amazement.

"Yes, child, she married Paul, and he has taken good care of her. She doesn't like to travel, so I haven't seen her in years, but we stay in touch."

"She asked the magazine to do the story on you," said Erica.

"She didn't think of it on her own, I think, but that is how it happened, yes. I wouldn't want her to feel that I disapproved of her, and if Graham knew her past, he wouldn't have been so belligerent about it, either."

"And you called her Dede to represent her two names?" asked Erica enthralled.

"Yes, that was the pet name my mum and I gave her. It helped avoid confusion, and I think Dede liked it. Shall we stop for now? I think we've gotten ourselves over the bad spot. Thank you for helping me get through it. Perhaps, you are going riding. I see Kyle is still here. And I must rest before Graham comes. It seems his timing is especially good this time."

"And I am to stay in his room?" asked Erica, cringing.

"It's good for him. Trust me. Now go help Kyle saddle up. You've finally been invited to ride, I understand. He's a fine fellow; not really your type, though. Not to say he's at all shallow, but not nearly deep enough for you."

Erica looked at Lottie skeptically to determine the intent of her remark, and seeing her sly smile, performed a servantile curtsy to the best of her ability and said formally, "Tomorrow morning, then, Mrs. Hill."

She could hear Lottie's distinct laughter all the way down the hall. Standing at the top of the stairs, Erica marveled to herself, I think I feel happy. How strange. It's perspective. That's what it is, and it's about time I had some.

Chapter Thirteen

That afternoon, after a great run on the geldings, Kyle and Erica headed back to the stables. The horses were eager to get home and were hard to hold back. Erica managed her steed very well, and Kyle praised her for it. As they neared Cairnview, they saw a taxi pull into the drive, from which Graham alit, grabbed his bag and stood happily staring at the house and grounds. He paid no notice as the taxi took off too fast, throwing pebbles and gathering a cloud of dust around it. He saw the riders coming in and waved a friendly greeting. They waved back, although after doing so, Erica felt a little embarrassed, realizing that the greeting had to have been intended for Kyle only.

The riders dismounted, and each went about dealing with their own horse. "We don't usually see Graham this often," said Kyle.

"He was smiling," said Erica in surprise.

Kyle rubbed his horse's neck affectionately. "He loves coming here."

"To see his grandmother or the horses?" asked Erica sarcastically, feeling immediate regret.

"Both, and to see Fran, of course," said Kyle watching her.

His brown eyes penetrated hers, but not with scorn—more like pity. "Sorry, Kyle," she said, shaking her head at herself. "I suppose I'm still sore about his reception of me when I first came here three weeks ago."

"Have you been here only three weeks?"

"Not even. I know; London seems like a lifetime ago."

"I could give you some advice, which you probably don't want, but will get anyway if you want to go out riding with me again."

Erica recognized the mischief in his eyes and laughed. "All right, advise me."

"Cut him a bit of slack. You're not very good at being unkind, anyway. You'll just feel badly later."

"I suppose you're right, but I'm already in trouble with him, Kyle. Mrs. Hill won't let me move out of his bedroom. She's taunting him through me."

Kyle laughed. "I suppose she takes her fun wherever she can find it."

"But her grandson takes it very personally. He won't be pleased to see me. I told him I'd refuse his grandmother's offer to stay, and then I stayed."

"Yes, but he knew that weeks ago. Plenty of time to get over it," said Kyle, raising his eyebrows comically.

Erica laughed again, and together they finished putting the horses away. She gave some attention to Fancy and apologized for not taking her along. "Sorry, old girl, we ran them too hard for you to keep up, or we'd have taken you with us. Maybe next time, right Kyle?"

"Whatever you say," he teased. "Here, take these bridles in for me. I'll bring the rest, just as soon as I tuck them up for the night."

Coming into the house alone to return the boots she'd borrowed and bridles to the tack room, she came upon Graham working on a saddle, taking them both by surprise.

"Oh hi," said Erica, hanging up the bridles in their proper places. Feeling awkward, she said unnecessarily, "Kyle is bringing the rest of the tack in a minute."

"Hello," said Graham, looking up from his labor momentarily.

"That looks like a saddle that's had some hard use and good care," said Erica amiably, taking Kyle's advice.

"This was my dad's favorite. I have no idea how

long it's been around. It's my favorite, too. It makes me feel like I'm part of the horse." He gave the saddle one last rub and stood back to admire it. "It probably doesn't need oiling this often, but doing it is part of my ritual in coming here. It is meaningful to me," he said, putting the oil and cloth away.

"I can imagine it would be. Your grandmother told me about your parents, and I do know how you feel, because I lost my mother five years ago. Her death was not sudden, though. It came at us slowly, and in full view, taking its time, relishing its power and our powerlessness."

"Hard to say which would be worse," he said quietly.

"Yes," said Erica.

He faced her and said, "Well, it's not like an ordinary problem one can solve, because you can't change anything. It's all about acceptance, and I suppose I'm not there yet. How's the project coming along?"

"It's coming. Your grandmother's memory is incredible. She almost transports herself to another place and time, and the memories seem to flow out of her. She's always tired afterwards, and we have learned that one session a day is enough."

"I just saw her. I'm expected to say hello and goodbye, and leave well enough alone, but she seems to be doing all right," he said, eyeing her.

"She is, in spite of the more tragic memories, of which there are so many. I find I'm overwhelmed by them myself. Nurse Martin says to do as your grandmother asks and let her decide what she can and cannot handle. I'm already finding it a little hard not to meddle or attempt to protect her from things. She won't stand for it, though. I know her well enough already to see that."

"Don't I know it," said Graham, shaking his head. "She mentioned something about there being papers of her mother's found in the attic. She thought they might interest me and suggested I help you with them in the library, later on."

Surprised for more than one reason, Erica asked warily, "Did she warn you there may be surprises?"

"I've figured out she's testing me, so I'll play along," Graham showed a hint of a smile. "I think something may have changed. It almost feels as if she's softened towards me. I'm sure it's had nothing to do with you."

Erica could tell he was teasing. How attractive he

is when he smiles, she thought. Seeing him smirking at her, she panicked that she might have said that aloud. "What?"

"Nothing; I was just going to say you look much healthier than when I last saw you."

She stared at him bewildered.

"That's a compliment," said Graham grinning.

"Did your grandmother warn you that I am still sleeping in your room?"

"No, Fran did, though, before she left a few minutes ago. Having grandmother playing games with people's minds is a pretty good sign she's in fair form. I think I can take it for a few days. She says the internet is up, so that gives me more flexibility with my work."

"Do we dare switch bedrooms without her permission?" asked Erica deviously.

"Absolutely not! That is just the kind of thing that got me in trouble in the first place. Listen, I've gained her trust enough to let me back into the library again, so I'd rather sleep in the stable than risk it."

"I hope you don't think I know anything about that. I couldn't help noticing the friction, though."

"I'm that transparent?" he asked, egging her on.

"In a word—yes."

"Let's find something to eat. Fran mentioned meringues. She outdoes herself when she knows I'm coming." Graham motioned her into the kitchen ahead of him. "I'm famished!"

After seeing the stew on the cooker, Graham and Erica decided to eat early and then take his grandmother's tray up to her themselves to make sure they knew what her instructions were concerning the work in the library. When they'd eaten, Erica fixed Lottie's tray while Graham went upstairs to offer Nurse an evening off, which she accepted readily. Graham met Erica as she came down the hall with the tray. He relieved her of the tray, and they entered his grandmother's room together. The nurse bustled about, gathering up her knitting and making sure everything was in order, and then, thanking them all and promising to be back in three hours, she left.

Silence filled the room after Joann's uncharacteristically frenetic departure, and Lottie looked from Graham to Erica and back to Graham. "I'm glad to see that you are able to be in the same room. Fran told me how it was with you two last time. Since I've decided to let you go through the papers together, it would be nice if you'd get along. Erica, please feel free to bring Graham up to date on our progress and discoveries, and we'll let him take on all things financial."

Erica jerked her head in surprise, locking eyes with Lottie to make sure she understood the directive. Lottie's barely perceptible nod told her everything she needed to know.

Graham moved into the room further and arranged the tray table for his grandmother. He placed her food in front of her, saying gently, "Fran's stew, tonight, Grams."

Lottie's eyes filled with tears, which Erica saw from her vantage point. Graham, standing over his grandmother could not see the tears collecting, nor was he aware that he'd even used his old pet name for her. It had appeared to come out of him, inadvertently, almost instinctively, thought Erica.

Diverting Graham's attentions, she moved toward the window and asked if the stables had been rebuilt recently. As she hoped, he joined her there, anxious to tell her about it. As he expounded on the taking down of the old stables and building the new ones on the same foundation, but with a new concrete floor, Lottie had time to collect herself and dry her tears with her paper napkin.

She looked at Erica fondly and smiled.

When Graham turned from the window, she was eating her stew. She looked at them, and said dryly, "Having one person to talk to while you eat is company—two seems like an audience."

Giving her no chance to expel either of them, Erica bolted for the door, saying, "Oh, excuse me, Lottie, I promised to call Andrea tonight. This will be the perfect time." She was gone before either could respond.

Graham's face showed surprise after hearing Erica's use of his grandmother's given name, but he held his peace. More tests, he thought.

Graham waited for his grandmother's invitation to sit—hoping, but assuming nothing. When she nodded towards the chair, he pulled it up closer to her and sat down. He felt so happy to be tolerated to sit her presence, he daren't say anything.

She said provokingly, "I'm insisting Erica stay in your room."

"I know that," said Graham.

"Well, that's where she started out," explained Lottie unnecessarily, "and it's updated, which is nice for a girl."

"I know—the en suite is very suitable for her."

"You've changed your tune," she said, goading him.

"I'm all right where I am."

"Well, that's good then. Glad you're not complaining."

"No, I'm not complaining. Can you tell me anything about the papers, Grandmother? What you want done with them exactly, and what they may contain?"

"They contain my mother's secrets, I assume. I think she wanted them to come to light, or why not burn them, rather than hide them?"

"Because she treasured them for herself and didn't have a chance to destroy them. But, considering she lived here until she died of natural causes, with plenty of opportunities to get rid of them after your father's death, or even have someone else get rid of them for her, I suspect she wanted them to come to light, eventually."

"Oh well done, Graham!" she exclaimed. "She may have treasured them, or thought they provided proof of something. But the very fact that she never destroyed them convinces me that she did want them to come to light. I just know it, and the time has come. I'm glad you came today, because I was going to send for you, anyway. The internet is up and going, thanks to you, and it is working very well. If you were to stay and work from here for a bit, would Erica have to be careful not to be online when you were?"

Graham didn't make fun of her. He didn't even smile, but answered, "No, not at all. It doesn't work that way."

"I don't understand how it works at all," said Lottie with awe.

"Neither do I, but if you'd like me to work from here, I can do that for a few days. I didn't bring enough with me to stay very long, though."

"But, your papers could be shipped, couldn't they?" she asked.

"Many documents are on file on my office computer. They could be emailed to me, if you want me to stay on longer. Are you sure you're feeling all right?"

"Oh, yes. Tired, you know, at the end of the day," she said pushing her plate away from her.

"Try a little of Fran's meringue. It's perfect," coaxed Graham tenderly.

Tears threatened again, but Lottie beat them back.

"I want you here because Erica and I have just barely had a sampling of what is in my mother's papers. She says much of it is financial, and I thought you should be the one to tackle that. But, you are free to see anything you wish. Erica will show you everything." She tasted the meringue, and liking it, she ate it with relish.

Watching her, Graham felt such overwhelming love, he wanted to tell her, but he refrained. Tread carefully, he warned himself.

"Are you sure you want me to see the rest of your mother's papers? Because, if you don't, I know I can handle myself. I won't go snooping where I don't belong. Nor would I ever let myself be drawn into a situation where I would trust someone else's judgment above my own."

"I believe you," said his grandmother, watching him. "I require Erica to call me by my given name, so I'm not jolted back to the present when I'm trying to remember. It's so difficult at my age."

"Not according to her. She says your memory is amazing."

"Well, she's just being polite," said Lottie. "I'm glad you don't mind her addressing me that way."

"Not for me to say, one way or the other," said Graham, smirking at her.

Lottie returned the look. "Well, glad to hear you think so."

It was Graham whose emotions got the better of him this time. He got up and walked over to the window. "It's getting dark. Would you like the curtains drawn?"

"Yes, I'll sleep for a while, I think. I will be fine until Nurse returns, so don't bother about me. Run along and help Erica, now. I'm sure she's in the library. Her telephone call was just a ploy to make sure that I'd let you stay, instead of her."

"Do you really think so?" he asked, surprised.

"Oh, I know so," said Lottie smugly.

Chapter Fourteen

Seeing the light streaming into the lower hallway, Graham made his way to the library. There he saw Erica sitting in the lamplight so deeply engrossed in what she was reading, she was not aware of him until he cleared his throat to get her attention.

He asked, "May I come in?"

Erica looked up surprised. "Heavens, yes! It is your home, Mr. Hill."

"Would you please call me Graham? If you can call Grandmother by her given name, you may as well do the same with me. I should think we've fought enough to elevate us to that level anyway, don't you?"

Erica laughed, "Probably. Let's start over then. I'm Erica Sinclair. Call me Erica." She stood and moved towards him, extending her hand.

He shook her hand. "And I'm Graham Hill. I'm pleased to make your acquaintance, and please call me Graham."

"It's a pleasure to meet you, too. Please come in. Like I said, it is your home."

"The one thing I have learned these past two years

is that this is Grandmother's home—lock, stock, and barrel—and she's perfectly capable of making her own decisions. I don't know if you noticed, but something happened today. I feel like she's starting to forgive me. And she even wants me involved in the project and to have access to the papers. That in itself is amazing."

"Some of it might take some getting used to, so I'm giving you fair warning. But I am glad to hear it.

"You are?" he asked.

Erica nodded encouragingly.

"Would you like me to tell you what happened between my grandmother and me to cause the rift?"

"Only if you want to. In the time I've been here— and I give you my word on this—no one in this household has told me what went on between you before I came. All your grandmother has ever said is that her grandsons thought her dotty. In your favor, she did say also that although you were easily influenced, she thought your cousin downright interfering."

"In that case, I want to tell you, because you probably imagine much worse. You see, my cousin John, his younger sister Elizabeth, and I are the all that's left of my grandmother's family. John is divorced, and Elizabeth lives with her significant other in London. Neither have children. Their parents, Frank and Karen, divorced years ago. I have no idea what became of her, but John's father died of lung cancer just a year before my mother and father were killed in the car crash. My grandfather George passed away in his sleep when I was only fourteen. He was eighty-nine. Good innings, as that generation would say."

"Good innings?"

"A long fulfilling life," explained Graham. "Wish that could have been said of my parents. I was bitter about their deaths for some time."

"I felt the same about my mother. I'm sure you knew your grandmother had lost her brothers in the war, as well as her mother's extended family," said Erica. "So much death, and yet she is so amazing. I sense no bitterness in her. Maybe it's all faded away through time."

"Only Aunt Dede is left," said Graham.

"I just learned Dede's story today, as a matter of fact. Do you know it?" she asked, proceeding carefully.

"I always believed her to be a distant cousin, although we called her *Aunt*."

"Come in, then. I'll fill you in on that after you have finished telling me what it is you want me to know.

Sounds like as good a place to start as any."

They pulled two chairs up to a card table, and sat down. Erica looked at Graham expectantly, and he began, "Well, it was my cousin John's idea that my grandmother wasn't handling her finances very well at her great age. He somehow convinced me—and I'm smart enough now to know that doesn't excuse my actions in the least—that I should come and gather whatever evidence I could, to determine if she was being cheated in anyway, by her solicitor, etc."

"I see," said Erica. "Good intentions—bad result."

"Exactly. Well, Grandmother had put a security system on the desk. She could activate it from her room. When I heard the buzzing sound from Grandmother's room above, I knew I'd been caught. It was horrible for me. The library door has been kept locked to me since then. Grandmother must have Nurse lock it before I come, because Fran apparently knows nothing about what happened, and for that I am very grateful. Anyway, I've been banned from the library."

"Until now," offered Erica encouragingly.

"Yes—until now. I think my grandmother has been waiting for me to stop making excuses for myself. She's wanted me to own up to my mistake and promise to make no more. That's not so hard. Why couldn't I have gotten there sooner? So much time has been lost."

"You may have never thought of this, but your cousin John probably had no idea that you could come back with anything useful. Sounds more like he wanted to ruin your relationship with your grandmother, of which he was probably always jealous. So, he was concerned that there wouldn't be anything left for him to inherit?"

"He told me it was urgent, or we could end up picking up the pieces after her death—stuck with all sorts of debt," said Graham. "Just hearing myself saying these words makes me feel so stupid."

"Perhaps, he was even aware of the desk alarm. Maybe he set you up," said Erica.

Graham shook his head. "I can't think that badly of him. Surely not."

"Well, perhaps I'm being a little dramatic. I watched too much television as a child," said Erica, smiling.

"Grandmother told me you just used your telephone call to Andrea as an excuse to leave us alone," said Graham teasingly.

"She's right, as usual."

"That's too bad. I was going to ask after Andrea's health," he said chuckling.

"I bet you were."

Graham laughed heartily. "Please tell me about Aunt Dede. I'm all ears."

The next morning, after sleeping later than usual, Erica found Graham in the kitchen making coffee. She greeted him cheerfully and asked, "How's your room?"

"It's a shambles. Not enough space to turn around in, but I'm going to get Kyle in here to help me take boxes up to the attic. We've used it as a box room for the past four years, so it's no wonder. Boxes of Christmas decorations and ornaments, and also children's books, are the ones I've tripped over, so far. It used to be my room whenever I came, but I've not wanted to sleep there since my parents died. I prefer their old room."

"And I'm in there, now," said Erica with regret.

"That's how Grandmother wants it, so that's how it is going to be," he said, smiling. "Her house—her rules."

"Where do your cousins stay when they come?"

"They haven't been here since my parents'

funeral."

"So, you've stayed in your parents' room ever since they died?"

"Well, I slept in my old room the last time I was here, if you recall," he said flatly.

Erica jerked her head to see his expression, not sure of his intent, and was glad to see him grinning. "Oh yeah, I forgot. In truth, though, I don't recall much, and I didn't know it was your room until the day before you left."

"Cup of coffee?" he asked with a wink. "Fran's is better, but she's not here, yet. She'll be along any minute."

"Yes, thank you." She sat down in the exact chair she'd sat in three weeks before, when she'd collapsed on the floor in front of him.

"Don't you think the concept of time is fascinating?" she asked, out of the blue.

He nodded. "Yes, and so do most people, or so many time-travel books wouldn't fly off the shelves."

Erica glanced around the kitchen that had become so familiar to her. "I came here just three weeks ago, and how long ago it seems."

"It does seem like a long time ago," he agreed.

"But, on the other hand, it's flown by. You know, although I've had just a handful of meetings with your grandmother—as it does take a toll on her, and we have to pace ourselves—I can tell when she's time-traveling. I've seen her transport herself to another place and time and speak of it as if it were yesterday, remembering details that amaze me. When she does that she almost takes me along with her. I'm sounding stupid now," said Erica, embarrassed.

"No, you're not. I read an article recently about time and humankind's relationship with it. It's all about one's perception of time. Childhood seems to drag on and on, like it will never end and then, as we get older, time accelerates accordingly."

"Memory is another amazing concept. One person remembers an event down to the smallest detail, while another, who was also there, remembers nothing of it," said Erica enthusiastically.

"And sometimes people remember the same event totally differently." Graham sipped his coffee and watched Erica's mind flit from thought to thought.

"Graham, I'm stalling," she confessed. "I think—

I'm sure—I was supposed to show you an important letter last night. When I see your grandmother this morning, she will have expected me to have shared it. I feel like such an intruder when it comes to things as sensitive as this, but your grandmother won't let me out of any of it."

"She likes you," said Graham, teasing.

"Well, she's put me on the spot this time—just like she did when she wouldn't let me give your room back to you."

"Mind games. She's a master at it. She gets away with it, too, because everyone loves her and trusts that her intentions are good."

"I trust her intentions, too, but it isn't exactly comfortable all the time. Anyway, here is the letter I found a couple of nights ago. It was written to Lottie from her mother and yet never given to her, although they lived here together and could have talked at any time. I can only assume your grandmother wanted you to know immediately, once it came to light. It may or may not be her intent to include it in her history, that's neither here nor there at this point, but I'm sure she wants you to know of it."

"She could destroy it, if she wanted to keep it a

secret," said Graham.

"But, it's not a secret anymore. I'm sure she realizes that if I know about it, so should you."

He looked at her askance and said warily, "No offense, but I assume you can be trusted with a secret, in spite of your disreputable occupation."

"Point taken. I know how you felt about my coming here, but it was the magazine's full intent to honor your grandmother, not humiliate her. We've had an agreement from the beginning that only she would decide what would get published, and just so you know, I am working for your grandmother—not the magazine—right now. And yes, she could, I suppose, destroy the evidence, but she did tell me she's not a runner. From my perspective, it's not damning, but proves she's human like the rest of us. She's made some tough choices, lived bravely with her mistakes, and carried the burden by herself for many years. I admire that."

"I suppose I'd better read it, then."

"Yes," said Erica, getting up and rinsing her cup. She placed the letter in front of him and took herself to the library, where she closed the door against the world. As soon as she was certain she was alone, she sank into the nearest chair and began to cry, having no idea why.

When she'd cried herself out, she looked out the window to the south and saw Graham on one of the horses, pushing the beast to go faster and faster, as if he were running for his life. Helplessly flung into a family drama that was not her own, with plenty of her own problems simmering on the back burner still waiting to be dealt with, she was about to collapse into tears again, when she heard a sharp rap on the door. "It's open," she cried shakily.

Fran peeked in, gave her a questioning look. "Look who's come to see you, dear."

When Millie stepped into the room, Erica flew into her arms and was received joyously.

As she backed out of the room, Fran said, "Looks like you came right when needed again, Millie."

When Millie saw that she'd been crying, she said, "And here I thought you were getting on all right. I had such a good feeling about you, and except for the red eyes, you do look much better."

"I am, Millie. It's just a little emotional setback that I couldn't explain if I had to."

"Well, Henry is waiting to meet you, and then we thought we'd get checked into the inn."

"Oh Millie, you've come at the perfect time. I need to escape for a few hours. Do you think I could come with you? I'm sure Lottie would be okay with it."

"I should say so, child. It was she who asked us to come. She rang last night after dinner, saying that you'd hardly left the place since you'd arrived and that Graham had come now, and she might need some time alone with him."

"I can't believe you're here. How did you manage it?" asked Erica, dabbing at her face with a tissue.

"I'm like a bad penny, you know, not too easy to be rid of. After I talked to Lottie, I told Henry about the wonderful golf courses in Scotland, and he was packed before I was. We were on the early train."

Millie and Erica sat down together and talked. It didn't take long for Erica to come out of her low mood. "Come now," said Millie, standing up, "Fran has invited us to breakfast. It's time you met my Henry."

As they came down the hall, arm in arm, they were surprised to see Henry coming out of the kitchen carrying Lottie's breakfast tray, with Fran leading the way. He said to them, grinning, "I'll be back in a moment. I've been summoned."

When he and Fran returned, Millie and Erica had already made up some more eggs and toast, and had arranged their breakfast in a casual buffet in the kitchen. They all sat down together and talked like old friends.

Erica fell in love with Henry instantly. He was Millie's other half in every way and had Erica giggling at his many stories. Kyle popped in for coffee, and Fran made him sit down and eat his second breakfast of the day.

Before leaving, Erica ran upstairs to put an overnight bag together. She decided to say goodbye to Lottie and arrange when she should be back. She tapped lightly on the door and entered, smiling timidly. As she entered, Joann smiled warmly, picked up Lottie's breakfast tray and slipped out.

"Hello, Lottie," said Erica.

"Oh hello, dear," said Lottie affectionately. "I saw Graham run to the barn, so I know you gave him the letter. I couldn't do it myself. I'm not so brave after all, am I?"

"I think you're plenty brave. You'll soon get to face him, while I'm running off."

"All is going as it should. He'll be all right. I have faith in him again. Take a day off to see the sights. There is much to see, and you've hardly sampled it. We'll start again on Monday. You deserve a break. You've done very well, Erica—very well, indeed."

"But we've had so few times to talk. We've met but a handful of times. I don't feel like I'm doing anything, really. We talk twice and I get five days off, it seems."

"Not as bad as that. We are right on course, child. You've worked very hard in the library, and we'll get the rest accomplished. Don't you worry now. I need to sort out Graham, but it will be all right. I wish I could show him the picture of his grandfather, though. I can't imagine what became of it. It is worrying me. Who moved it and why?"

"Like I said, I'll look through everything again," assured Erica. "Your mother knew of it, and she also thought your hiding place was less than adequate. It's my bet that she hid it for you. I'm going to give it a rest, and when I come back, we are going to figure this out. I promise."

"I believe you, dear," said Lottie. "Graham looks a lot like Elliot. I wonder if that is has anything to do with why I've been so hard on him. That wouldn't make much sense, would it?"

"It might. I think you'll have to figure that one out, though," said Erica with empathy.

"Elliot was the love of my life, and this is the first time I've said it out loud in more than seventy years. He was such a wonderful man, and Graham is his only grandson. He has such potential, if only he could see it and live up to it."

"It's none of my business," began Erica carefully, "and I'm just a fly on the wall in all this business…"

"But?" asked Lottie intuitively.

"I hope you'll go easy on each other. This can be what brings you back together—you mustn't let it push you further apart. If it does make things worse, I'll feel terribly guilty. I know what you're going to say, but that's how I feel."

"Well, thank you for telling me," said Lottie. "I think that took some courage."

"If I may ask, how do you feel about your mother having known about Elliot?" asked Erica.

Lottie gazed wistfully out the window at her view. "I feel quite relieved that she knew of him, now that I've had time to think about it. It makes him more real to me, for one thing. It's going to take some time for me to get used to the idea, though. It's like I have to rethink my whole relationship with her. But, I think her letter has given him back to me, and I'm grateful for that."

Erica was relieved. "I was hoping that was the case."

Changing the subject, Lottie said, "I just met Henry. He is certainly a fine fellow. I'll speak to Millie, too, before you leave with them. While you are enjoying their company, Graham and I will sort ourselves out, and all will be well when you return. You will return, won't you, dear?"

"Yes, Lottie. I can't quit now. I have to know the rest of the story. I think Graham is still out riding."

"I know; I saw him. Hell-bent for leather, whatever that means."

Impulsively, Erica rushed to the bedside, planted a quick kiss on Lottie's cheek and dashed out, before she could be accused of being dramatic.

Chapter Fifteen

The sightseers were gone by the time Graham came back. He rode back in at a leisurely pace. The horse was well-lathered, indicating he'd had a hard run. Leading him into the center aisle of the stable, he found Kyle cleaning the stall.

"Don't worry, I didn't hurt him any," said Graham grumpily, as he released the girth of the saddle.

"I didn't hear myself breathe a word of criticism," said Kyle. "Besides, with one animal out, it seemed the perfect time to do some serious stall cleaning. Before I go, I'll give the other one a short run. That's not the saddle you normally use."

"I was in a hurry." Graham reached for the brush and ritualistically rubbed down the animal, while whispering in his ear, "You're going to love this, Dandy Boy." When the horse was dry and cooled down, Graham led him to the water tank and watched him drink eagerly. He then let him loose in the back pasture to graze from the new grass for the rest of the day.

When Graham said he was going in, Kyle wandered over to him. "My mum told me that Erica had a really bad time the day she came up here. Millie, you know, the lady who came to look after her, told my mum all about it. She didn't want to tell anyone in the house, because Erica was possibly going to be staying on and working here, but she did talk about it with my mum and Arlene Smith one day when she went to the Smith's for tea. Erica's friend in London told Millie all about it on the telephone, hoping it would help."

"All right. Get on with it." Graham bristled. "If you've got something to say, just say it."

"Well, it turns out, that when Erica went home early from work to pack on the day she traveled up here, she found her boyfriend cheating on her. She stuffed everything she possibly could into her suitcases, which became a huge burden to her, of course. She and Millie met on the train, and Millie helped her manage the luggage at Newcastle when she switched trains."

"All right, so her love life is a mess and she learned to travel light the hard way," said Graham. "What's it got to do with me, especially?"

"It's just that when she finally got here late at night, her taxi couldn't manage the muddy road in that storm that came through, so she tried to walk to the inn from Polmaise Road, and before she got very far, the electricity went out. All she had to see by was a little torch. She finally managed to get to the Smith's cottage, so they looked after her. She was getting ill already then, although no one knew it, yet. The whole neighborhood knows all of this, but I suspected you didn't. You were gone by the time we were learning it all through the rumor mill. I didn't think it was fair for everyone to know the whole story, except for you, so there you are."

"There I am," said Graham, remembering the text he'd gotten from Andrea Frey, asking him to be kind. "That does sound terrible. I suppose that's what you call a really bad day. By the time I was interrogating her in the kitchen, she was at the end of it, so to speak. All right, I am glad you told me, Kyle. I doubt my grandmother would have, and Fran and Nurse live and work here and probably wouldn't have dared."

"If you wonder why I dare, it's because, well, because I do. Just thought you should know."

"It's been quite a day for revelations. You don't know the half of it."

Kyle was intrigued. "Want to tell me?"

"Another day. I have to see my grandmother now.

You're afraid I'll be hard on the girl, aren't you?"

"It did cross my mind. You were pretty brutal to her last time. Fran forgot herself and told me that, but my mum had heard it, too," said Kyle shamelessly. "You can't keep a secret in these parts."

"Suppose not. Well, I'm glad everyone knows what a cad I can be. You're a little sweet on her, I think, aren't you?"

"Not me. We're friends, though. She's good with the horses. I'm dating a pretty little redhead that's been doing your cleaning here. I see her on campus, too."

"Since when has she been cleaning here?" asked Graham, remembering his encounter with a redhead.

"The first time she came was the same day that Erica showed up. In fact, Fran mistook poor Erica for the cleaning girl, at first. Her name is Danielle. She's really quite something."

"You're right, she is. I saw her that day. Just tell her I'm sorry when you see her next," said Graham. "It wasn't my best day."

"She didn't say a word about it, mate, but I'll tell her. I hope it's all right that I told you all that. I don't want to get anyone in trouble. I just thought you ought to be in the know," said Kyle walking away. "It's always better to know."

Graham walked toward the house and muttered to himself, "It's always better to know, is it? I wonder."

Joann had helped Lottie to her chair by the window right after Henry and Millie had come and gone. As Lottie enjoyed her view, Joann had changed out the bedding and done a thorough cleaning of the room. Making light conversation as she normally did while working, she said, "You looked very nice for your visitors this morning. Your new pink bed jacket brightens your complexion and brings out your eyes."

Lottie nodded, absently gazing out the window.

Joann said, "There you are, all nice and clean again." Still getting little more than a nod from Lottie, she asked, "Are you worried about your horse? I saw your grandson ride out. Which horse is it?"

"It's Dandy Boy—Graham's favorite. He's a good rider. No, I'm not worried for the horse."

"That's good, then," said Joann.

Lottie sat quietly. "He'll be back soon, and we'll talk. It could go either way, but Erica counseled me to go easy on him."

Joann said, "All you can do is hope for the best, then. Sometimes, that's all we can do."

"I won't know until I see him," said Lottie. "I've had the truth tucked away for so long; I've nearly erased his grandfather. I never meant to do that. I was only trying to protect the feelings of the living."

"I'm sure you did right," replied Joann, reminding her patient that she was still in the room, in case she was talking about things not intended for her ears.

"Will Graham understand that, though?" Lottie whispered.

"He'll be back soon," said Joann. "I can put you back in bed now. You've been in your chair quite a while."

"I don't want to be in bed when he comes in," said Lottie. "He'll be along soon. Surely, he'll be along soon. You can leave me now and see to other things. I'll just watch and wait."

"If you're sure," said Joann, gathering the linens and moving toward the door. "I'll be nearby if you need me."

When Graham finally came up to her room, he had

showered and made himself more presentable after his breakneck ride. He'd needed the time to think. He checked with Nurse to see if it was a good time to disturb his grandmother and was told that she had been waiting for him.

He did his little tap and entered, surprised to see her still sitting up in her chair. "I'm here, Grandmother. Were you waiting for me? I would have thought you'd be napping or at least lying down by now."

"Well, I was just too riled up about everything," she said wearily. "I saw you come back, and I wanted to talk to you before I slept. At my age, sometimes you hate to go to sleep, even lie down, for fear you may not wake up again."

"Oh, don't say that. It's going to be all right. I'm here now, but let's put you back into bed, first. We won't bother Nurse. I can do this. Fran taught me how to do it ages ago. He raised her up and let her stand momentarily with his support, because she took pride in that she could stand for a few seconds. When her legs buckled a little, rather than moving her into her wheelchair as the nurse did, he gently picked her up and put her on the bed. He carefully straightened her legs, covered her lovingly and fixed her pillows. He pulled a chair up close to her bed, and then he waited.

"Aren't you going to talk?" asked Lottie expectantly.

"I'll let you say whatever it is you waited up to say to me, and then you're going to rest. See? I can be bossy, too," he replied affectionately, his voice breaking with emotion. She had let him put her to bed. It had been so long since he had even touched her, his heart was pounding with hope.

"Oh Gram, darling Gram, I've been so hard on you," said Lottie, starting to weep.

"Oh, Grams, please don't. It's all right; I'll do the talking then. I'll tell you what I've been thinking about while I showered and changed. It's all right, Grams, really. Here," he said handing her a tissue. "I've been thinking about so many things. I would start to wonder about something, trying to process the new information, you know. I worried it around and around, and finally the answer just seemed to come to me. For instance, I know that my dad was never told what I just learned. I knew him, and I know he wasn't in possession of this information. Just nod, Grams, if I'm right. You're too tired to talk right now."

She nodded sadly. "I couldn't, could I?" she asked, dabbing her eyes with the tissue.

"I'll talk, Grams, just rest. In my gut, I don't think Granddad knew, either, and I'll have to hear about that later. Right now, I want to suggest that you loved two men very much. You were *in love* with the first—who, I assume was killed in the war—and you simply loved the second, which was most likely good enough for Granddad George. I mean, he probably didn't know the difference."

Lottie nodded again.

"And you've never told a soul, not one," said Graham. "To me, that's the astonishing part."

"I know. It was difficult at first, but I got used to it over the years. Just let me say that the great lesson I learned from the burden of it was that when you hurt someone, apologies are necessary and good, but when no one is hurt, and your apology is for yourself only and will do more damage than good, then you must be strong enough to be still about it and carry the burden alone."

"Did you ever come close to telling anyone, Grams?" asked Graham in amazement.

"Just once. When George died, your father and I

sat down and had one of the best conversations of our lives. We were both hurting, and I suddenly felt like opening up. I even went so far as to ask him to bring me my sewing box. By the time he got up, retrieved it, and gave it to me, I had come to my senses. I took my little scissor from it and trimmed some imaginary loose threads from my skirt. I had waited too long to say the words and didn't know how to start, and I realized I was just being selfish, anyway. You read his name in the letter, but I want you to hear it from my mouth. Your real grandfather's name was Elliot Gregory, and we loved each other very much. It feels so good to be able to say those words. Erica discovered the letter and deserves to know the rest of the story. She's worried that she did—well, not wrong, but perhaps harm, in showing it to me. I have to trust her to tell me everything or there is no point in anything we're doing. I'll tell you and Erica all about that part when she gets back."

"She's gone?" asked Graham, taken aback.

"Just until Monday. In the meantime, you and I will spend some time together. You'll get used to knowing about it, and I'll get used to having you know." Lottie smiled, but Graham could see the toll the whole ordeal had taken on her.

"You're going to rest, now, Grams. I trust you still have the photo. Do you think I could have it for a while?"

"It seems to have gone missing. I can't really remember the last time I saw it. Many, many years, to be sure. We'll worry about that later, but Gram darling, if I should pass before I see her again, will you tell Erica that I'm so grateful for her help and tell her how sorry I am that I took the easy way out and let her be the one to inform you."

"You're not going to go anywhere. I won't let you. I just got you back." Emotion got the better of him, and he turned to the window. When he'd composed himself, he said flatly, "She just handed me the letter this morning in the kitchen, and then she bolted. So she's not so brave, either."

Lottie laughed tiredly. "I suppose I shall have to rethink suggesting you marry her, then."

Graham looked at her askance. "I'll pretend I didn't hear that, Grams. I'll see you again today, or maybe wait until tomorrow, depending on what Nurse says. Please don't worry about me. I promise you I will be just fine with my new knowledge. It will just take a little getting used to. Promise me you will rest."

Lottie nodded.

At the door, he turned and said, "I love you, Grams. I always have. I'll make no more excuses for myself. I'm just terribly sorry for what I did, and I won't ever let you down again."

He walked back to her bedside and placed a kiss on her cheek.

"All is well now, Gram," she said. "We got through it. I'm so proud of you for learning these important lessons. You will be my heir, and I had to know that you were trustworthy and loyal and humble. I have a sum of money put aside for Elizabeth, and John has already gotten some of his. He's been trying to get more lately, and I suspect he actually thinks I will give the bulk of it to him, simply because he's the eldest. That will never happen."

"I've always thought the same, because he is the eldest grandson," said Graham, stunned by the revelation.

"I repeat. That will never happen," she stated firmly.

"Just rest, Grams. All I have ever wanted was your love and approval."

257

"I withheld my approval for your own good, but I never stopped loving you, Gram. There is just one more thing I want you to learn from me—not my solicitor—in case I die." She put her hand up to keep him from speaking. "I just want you to know that the estate is very large. John has no idea. I've been grooming you for this, Gram, and I can die happy knowing you are ready for the responsibility. I'll rest now."

Graham exited quietly and thought she was already asleep by the time he closed the door. He crossed the hall to the nurse's apartment. The door was slightly ajar, and he could see her sitting on her little sofa folding clothes. He tapped lightly on the doorframe. She motioned for him to come in.

The room she was in was once considered the dressing room for the master bedroom. It had just enough space for her television and comfortable seating. The whole suite, though, was perfect for the nurse. The bedroom and bath had been updated for her and were far larger, but she used the smaller dressing room as her little sitting room, as it was directly across the hall from Lottie's bedroom door. Lottie had refused to have a bell to call for assistance. She disliked the idea and had made herself clear on that from the start.

The suite had originally been Lottie's father's. Lily had once occupied the bedroom that Lottie was in now, and when she died, Lottie moved into it. George had not been offended by her move, as he was up a lot at night and hated disturbing her.

The dressing room—now Joann's sitting room— had brown, geometric wallpaper, much faded from the harsh morning sunlight that had poured through the large window for decades. It oversaw the same view to the east as his grandmother's room.

Joann stood. "Is your grandmother ready to be put back in bed?"

"I put her in bed. She is sleeping already, I think. Are you aware of the bit of drama that has come about because of the memoirs project?"

"Not entirely, but I can't help but know more than I probably should," said Joann carefully.

"That was tactfully put," said Graham.

In a kindly voice, she said, "I have a job to do, Mr. Hill, and it does not include sharing my patients' secrets. You can trust me on that score."

"I already knew that about you, Nurse. I've known

that for a long time." Moving towards the window, Graham could see that Kyle had let the other horses out in the far pasture. He said, "She loves those horses. I hope I'm still passionate about life if I ever get to be her age."

"She's a grand lady," said Joann, joining him.

"You will know better than me, Nurse, but I think she looks especially exhausted today by the whole thing. Did she have her lunch, yet?"

"I offered her something a while ago, when I fixed myself a snack. She'd eaten little of her breakfast, but she refused it. She'll be ready to eat when she wakes, I'm sure. I will sit with her now and keep a close eye. Don't worry, Mr. Hill."

"You know enough about me to call me Graham, I think," he said with a wink.

"Perhaps," said Joann dryly. "Have you noticed how everyone is calling everyone by their given names? The girl's friend, Millie, was a catalyst for much goodwill here. You may as well call me Joann, too."

"Thank you. I would be honored to," said Graham. "You've called my grandmother by Mrs. Hill all this time. Is there a reason you don't call her Lottie?"

"She knows I'm her friend, but her dignity is

spared by having me address her formally. As her nurse, I take care of her most personal needs. I'm a professional. It has to be that way."

"I think I understand," said Graham.

"Dignity is sometimes all that one has left, and if that is taken, too, well, let's just say I guard it. I don't see her as an aged patient. She is the lady of the house. Fran and Kyle address her that way, too, and probably for much the same reason."

"Thanks for explaining that to me."

"It is good that the girl came, you know, Graham. Your grandmother has been living more fully the past few weeks, and that is wonderful, even with all the drama. It's all right. She's living and remembering, and there is always a little suffering when that happens, but it is part of life. Why shouldn't she have all of life while she yet lives?"

"I just want her a while longer now that things are sorted out between us. All I had to do was quit making excuses for myself. Why couldn't someone have told me?"

"I didn't know what she was waiting for. I'm not sure even she knew consciously. She didn't talk to me about it, but I assume she wanted you to get there on your own. She's very pleased you are here. I have noticed that," said Joann.

"Things are finally fixed between us. I'm glad time didn't run out on me before I got it right."

"She never stopped loving you, Graham," said Joann kindly.

They moved to the door together, and Graham waited for her to go out ahead of him. "When do you ever get a break? You are always here."

"Other nurses come sometimes, but mostly Fran spells me now and then. I've wanted to stay put while so much is going on. My patients come first."

"You're a good egg," said Graham. "Friends?"

She turned. "Friends. I always knew you were a good fellow. The apple doesn't fall far from the tree, you know."

"I can think of no greater compliment."

Chapter Sixteen

The first thing the sight-seeing party did was to check into The Little Scottish Inn, where Henry insisted on paying for Erica's room. It was an ancient stone edifice, but upon entering the small reception area, Erica could see that it had been completely modernized. The walls were all painted a creamy white, drawing one's attention to the heavy, dark woodwork and the old paneled wainscoting that had been polished to within an inch of its life.

When the clerk heard Erica's name, he looked at her so intensely, she finally said, "Yes, it's me. I'm the one who got lost in the storm trying to find you."

"If only you had rung us first, we could have met you," said the clerk apologetically.

"It was the end of a long day, and no one is to blame, but me. I'm sorry I gave you so much trouble."

The clerk smiled and told the others in the office to come say 'hello' to her, before he finished checking them in. They were shown to their quaint, but comfortable, rooms that offered all the amenities of more modern accommodations. Erica was pleased with her room that was decorated in yellow and green and featured an old four-poster bed. Millie's and Henry's room was done in blue and white and was equally as inviting.

On their way out to the car again, Erica spotted Ian Smith, who had been so kind to her upon her arrival. She insisted that Henry and Millie meet him. Of course, Millie already knew Ian's wife, Arlene, so small talk of every kind ensued for some duration. Before parting, Ian promised to tell Arlene that they were invited to tea at the inn the following day, and finally, the sightseers were off.

Erica had little time to dwell on the events of the morning, because Henry and Millie kept her mind occupied with their constant chatter. She knew how it was going to be when they fussed at each other about the best route to the National Wallace Monument atop Abbey Craig. It certainly wasn't fighting, or even bantering, but more like a gentle teasing that went back and forth to Erica's amusement.

Once parked, Millie hunted for her guide book and read the full history of the monument, and then and only then, were they allowed to emerge from the car to begin the experience. A bus took them to the monument, saving their strength for the climb to the top of the tower.

Although Erica was nervous about the climb for

herself, she was even more so for her elderly companions, but they were determined to do it. As they made their way slowly up the nearly two hundred fifty steps of the spiral staircase to the top, they stopped at each chamber to catch their breath and take in the marvelous views. Erica praised them, telling them they must come to Mt. Rushmore in South Dakota and climb the steps of the President's Trail. Although panting from their exertions, Henry and Millie assured Erica that they were managing just fine and would gladly take on the President's Trail one day if she would go with them.

Erica received a "poor you" look from a young male tourist they met coming down the steps, and Erica laughed to herself. She understood his message, but also realized that she truly wasn't the least bit impatient with her companions. Their pace matched her strength. She thought they were adorable together. They had become her family.

Overlooking the scene of Scotland's victory at The Battle of Stirling Bridge, the view from the top was as breathtaking as had been promised. They were simply awed.

Erica was delighted when she spotted bits of

Cairnview and the inn, peeking out from beneath the trees, and she pointed them out to her companions. She said, "This really is the 'Gateway to the Highlands.' What did the guidebook say about Stirling, Millie?"

"It's the 'brooch which clasps the Highlands and the Lowlands together,'" replied Millie proudly.

Henry was more practical."That's all well and good, poetic even, but it was built as a fortress and strategically speaking, its position as the nearest crossing of the River Forth, made it the only viable connection between the Lowlands and the Highlands. There has been fortification on the rock since 1000 BC. Its importance in the wars of Scottish Independence can't be overstated."

"Where did you learn all of that?" asked Millie indignantly.

"You read it to us, dear, before you let us out of the car," teased Henry.

"Well, I don't remember that part," she said, laughing. "I thought the brooch part more memorable, I suppose."

They descended again, slowly and carefully, and then took multiple pictures of each of them separately, Millie and Henry together, Millie and Erica together,

Henry and Erica together, and one of all of them, taken by a kindly guide. Having done that, they decided a bit of refreshment was called for and made a visit to the café and gift shop, where they had an excellent lunch and Erica bought a few postcards.

By the time they'd visited Stirling Castle, which took far longer than they had anticipated, the exhausted trio determined they had accomplished enough for one day. Millie insisted that Erica must rest for an hour before tea, so they returned to the inn.

Back at Cairnview, Joann sat by Lottie's bed, watching her sleep. Her breathing had been so shallow at times, that Joann had situated herself as close as possible. Her patient was comfortable, so there was no reason to call in the doctor. Lottie had been through this before.

Graham was very concerned, but Joann had reassured him before he'd left her that she wasn't going to sit there with her fingers poised to dial emergency, but rather wanted to be on hand if needed or to simply be with her patient if she passed peacefully. She said, "As long as she's comfortable, there is no emergency. I know this will sound very strange to you, Graham, but death can be very sweet, sometimes, and it should be."

Graham had asked her how many patients she'd seen out of this world, and she'd replied that she couldn't really say, but they had become her closest friends.

Sitting there, Joann occupied herself by working on a pale blue cardigan she was knitting for her yet unborn grandchild.

Graham relieved her two hours later to have some tea and eat the sandwich he'd made for her and set out on the little table in her sitting room. Then he sat with his grandmother, listening for every breath and looking nervously out over the view she loved so much. "Please don't die yet, Grams," he whispered.

He put his mind once again to the possibility of the lift that he'd wanted to put in earlier. He didn't need John's permission if he used his own funds. Knowing what he did now, he could go ahead on his own.

He could barely take in the significance of being chosen to be her heir and was overcome with much emotion by it, but in terms of coming to grips with the actual monetary aspect of it, he was far from absorbing it. It would take some time. He couldn't bear to think of it now. He couldn't bear to lose her, now. "Please give us more time together, Grams," he whispered.

He so wished he had the photograph of his grandfather, Elliot Gregory. He'd been online earlier, and by signing up at a genealogy website, had been able to find his grandfather's line with ease. The Gregory family of Inverness had a pedigree that stretched out before him, and if he hadn't been already convinced, there was no escaping the truth that was outlined so meticulously by some conscientious distant cousin. He was very disappointed no one had submitted any photographs of his grandfather and was determined to find the one that was missing.

He wondered what would happen if he crashed a family reunion and announced himself as a long-lost Gregory. Seventy years ago, it would have been highly discouraged, but today things were so different. He'd have to think about it. His children, if he ever did have children, would have a right to their proper heritage, wouldn't they? And yet, he knew his Granddad George had been a good grandfather, and he would wear the name of Hill with pride all of his days.

As the hands of the clock moved slowly around, all these thoughts and more ran through his head. Then, feeling his grandmother's gaze upon him, he looked at her.

She asked shakily, "Elliot?"

Graham leapt to her side. "No, Grams, it's just me, Graham."

More alert, she winced from pain. "Get Nurse for me, darling. She'll know what to do."

Worried, he ran downstairs and found Joann sitting outside under the same tree that had hosted the picnic not long before. "Grandmother is in pain. She asked for you," he said urgently.

"Don't worry, now," she soothed, as they hurried back inside together. "She's often in pain at this time of day. She needs to eat and have her pills. Her schedule got off today, but don't worry too much. Her body is wearing out, like it was designed to do. Think how awful it would be if we didn't wear out and die. Go have some tea and stop worrying."

As they parted, she scolded him, "You're worried for her, but you are also worried for yourself, you know, Graham. You are frightened by it, but I assure you, your grandmother is not. She will die one day soon, and it will be all right, because she has lived a good life. For your own sake, your mission is to make the most of each day she is still here with us. There will be a hole when she leaves us. That's for certain."

Graham fixed himself a pot of tea and cakes and took it back to the library. He decided to make sense of all the financial papers, so he could get that out of the way. He doubted there would be much of real significance to be found there, but his grandmother wanted it done, so it would be, before it was too late.

He spent the evening pouring over the financial information and found that it was more revealing than he had anticipated. He hadn't been asked to tackle the more personal papers on his own, and he'd rather die than make a wrong move with his grandmother, so he left those untouched. He kept thinking about the nurse's counsel that there was no tragedy here—just a life well-lived, coming to an end and a deserved rest.

He looked at his mobile phone and wondered who might have Erica's number. The day had been so full, he was bursting and desperate to talk to someone, and she was the only other person who knew what he knew. Remembering she was staying with the Wells couple at the inn, he reached for the phonebook, but caught himself in time, realizing it was after midnight.

He tidied up the library and made his way to his

room—his old room—where he'd always been so happy as a child. For the first time in years, he felt peaceful again. It was a kind of happiness he'd never experienced. It was a mature kind of happiness, he thought. It had nothing to do with pleasure and everything to do with joy.

By Sunday afternoon, after having a nice tea with Arlene and Ian at the inn, Erica encouraged Henry and Millie to take their walk through Stirling's Old Town without her. She wanted to get back to Cairnview, and they understood.

On Tuesday, they had decided to go to Inverness for a week, so Henry could golf and Millie could see the one place on earth she'd wanted to visit her whole life. They promised Erica they would stop back for a few days on their way home and would come see everyone at Cairnview.

Erica was refreshed and ready to go back and face Graham after leaving so abruptly upon presenting him with the letter. Although Henry offered to drive her back, she opted to walk from the inn, something she'd wanted to do. The innkeeper told her where she could climb a stile that provided her a shortcut to Cairnview across a pasture.

He assured her that it was allowed and that the cattle were used to people passing through. This time she had packed light and carried her things easily in her carryall. It felt good to stride out. She felt as good as new again.

She marched along happily, thinking of all she'd learned from Lottie in a very short time. She knew the experience was changing her and making her grow, and she was glad. She gasped when she stepped in some fresh cow dung, and thought of Andrea's prediction immediately. Laughing at herself, she quickened her pace and made for the house, skirting the pasture where Lottie's horses were grazing in the afternoon sun. Kyle had come back to call them in, shaking a pail of oats.

They know the drill, thought Erica happily, waving to Kyle from afar.

She saw him driving out as she arrived at Cairnview. She made for the tack room door, where she'd seen everyone leave their dirty work shoes. She got her offending walking shoes off—her old ones, for which she was more than grateful—and left them outside. She had just stepped into the kitchen, when her cell phone began ringing. Digging her phone from her carryall, she looked quickly at the screen, and seeing Dean's name, decided to buck up and answer it. "Hello, Dean," she answered wearily.

"Hi, babe," he said. "I thought you would have come back to London by now. I was hoping we could sort things out. I know I let you down, but I've learned my lesson. It was a weak moment, and I regret it more than I can say. I just want you back."

To her own surprise, Erica felt nothing for this pitiable man on the other end. "I know you are banking on me being pathetic and running into your arms, crying that life without you wasn't worth living, but that won't be happening. Neither will I be coming back to London anytime soon. I'll be working up here for a few more weeks. My assignment took an interesting turn, and I'm settled in quite nicely. It doesn't matter when I come back, though, because you must know that you and I are finished."

"Don't say that. Please, don't say that," he pleaded. "Okay, I'll beg if you want me to. I need you so badly. I don't think I can go on without you."

Hearing what must be his idea of the weeping, repentant man, Erica suddenly felt nothing but revulsion for him. "All right, Dean, you can stop the act. I may have been stupid and gullible before, but no longer. You see, I'm not buying it."

"Have it your way," said Dean, cynically. "The thing is that you and I had a verbal contract that you would pay half of the expenses for the flat. If you don't come back and be a couple with me, you leave me no choice, but to take you to court."

"How dare you?" shouted Erica. "I will never come back to you, and you will get nothing from me, ever again. As it is, I unknowingly sold myself to you for what I thought was love. Don't you dare call me again, Dean. Don't you dare!"

"Look Erica, just loan me some money, then. I'm in a really bad spot, and it could look like jail time for me if I can't pull some money together quickly. This is all Marshall's fault, anyway."

"Looks like you've come to the end of people to use. Maybe you'll have to start doing things the old-fashioned, honest way and get a real job, or how about selling your car?"

"I never actually had a car," he said.

"So I paid for everything, so that you could have repairs done on a car that didn't exist? No wonder I couldn't get you to take me for a drive in the country or anywhere else, for that matter. You are even lower that I gave you credit for."

"I'm serious about taking this to court, Erica. We had a contractual agreement, and I intend to see you hold up your end."

With shaking hands, Erica pushed the *Off* button to end the call and quickly set her phone on the table, as if it was partly responsible for what had just happened. She sunk into the nearest kitchen chair, and putting her head in her hands, began to cry.

When she was touched on the shoulder from behind, she knew that Joann had come to comfort her. She turned slightly and leaned into her friend, seeking comfort. As her head was gently stroked, she cried heartrending sobs that shook her whole body. When calm enough to speak, she said, "Oh Joann, I have wept more in the last three weeks than ever before in my lifetime. I can't seem to turn off the waterworks."

She mopped her face with the paper napkin at hand, and sighing heavily said, "There—done."

She picked up her telephone and was about to stand, when her comforter said, "It will be all right, you know. It can't be that bad, can it?"

To her shock and horror, it was a male voice, and it was not Kyle's, because she'd seen him driving off minutes before. Unsure of what to do, she simply froze.

It was left to Graham to end the suspense. "I didn't hear much, but I think I can help. Let's pretend we haven't had such a rough start and be friends. Come now, let's go sit down and talk it out."

He reached down, and taking her hand, pulled her up. He put his arm around her shoulders and led her from the kitchen, down the hall and across to the sitting room. It was getting dark, so he gently guided her to the sofa and turned on a couple of lamps before joining her there.

"Now," he said tenderly. "Tell me all about it."

Chapter Seventeen

The next morning, Graham invited Erica to ride with him, but she declined, knowing that her first order of business would be the cleaning of her shoes. "As Mrs. Smith would say, my *clarty* shoes can't be sitting on the step when Fran comes," she said, smiling. "I suppose I could hide them in the tack room, but Kyle would have my head on a platter for that. Or," she added mischievously, "I could just throw them away."

Seeing disapproval in Graham's expression, she sighed and said, "You go and have a good time for both of us."

When he came back in, he noted the offending shoes were gone and entered the kitchen through the tack room, hungry as always after a ride. Erica was there with Fran and they were organizing Lottie's breakfast tray. He said, "Let me take it up to her, Fran. I want to see for myself how she's doing this morning. I'll just wash my hands real quick."

"Fine by me." Fran chuckled. "Those stairs are going to be the death of me."

He thought again of the value of a lift, for

everyone's sake, as he climbed the stairs with the tray. He got a nod from Joann that they were ready for him and entered the room. His grandmother looked even frailer to him than before, and he was truly worried about her. He looked questioningly at Joann.

She nodded reassuringly. "Doctor is coming to see her this afternoon, but she's doing much better this morning. Aren't you, Mrs. Hill?"

"I'm still here, if that's what you mean," said Lottie brusquely.

"Happy to hear you've still got sass, Grams," teased Graham.

She laughed weakly, and Graham breathed a great sigh of relief. She had gotten through another rough spot.

"Now," she said, "I want you and Erica up here in a half hour. Can you manage that?"

"I think so. I'll grab a bite of breakfast, I have a few emails I have to answer and then we'll be up. Eat up, Grams."

Half an hour later, Graham and Erica tapped on Lottie's door and went in, ready to hear her out on whatever subject she chose. Each were hoping she'd tell them all about Elliott, but knowing how she got her fun, they weren't sure she'd be forthcoming, just yet.

Erica decided to leave the recorder downstairs and brought up only a folder to take handwritten notes. This was becoming personal to her, and she didn't want to stare at a computer screen. She wanted to see Lottie's face as she listened to her story. That was all that mattered now.

When they were seated in two chairs by the window, Lottie said, "I like seeing the two of you together. You are the only living souls to know my secret. It feels so strange not to carry it alone anymore. I think the release of it all made me a little ill yesterday."

"We were worried," said Graham.

"I know you were. I'd better start by telling you all about the war years. I've told Erica about my going to Shrewsbury to help at the school for girls before the war. It was actually a happy time for me. I was out of the house and away from the fighting and unhappiness. It did me a world of good. Of course, when I learned the plight of the Jewish people, I was sickened. I kept wondering why we weren't doing more. The English people desperately wanted to believe that some way, somehow, a war might still be avoided. Acknowledging the Jewish problem didn't help that cause, so it was ignored by many. Did Erica tell you about your Aunt Dede, Gram?"

"Yes, I had no idea at all. I was pretty irritated with her when I heard it was she who'd set up the interview for you, but I can't be irritated at her for anything, now."

"Oh, she lost absolutely everyone in her family. My mother spent some money after the war, hiring someone to try to find any of her people, but no one was found. There must be someone out there that knows Dede from her early life, but we quit looking when she asked us to.

"When my mother's family was killed, Dede was very sympathetic. She said little, but did much, if you know what I mean. She was a great support."

Lottie took a drink of water. "I want to tell the both of you about Elliot and me. It was my father's fault that we met at all. He insisted I go to Liverpool to see my grandparents as often as possible. He thought that a girl out on her own was asking for trouble, so to appease him, I took the train to Liverpool regularly. The trains were packed with military personnel, and I felt guilty traveling as often as I did and tried to ignore the posters that discouraged it. As often as every month, I went to Liverpool, which was in itself a bit of a risk for a girl traveling alone, but as long as my grandparents could lay eyes on me from time to time, my father was appeased, so it was worth it.

"I met some girls on my excursions there, and my grandparents had no problem with me going out with them at night. Even at my age, I always asked my grandparents for permission to leave the house, so that my father wouldn't get word that I was being difficult in any way. My friends and I were regulars at the Grafton, a big dance hall. It was the place to go to meet people, and my friends were always looking for anything in trousers. Excuse me if that sounds crude, but they talked of nothing but men— quite tiring after a while.

"Sometimes we'd go there, and you wouldn't believe how many people were packed in there. More than a thousand, sometimes, all of them smoking, of course— even me. It's what everyone did to be more like the movie stars.

"I was always nervous going there, because I knew my father would kill me if he found out. He'd have had all kinds of names to call me for going to such an establishment unescorted. I was always looking around the crowd, fearing someone that knew my grandparents would see me there and snitch on me. It was a younger crowd that went there, though, so I needn't have worried. If you wanted to meet someone young—that was the place to go."

"Is that where you met him, Grams?" asked Graham.

There was a long pause, although not uncomfortable. Both Graham and Erica watched on as Lottie's facial expression softened as her thoughts turned to love. She seamlessly slipped into another time. Erica looked at Graham, hoping he wouldn't say anything to bring her back from her happy place.

Leave her there, thought Erica.

Graham caught her eye and nodded his understanding.

Moments later, Lottie began to tell the story she'd kept inside for decades. "I went to the Grafton several times and decided one night that it just wasn't for me. I had never had much of a social life, so I couldn't pretend to be the life of the party. I didn't like crowds, and why would I, with my upbringing? I told one of the girls I was with that I was going to get a taxi and go home to my grandparents. I got as far as retrieving my light wrap and hat from the cloak room, when a man bumped into me."

Lottie smiled at the memory and paused to allow herself to stay there for a moment. "He bumped into me, making me drop my hat, and before I could pick it up, two or three people had stepped on it, squashing it beyond repair. It was simply ruined, so I left it. It was so crowded there that night, I remember. Elliot apologized over and over for the loss of my hat and offered to buy me something to drink. I thought he was sweet, so I accepted his offer." She laughed, and said, "I was stuck wearing my drabby wrap the rest of the evening and remember wishing he could see my pretty frock underneath it. As the night was rather cool, my grandmother had insisted I borrow it, and I couldn't risk losing it. I could have returned it to the cloak room, but there was no way I was going to risk missing my chance to talk to Elliot."

Lottie paused dreamily and said, "I think I was smitten immediately. We both were, but he was shy and so was I, so it took some time to admit it to each other. We fell in love terribly fast, but there was nothing unusual about that in wartime. It was still early in the war, though. Everyone called it the phony war, because for months and months nothing happened.

"In the spring of 1940, before I'd met Elliot, the Germans took France suddenly and our defeat at Dunkirk happened. It was nothing short of a miracle that so many of our men were picked up off the beaches. German planes were sweeping out of the sky to strafe the thousands of men of the British Expeditionary Force, who were trying desperately to get to the boats. Of course, the larger ships couldn't get in close enough, and if the men were taken out to the large ships, it didn't mean they were safe, either, for they were sitting ducks in the water.

"I tell you all this, because Elliot was there. He made it to a little boat belonging to an ordinary Englishman, who, like so many others, came out in force to bring the soldiers home. For days, back and forth they went across the rough channel to save the desperate men.

"Elliot was helping his wounded friend get into the boat, and that's when he was hit in his left leg. He felt the searing pain and then saw the blood in the water. He told me that he'd since had terrible dreams about those few days of terror. Of course, France fell to Hitler and it was a terrible defeat to our forces, but the miracle of bringing so many thousands back safely gave the country new hope."

Lottie stopped speaking. She was somewhere else,

entirely. She wept quietly, seemingly unaware that Graham and Erica were still with her.

Concerned, Graham finally asked her gently, "How are you doing, Grams? Want to stop for a while?"

Lottie replied, wearily, "Just a short break. I must finish, though. Come back in a few minutes."

"Of course," said Erica and Graham simultaneously.

They went to the kitchen and made some tea. Graham looked in the refrigerator. "I know there is some cake here somewhere. It's early, but I can always eat cake. Fran had to go home early today, but she goes the extra mile when I'm here. She hides the desserts, though. She and Nurse have conspired against me, ever since I ate a whole cake single handedly one Christmas."

"Are you a growing boy?" teased Erica.

"Not exactly, but I've always had a good appetite," said Graham, "especially at Cairnview. Does it do that to you?"

"No, thank goodness. I'm pleased with the weight I've lost, and I'd like to keep it off."

"What?" exclaimed Graham. "You don't want to be thin. No girl should look like the girls in magazines.

They look like skeletons wearing skin."

Erica laughed. "My dad poked at me because I was curvy. He was always encouraging me to drop a few pounds."

"Nice guy, your dad. You looked perfect when you first got here, before you were ill and lost it all."

"Well, that isn't exactly a compliment, but your honesty is certainly refreshing, I must say," said Erica, blushing now.

"I didn't mean you look bad now," said Graham, flustered. "I think you're lovely."

Not knowing what to say, Erica changed the subject. "What was your grandmother like when she was young?"

"She was lively. As a young woman she was striking, intriguing even. I'm thinking of one photograph in particular that I haven't seen in a while. It's not in the library. I've looked. I'd like to show it to you."

"I'd like to see it." Looking into her cup, Erica said, "I've never drunk so much tea in my life."

"Tea is what we do when life is upset by something as small as one's cook quitting suddenly or as tragic as a death in the family. It's the universal solution."

Chapter Eighteen

Erica took Joann her tea and cake and joined Graham as he delivered Lottie's. They found her eagerly waiting for them, and she thanked them for bringing tea. After a few restorative sips, she tasted a little of her cake. When she was satisfied, Graham took her tray, and she began her narrative exactly where she had left off.

"Before I say anything more about Elliot, I should tell you about the matron at the school in Childress where I taught. She wasn't much older than me, and she and I weren't really friends, because, well, she was my boss, and we couldn't go to the cinema together or anything. Someone always had to be at the school. Already in '38, when I got there, the staff was beginning to thin out. Our gardener enlisted shortly after I got there. He was adamant that signing up early was the right course to take. He could pick the arm of the services he preferred, and he chose the Royal Navy. I never heard if he made it through the war."

She looked blankly at Graham, and he coaxed her, saying, "The matron?"

"Oh, yes," said Lottie. "She had a cousin who worked and lived nearby. I think he was considered unfit for service, although we never talked of it, as it was a sensitive subject. The matron thought he and I made a fine pair. She invited him to Sunday teas, but we were just friends. I was very fond of him, but no more.

"Then I met Elliot at the Grafton early in August of 1940. I had eyes only for him after that. He still limped from his injuries, but he was insistent that he would soon be on active duty again. He wasn't really ready to go to work, either, but he was eager to be doing something again and looking for any kind of work, rather than going home to Inverness. Do you know where that is, Erica?"

"It's in northern Scotland. I only know about it, because Henry and Millie decided to go there this week."

"Yes, it's a lovely city in the Highlands. Elliot wanted to take me there after the war. He loved his home very much, but he couldn't bear to sit out any of the war up there. It had become personal to him. He felt he had to stay in the thick of it, and Liverpool was as good a place as any for that.

"Once we'd met, we were desperate to see each other every day. I'm ashamed to say that I left my grandparents' house each day with my girlfriends, but they were just a willing decoy. Elliot and I spent many wonderful days together. We knew we were destined for each other, and it was exhilarating to meet him secretively. Remember, I was twenty-eight years old, so if I'd had a normal upbringing, I doubt I'd have sneaked around as I did, but then you didn't know my father. I was willing to take many a risk to avoid confronting him about Elliot. I felt there wasn't enough time to have my father look into his prospects, or his family, or anything. The war did that to people. Of course, Elliot thought it humorous that I was sneaking around at that age, but that is how it was.

"I should back up a little. When the school broke for holidays that July, the students left and the staff remained for the rest of the month to get ready for the next term. I had the month of August off completely and wasn't required to be there unless I wanted to. In that case, of course, I was always welcome. It was the best situation I could have hoped for during the war. Teaching school was a reserved occupation, so I didn't have to look any further for war work, and I loved it.

"I thought Dede should have a real summer holiday, so I brought her to Cairnview. Of course, I had to go back, but as I'd hoped, Dede loved it here and hit it off with my mother.

"As planned, I went to Liverpool early in August for a few days to see my grandparents. I had intended to return to Cairnview for the remainder of my holiday and to take Dede back to school, but after meeting Elliot and hearing how well Dede was getting along, I decided to stay on.

"My grandfather had given me a good excuse to stay on when he heard that his daughters Anna and Isobel were taking their grandchildren to Northumberland from London and were going out of their way to enable them to stop in Liverpool for a night. Grandfather wanted me to see Isobel, in particular, in hopes my mother and Isobel might begin to heal the hurt between them that had happened because of my father after the first war. Erica can fill you in on that, Gram."

Graham said, "Of course."

Lottie rested for a moment. Then she said, "Talking is tiring business."

"We could break again," offered Graham.

"Not yet, I must keep on. Dinner that night went very well. I talked with my Aunt Isobel, and we had a very friendly visit. We did not discuss my mother or father, but it was a beginning, and I could tell that my grandparents were hopeful for a reconciliation between their daughters one day.

"My grandparents' home was in Woolton. It was a very elite neighborhood at that time. It is less posh now, I've heard. Only makes sense that more houses should be squeezed in. My grandparents had more garden than they knew what to do with. To their credit, they gave out allotments to people who didn't have any space to garden during the war. All sorts of vegetables were ready to harvest all around the Anderson shelter, where it was half-buried there. I remember that vividly.

"We all went to bed as usual that night, on the twenty-eighth of August, but I had made plans to sneak out to meet Elliot. There I was at my age, sneaking out of the house like a teenager. That sounds so silly, now."

Lottie's face paled, but she continued. "While Elliot and I were walking the streets together, the sirens began wailing. The first thing I thought of, and I'm ashamed to admit it, but I panicked that I would be missed and my father would find out about Elliot and me. We found a shelter and waited out a long night of bombing. I was terrified to go back and face my grandparents the next morning, but then, I didn't have to, did I? Elliot walked me back after the all-clear sounded. The house was in ruins, the bomb crater was in the vegetable garden, with the shelter just to the side of it. No one had made it out. All twelve bodies were recovered, including my grandparents, my two aunts, their five grandchildren, and three servants. I still cringe to think how my grandfather must have been both worried about me and angry with me when he died."

Lottie looked at Erica affectionately. "I've shared much of this with you, already, haven't I?"

"Yes," said Erica.

"And how are you doing? Better than last time?"

"I think so."

"Here, Grams," said Graham gently. "Have a little tea."

She accepted it gratefully before continuing, "My father was very busy in Glasgow, so when we talked on the telephone, I offered to deal with the funerals on my own. He was very relieved and said he could see no reason for Mum to come down, either. I talked to her, too, and she was willing for me to take care of it all. I was relieved she wasn't coming. It was too dangerous there, and I suppose I was trying to protect her from the ordeal, which was immense.

"Elliot helped me arrange everything. Strangely, my father never questioned why I wasn't in the shelter with the rest of the family at that late hour. I don't think he ever put it together. My mother did, as seen in her letter. Have you ever noticed that those who brag about how smart they are, often aren't at all?"

Lottie looked at Erica and Graham, who were sitting as still as statues. "Are you two doing all right?"

Graham spoke for them, saying, "Of course. Please go on, Grams."

"I tried to come home to visit my mother afterwards and take Dede back to school, but in the end, I didn't. Time was getting short for me to get back to school for the next term, and Mum encouraged me not to come. She said she'd put Dede on a train, which worried me a great deal, but she made it there, all right. She was awfully glad to see me at the station, though.

"My mother assured me that she had friends coming to be with her. I was amazed that she had finally made some friends. When I first spoke to her on the telephone, she wasn't as distraught as I thought she would be, which was confirmed by the letter. I later spoke to her friend, and she assured me that I'd done enough with the funerals and all, and that she and her husband would see to my mother's needs.

"It must be hard for you to imagine, but it was simply too much to take in. With so many of the family dead, I felt like I had to live in the present, because there might be not be a future. The bombing of London began soon after the family was killed in Liverpool, which I'm sure was a boon for Liverpool, for as long as London was getting it, Liverpool was not.

"Everyone was determined to live fully, while we yet could. I know that sounds very strange to you, but it was truly like that. Elliot got a job late in September. He wasn't fit for active duty yet, but he'd found work and was happy about it. He was working as a firewatcher for the Waterloo Grain Warehouse in Aigburth, a suburb of Liverpool. The warehouse was right on the docks, of course.

"Once he'd saved some money, we met at a halfway point, getting separate accommodations in October. On the first of November, we met again, and to put it simply, we got but one room and had decided we would marry. I got pregnant then, but Elliot never knew about it. By the time I was sure I was pregnant, it was only two weeks until we were to meet for Christmas, so I decided to wait to tell him then. I wasn't worried, because I knew we'd get married right away."

Lottie's voice got so quiet, Graham and Erica had to lean forward to hear her. She said, "He was killed on December twelfth, when the grain warehouse was bombed. I never saw him again. I knew he was injured, or worse, when he didn't telephone me as arranged. One of my friends rang me a few days later when she saw his name on a list of the dead, but I never heard what arrangements were made for his burial. I was too sick with morning sickness at the time to find out. I always hoped I'd find out what became of his body, but never did. I assume he was buried with the other victims. When so many were killed at once, the logistics were insurmountable, at times."

"Perhaps, I'll do that, Grams." Graham handed her a tissue. "I would like to do that one day. Do you want to take a break again?"

"No," she said, shakily. "I must finish."

"All right. We won't leave. Just rest a second, Grams."

Lottie took some deep breaths and went bravely on. "When most of the children left for their Christmas holidays—we still had the Jewish children and any others that had nowhere to go—Emma's cousin brought a friend of his to meet me. I had told no one of the pregnancy, of course, and hiding my grief for Elliot was a terrible burden. The fact was, we were there for the children and had to be strong. I didn't even let myself cry at night, because Dede was always with me. Emma, the matron, once asked me if I was all right, but I assured her that I was. It only made sense that I'd be traumatized by the deaths of my grandparents and the other relatives, not to mention the task that had been mine to see to their funerals. Emma had problems of her own, of course, so she never did learn of my pregnancy. The cousin's friend was.."

"Granddad George," exclaimed Graham.

"It was," said Lottie. "He fell in love with me. I think he saw my sadness and vulnerability and wanted to take care of me. He asked me to marry him within the week—a common occurrence during war, and I said I would. He was finishing up some special training and was to ship out before long. He gave me an engagement ring on my birthday and we were married immediately by special license. His picture is right there beside the clock,

Graham. Would you get it?"

He got it quickly and handed it to her.

Putting on her glasses with shaking hands and looking at his picture fondly, she said, "I didn't use him, if you think that. Well, maybe I did, a little. The pregnancy definitely was a factor, I admit. I was very fond of him, though, and with Elliot gone, I knew I'd never love again. If I couldn't have Elliot, I knew I needed George. Said out loud, that sounds terribly selfish. What I'm trying to say is that his love for me made me want to love him. And, of course, I grew to love him more with each passing year."

"You don't have to explain anything, Grams. We just want to hear your story."

Lottie nodded and continued, "We married without contacting either of our families. I resigned from my job at the school, and leaving Dede there, George and I enjoyed a few weeks together. We boarded at a large house called Greystone Manor, just outside of Nuneaton. George knew the family from some connection or another. The lady of the house was very kind and gracious, and it was very comfortable, in spite of being full of evacuee children.

"My father was angry at not being told we were marrying, but he liked George—on the one occasion they met in February. On our first visit as a married couple to Cairnview, my pregnancy wasn't showing yet, and although George knew I was pregnant by that time, we had agreed to keep mum about it. My mother made a big fuss over our arrival. She, too, liked George right away. He was so likeable, one couldn't help but love him. He had some money from a small inheritance, which he had invested here and there. As we were already married, my father could only approve.

"George's unit was shipped out to Africa right after our visit to Scotland. I collected Dede from the school, where she'd done poorly during my absence, and took her home with me with my mum's blessing. My father was not happy about keeping her on a permanent basis, but my mother stood up to him for the first time, telling him that other children would soon be coming to live with us, so Dede was only the beginning. I'm not sure why Cairnview didn't house children before that. It may have had something to do with the loss of my mum's family at the time they were getting shipped out of London again. They had already done it once, but many of the children had gone back to the cities when the war didn't get going. Anyway, the children did come, and my father stayed in

Glasgow, which suited us just fine.

"My father never knew I was expecting a baby. I had finally told my mother, and we were going to tell him the next time he came home, which he never did. He was killed in the Clydebank Blitz in March, of 1941. A stray bomb was dropped on Stirling that night, too. People must have thought my mother and I were in shock, because we didn't exhibit any grief. We never talked about our lack of grief at the time and did our best to show appropriate sadness when around the minister and our caring neighbors, but when alone, we went about our business unfazed by his death. We didn't talk about it. It just was."

Graham interrupted, "Grams, you look so exhausted. Why don't you take a minute. We'll wait right here. Just take a few moments."

Lottie nodded her head and closed her eyes. Graham looked at Erica in alarm, and she whispered, "She's all right. I've seen her do this before."

Minutes later, Lottie opened her eyes, smiled at her listeners with affection, and went on. "Your father's early birth in August seemed to surprise no one, and he wasn't a big baby, which went in my favor. The emotional trauma of losing Elliot early in the pregnancy may have had something to do with his small size, but he was healthy and thrived—and most importantly—no one ever questioned his paternity or the timing. If people were counting months with their fingers, they'd have to have had a wedding date to go by, and I just told folks we were married in December, which was true.

"I don't think George was naïve, nor was he a simpleton, but he never questioned me about your father's early birth. I think the fact that he wasn't here helped with that. Also, it was in his nature to be trusting, and he simply didn't think of it as a possibility. He had no reason to suspect anything, so he didn't. I loved him for that, and I determined never to hurt him by telling him. He was too good to do that to. He loved me that completely, and I loved him, too. I never loved him in the way I had loved your grandfather, Gram, but there are different kinds of love.

"George came home on leave in the fall of 1943. He stopped in Yorkshire to see his parents for a day and then came to me and your father at Cairnview for the rest of his leave. Frank was born in 1943, and was two before his father ever saw him. I was always worried that George's parents had put two and two together about your father, but I never once saw any indication of it. They weren't ignorant. I don't want to leave that impression, but if they did suspect I was pregnant before marrying, they had no reason to think it wasn't George's baby. And thankfully, they were too polite to ever bring it up to George.

"I shouldn't be surprised that Mum knew I was pregnant all along, but she never said anything to make me think she knew. I wonder now if I had never given her enough credit. I now think that she must have known I was pregnant early on and made sure that the house was filled with evacuee children to keep my father in Glasgow. She was probably nervous that he'd have been be the one person to give me trouble over it. The fact that he was killed didn't hurt my cause, either, but I try not to think about that. When life is unfair, I try not to question it, and when it is fair, well, it's only sensible to do the same."

She looked at her listeners with a sly smile, and Graham returned the smile, saying, "We understand."

"My father's body was recovered and brought home for burial. Once all that was handled, we went on with our business. Dede was a great help to my mum and me. She helped tirelessly with the evacuee children, and after my boys were born, she was devoted to them."

"And Dede never knew about Elliot, either?" asked Graham.

"She was much younger than me. I never shared my troubles with her, because her load was enough for her to bear. She was fragile that way. She may have been old enough to know about the birds and the bees, but she never gave me any reason to think she knew about me. It seemed I had gotten away with it.

"We were a household of women, with the exception of the youngsters, and we managed very well. We had good neighbors, like the Smiths. Ian Smith's parents and grandparents were devoted to my mum and were always on hand to give assistance to us when needed. We found our pace and we just kept marching, until the unthinkable happened.

"Your brothers were killed," offered Graham solemnly.

"Yes, both of my brothers were killed in the final year of the war. They had both joined the Royal Navy. Robert wanted to be with Edward to look out for him. My father was furious at both of them for signing up when they had a ready excuse to stay home, being in the shipping industry. As neither of them wanted anything to do with my father or his company, they'd signed up early on. My mother was sad when she learned of it, I'm sure, but I was already gone from home. She supported them in their escape from our father, though, I believe.

"We saw them only once, when they came home together for a long leave after their training, early in the war. I was able to get here at the same time, so it was a real family reunion. My father was even civil, which was noted by all of us.

"My brothers were both officers on the HMS Aldenham. It was an escort destroyer sunk by a mine in the Adriatic Sea off the coast of Croatia. Some of the crew was saved, but neither of my brothers made it. I have often wondered if Robert was trying to look after Edward, even in death. They were lost with the ship and their bodies were never recovered. I heard on the news a few years ago that the ship was found, broken in two on the sea floor, and deemed a war grave for the many lost. To be found after so many years was remarkable to me. Closure, I suppose." She looked up to see that Erica was weeping silently in her chair by the window.

"What is it, child?" she asked.

"I don't see how you could bear the loss of so many. I know loss, but I can't imagine how it was for you and your mother to lose so many."

"Well, dear, put simply, it was awful—and we wondered at times if we were holding up. But, you see, we had to keep going. We had the evacuee children to look after and my two little boys to love and care for. And we had Dede here, who had lost everyone. Who were we to complain in front of her? I know my mother wept at night after my brothers were lost. By that time, I was becoming numb to it all. Nothing made sense anymore. Neither of us coped as well as we'd have liked, but we did keep going. We didn't speak of it, and to tell you the truth, I think that helped.

"We were so happy when George came home to us safely. He fought first in the North African Campaign with General Montgomery, escaping death miraculously, at times, and later on he fought in the mountains of Italy and throughout Europe until it was finished. His safe return marked a new beginning for all of us."

Lottie paused for a drink, and Graham handed her the water glass, certain the tea was cold by now.

Graham took the opportunity to ask, "Grams, my

parents had a small copy of a portrait of you when you were a young woman. Your wavy hair was cut rather short. I can't describe it much better than that. Do you know the one I mean?"

"I do. It was taken before I left home to teach at the school. My mother wanted it taken, especially."

"Was there ever a larger one that I could have?" asked Graham.

"Yes, but I haven't seen it in decades. It's around here somewhere. I haven't thought of it in decades, either. Out of sight—out of mind, you know. Perhaps it will come to me if I give it some thought. You know, come to think of it, a portrait quite like that of my mum used to always sit on her bureau, there," she said pointing at the antique chest of drawers. "I haven't seen it for a long time, either."

"If it's all right, we'll look for it, too," said Graham. "I'd like to have the one of you, especially, if I could."

"Well, don't tear the place apart."

"Don't worry, we won't," promised Erica.

Lottie took another drink of water and said, "Well, of course you may have it, Gram darling. Who else would want it?"

She laughed the tinkling laugh that both Graham and Erica had come to identify her with. They looked at each other, knowing that each had appreciated the moment in the same way.

Lottie continued, "My mother had several smaller ones of me made up—wallet-sized, they called it. She gave each of my sons one many years later—like the one you'd seen that your parents had, Gram. She wanted them to each have one, and of course, I had given one to Elliot soon after we met. I was glad my mum made me take some with me to give to family and friends.

"She was funny about things like that. Pictures were very important to her. She liked to take pictures, too, I remember—not that they turned out particularly well. She had a little Brownie camera, I remember. I wonder what became if it."

Lottie was still for a moment and then said, "Elliot promised me an engagement ring the next time we met. I like saying his name out loud, now that I can."

"I am so sorry you lost him, Grams. You couldn't even talk about him to anyone. It would have been a good thing, don't you think, if your mother had given you the letter, or better yet, spoken to you about him?"

"I think I know why she didn't, but let's save that until tomorrow. I admit I am very tired."

Looking at his watch, Graham exclaimed, "It's past time for your lunch. Fran made us a nice soup."

"Oh, but I had a little cake," she said. "I'm fine."

"That's even worse for us if the doctor finds out. He'll ban us from seeing you, for sure."

Joann showed up at the door, sleepy-eyed and embarrassed. "It seems I went to sleep for a few minutes. Your grandmother hasn't even had her lunch. It was that cake and tea that did it. Now, we're all off course."

Lottie insisted, "To the contrary, dear nurse, I think we are completely on course. I had to get it all said. I couldn't have rested easy until I did."

Chapter Nineteen

Having seen the doctor late in the afternoon, Lottie agreed to rest the following day. Erica and Graham decided to use the time wisely. They met in the kitchen for an early ride, after which, they ate the huge breakfast that Fran had prepared for them. Together, they delivered Lottie's breakfast to her to save Fran's legs.

From her bed, Lottie said, "I saw you ride out this morning. Nice of you to take Fancy along on her lead. She feels so unwanted when the others go on living life to the fullest, as she wiles away her time behind the fence."

"If you don't mind that I read a little into that, it sounds like you'd like to get out of your bedroom," said Graham.

"Maybe sometime," said Lottie, smiling weakly.

"Of course," he assured her. "You are to rest today, remember?"

She nodded.

"One day, though, Kyle and I could carry you down in a chair. You'd be very safe, I promise. We could go for a drive in the country, Grams."

"You can't see much from the roads, and you have

to keep moving or get out of the way," said Lottie, pessimistically. "All that traffic!"

"It's not so bad around here," coaxed Graham.

"Bad enough for me."

"The lookouts are worth getting to. I think you'd like it."

Lottie only shrugged.

"Or we could take you around the property in your wheelchair," offered Graham eagerly.

"Not without cracking every bone in my body," said his grandmother, matter-of-factly. "Nurse would have plenty to say about that."

"It would be jarring," said Erica. "We'll think of something."

That afternoon, Erica put her mind to reading again all the personal letters, and Graham finalized his assessment of the finances. They took turns reading out loud any intriguing parts to each other, and by the end of the day, they'd learned a great deal more.

Erica said, "The couple that sent these piles of letters from abroad are, I'm guessing, the same friends that came to Lily when her family was killed, but there is no proof. They took turns penning the notes, but always signed them, 'W' and a small red hand-stamp of a rose."

"How cryptic they were. I wonder why. Love letters?"

"Whatever, Graham! Seriously—and I quote, 'my wife did this, my husband did that.' Does that sound like a love letter to you? Maybe that's how they wrote all their correspondence."

"Yes, but notice, they didn't use any names in the letters, either. That's telling, and it's a little corny, don't you think?" he asked playfully.

"I thought it was sweet," replied Erica defensively.

"Dates?"

"None, but we can assume they were all before the war, as there was no need to hide anything after that. Strange that she'd have to hide the existence of her friends."

"We'll ask Grams about it."

"What have you learned?" asked Erica.

"In a nutshell, Lily had an inheritance from her grandmother that had been put in trust for her when her parents married her off to Gordon Jackson, jack-ass and all-round scoundrel."

Erica nodded her agreement on his assessment of the man.

"The money was to be kept a secret from Lily's parents, as well as from her husband, according to one letter, which I found interesting. I think we'd have liked Lily's grandmother. She would be my third great grandmother, right?"

"That sounds right."

"It indicates in these letters that by the early thirties, Maitland Shipping had taken some hard hits. Maybe from mismanagement, maybe from the crash of the stock market, or both—hard to say without further study. But, if he'd have found out about this money of my great grandmother's, he would have wanted it. He reminds me of my cousin John, or more correctly, John takes after him. But, if he'd known of the money, life would not have been easy for Lily."

"I'm sure Lottie has it now, however much it was or is left of it," said Erica, without thinking. "Oh, I'm sorry, Graham, that was thoughtless and tactless of me."

"We were already talking about money, Erica. You didn't offend me."

"I'm glad. In one of our first sessions, Lottie told

me that her parents fought continually when she was about seventeen. Let's see, that was 1928. Does that correspond with the papers?"

"It does with the beginning of the problems, which only got worse going toward the 1929 crash. He might have had suspicions that she had money of her own. She must have had these communications and bank statements sent to a different address, or she'd have been found out."

"Weren't there a couple of envelopes?" asked Erica, remembering seeing them.

"Here." Graham held one of them to the light in the late afternoon. "Addressed to Mr. and Mrs. Boyd Smith, Smith Cottage, Cambusbarron. Erica, that's got to be Ian's parents, possibly even grandparents! They received the correspondence and passed it on to her when the ogre wasn't around. How amazing! Grandmother will love this!" exclaimed Graham excitedly.

Looking at Erica, he could see that she was miles away and asked, "Are you all right?"

"Just worrying a little. Do you really think Dean's threat to me was hollow?"

"I do, but I'll go one better. Our office has a solicitor. There's no defense like a great offense. He mentioned jail time to you, right?"

Erica nodded.

"Well, if he wasn't lying about that, too, he won't want to be in the courts under any circumstances."

"Would you really do that for me, Graham?" asked Erica tearfully.

"Well, not if you cry." He put his arm around her shoulder. "I'm just teasing. You can cry if you need to. Kyle told me all that happened to you before you got here. That was one very bad day. I'm so sorry I made it worse."

"I've put it all behind me. I was never in love with Dean—no more than he was with me. It was stupid of me to think I was. All that remains is that niggling fear that I'm going to be called into court."

"Well, it's time to put that to bed, too." He handed her a sheet of paper, "Write down his name, number and anything else that might be useful. I will make a telephone call. After which, would you like to go for a walk?"

Erica hurriedly wrote down the needed information. "Sure. It will feel good."

"You can wear those neon walking shoes you were wearing the first day you came," he teased.

Erica stood and stretched. "I think I'll wear my

matching jogging suit, too."

"Whatever pleases you," he said, laughing. He took the paper Erica handed to him. "I'll tell Nurse we're leaving. Then, I'll make that telephone call to Newcastle, and I'll be ready. Let's walk over to Kyle's place and see if he has a solution for us for getting Grams out of the house for a few hours. If I know her as well as I think I do, I think she'd like to wander around in her own neck of the woods, maybe make some surprise calls on neighbors. I have a little idea."

By the time they got back to Cairnview that night, Lottie and her nurse had already had their dinner and gone to bed. Erica and Graham had eaten with Kyle's family. They were terribly excited to present their idea to Lottie the following morning. In fact, they were too giddy to go to bed, so they found a movie on television and watched it together.

The television was secluded in a corner of the tack room across from a beat-up leather sofa. Tucked behind a wall of shelves, Erica hadn't noticed it. Amazed, she asked, "You pay for all this and don't even watch it?"

"Pretty strange, I admit," said Graham. "Especially

so, considering Grams wouldn't let me get the internet—not even if I paid for it myself. She's not tight. She was still teaching me a hard lesson."

"But who watches television?" Erica asked incredulously.

"Well, the one down here is for Kyle and me, although we rarely use it. Grams lets Kyle bring a date to watch a movie, occasionally. He calls it his cozy corner, but the real reason Grams hooked it up was so that Nurse could watch her programs on her television in her suite upstairs."

"Of course," said Erica. "Your grandmother once said she'd watched a movie with her."

By the time their movie had ended, Erica was asleep. Her head had fallen over on Graham's shoulder, and he didn't mind. He turned off the television with the remote and listened to her quiet breathing as she slept. When his arm fell asleep and his stomach growled hungrily, he carefully stretched her out on the sofa and covered her with an old knitted afghan, which was none too clean, but served its purpose.

Hating to leave her there, he went to the kitchen to see if Fran had hidden anything delicious from him. There was still some cake remaining, so he helped himself to a large portion. After washing it down with cold milk, he went back to the tack room to check on Erica.

He knelt on the floor beside her to wake her gently. It occurred to him to leave her be, but he feared she'd be afraid or disoriented if she awoke there by herself in the middle of the night. He bent close to her, and without thinking, impulsively kissed her lightly on the lips. She didn't pull back, so he kissed her again, ever so gently. She responded this time, and after a long, tender kiss, he made himself stop. He was starting to have feelings for her, and realizing this, he simply could not take further advantage of her while she slept.

"Erica," he whispered. "Let me take you up to bed." She nodded and he led her, half asleep up to her room, where she crawled between the sheets with her shoes on. He took them off for her and covered her up properly before leaving her.

He went into his room and, maneuvering his way around the boxes that were still strewn about, got ready for bed.

He fell asleep, but not until he dissected what had just happened between them, worrying especially that he may have been the only one to experience it.

If she doesn't remember it, I'll take that as a sign, he thought.

They met in the kitchen the next morning, as usual. Upon waking, Graham decided to act as if nothing had happened. If she hadn't noticed what had passed between them, well, then she hadn't noticed—period. No sense talking about something awkward that only one of them was aware of. Or, if she had noticed and thought it unimportant, he should do the same.

She looked rested and relaxed, reminding him to follow up on his telephone call of the day before. The sooner she knew that Dean couldn't hurt her, the happier she'd be, he thought.

She chattered on about the surprise they had in store for Lottie. She couldn't wait to unveil their plan to take her in the Johnson's open cart. It was 'well-sprung,' a term used by Kyle, promising a smooth ride. It also had air-inflated rubber tires to make the ride even smoother.

As she chattered, Graham watched her with new eyes. Unobserved, he noticed her every move—every nuance of expression reflected in her dark eyes. He watched her mouth as she spoke, sometimes fixating on it until he was sure that she'd seen him. He looked away embarrassed, but she gave no sign of discomfort.

After a half hour of waiting for her to give any kind of indication that she remembered the kisses, he determined that either his kisses meant nothing to her, or she'd been completely unaware of them. So, end of story, he thought.

Erica looked at him and said, "Graham?"

"Yes?" he asked hopefully.

At that moment, Fran entered noisily through the kitchen door, fussing that she was later than usual, putting an end to their exchange.

Meeting with Lottie after her late breakfast, both noticed how small she looked in her bed.

She's shrinking, thought Erica sadly.

Erica announced to her cheerfully that they had discovered a few tidbits of interest. Graham first told her about the findings of the financials. He said, "Your mother had her own money bequeathed to her from her maternal grandmother. She kept it hidden from Gordon. Did you ever suspect that?"

"Mum always spoke affectionately of her maternal grandmother. She once said that her grandmother Scott was the one person in the world who saw her as an individual," said Lottie.

"So that's one big reason, right there, Grams, for Lily to have the attic stash. She was protecting her assets for you and your brothers."

"And in the end, it was only me. I did get a separate, special legacy from my mother, but I didn't realize the meaning of its separateness. The rest of her estate included money from the sales of the shipping businesses in both Liverpool and Glasgow. She sold them immediately. As they were critical in time of war, she sold them to the interested parties for much less than her father or her husband would have approved of. She felt it was her patriotic duty.

"Years later, she sold the Liverpool property in Woolton to a buyer, who was going to build several houses on the empty lot. It relieves me to know that Mum's grandmother gave her some sense of independence while my father was yet alive. She was wise to have hidden it from him, brave even. It makes sense, though. If he'd had some financial bumps along the way, he'd have eaten it all up, one way or the other.

"She was generous with her money, and wise, too. She helped rebuild the council houses in Stirling in the fifties, I believe, and she also donated to the city of Glasgow for rebuilding the bombed areas after the war."

Graham said, "There's more, Grams. It doesn't appear to be terribly important, though." He nodded to Erica to tell her part.

Erica held up one of the letters from 'W' and said, "Letters came from 'W' and companion from all parts of the world. Do you think they could possibly be the friends who came to stay with your mother during the war?"

"They were never here when I was here. I talked to the woman on the telephone once, but I don't remember her name. Oh, why didn't my mother write some of this down?"

"I don't think she had to, Grams," offered Graham. "She's giving it to us now. She led you to her stash, and we'll get the rest of the story, if there is one. This might be it. She had money that needed to be protected. Oh, by the way, her correspondence dealing with her money went to the Smith Cottage. They were her friends."

"How exciting a find! I always knew they liked my

mum. And she liked them, too. It took her some time to feel at home with the locals, being English herself. She had to earn their friendship, which she did. The Smiths died a few years before she did, if I remember correctly. Ian is their grandson, of course." She looked at Graham questioningly and asked, "What do you mean by, 'she is giving it to us now?'"

Graham was embarrassed. "You both will think I'm crazy, but we have talked about how certain we are that Lily wanted these things to be found. Well, it occurred to me that she helped you find it, that's all."

Both Lottie and Erica looked at him quizzically. "I didn't expect you to say that," said Erica. "When I first came and was told about the papers found in the attic, it occurred to me that perhaps Lily's great desire to have them found were part of the reason why they were found. I'm not thinking paranormal, really, but Lottie, you did say it was a vivid memory that came out of the blue."

"Yes," said Lottie, humoring them.

"To change the subject, since you are mocking us, Grams, you mentioned that if your mother had hidden the picture of my grandfather, that you might know why. Maybe if you know why, you'll know where."

"Interesting theory," said Lottie. "I think she hid it simply so that George wouldn't find it. She was protecting my marriage. I think it's as simple as that. I think her reason for never talking to me about it was for exactly the same reason. She was afraid of being the wave that rocked our happy boat. I really think that's all there is to it."

"There is one more thing noteworthy, if I can get back to the letters," said Erica, concentrating. "Some of the letters from 'W' were signed with his initial only. They were particularly cryptic. There must be something to it, but the notes give nothing away. 'Hoping you are well. Wishing you a happy Christmas. Take care of yourself.' Nothing at all is given away as to how he was connected with her. The other notes I mentioned were from two people sending their joint greetings, often from their travels. Those were signed with a 'W' and a small stamp of a rose in red ink. My guess is that her name was Rose, but I'm sure Graham thinks that's corny."

Graham grinned. "I have no room to talk, since I'm the one asking Lily to lead us by the hand to my grandfather's picture."

"All very interesting," said Lottie. "Nice guess, Erica, but I knew no one by the name of Rose. Can't think of who 'W' would be, either. It appears that the motive of my mother's stash was so that she could have friends of her own and money of her own, too. The meaning of her letter to me was to let me know that she knew about Gregory's paternity and perhaps to warn me that she might hide the photograph for my own protection. Now, what is left to go through?"

"A few miscellaneous items and a very few photographs," said Erica. "I've shown you most of them already. I've since looked through them twice, in hopes of finding the lost picture, but Graham and I will go through them again and an address book, where we might just find out who 'W' was. I've paged through it. Nothing stood out, but I'm looking for something specific this time," said Erica enthusiastically.

"Well, done! What good sleuths you are!" praised Lottie.

"I suppose that does pretty much tie things up," said Graham.

Lottie beamed at the two of them. "So that is the crux of the matter, or is there something else to be learned, I wonder?"

Lottie paused to think and then announced, "Now,

Erica, I believe you could begin writing. I still haven't decided how much of the delicate subjects to include, but one thing I am sure of. I would be pleased if you would write the introduction to my memoirs from your own perspective. That would please me very much."

Erica said, "I'd be glad to. Thank you for trusting me with it."

"Oh, you're a good girl," said Lottie.

"We are going to let you rest, Grams. We'll talk again tomorrow." Before leaving the room, he kissed her on one cheek, and impulsively, Erica kissed her on the other.

She laughed at them and said teasingly, "Go kiss on somebody else."

Graham's face reddened, but Erica seemed oblivious.

End of story, thought Graham, disappointed.

Back in the library, they looked through the address book but couldn't find anyone named Rose. They did find a Wilbur, her doctor; a Warren, her solicitor; and a Weylan; her retired stable man. Last names starting with a 'W' were there, but gave them nothing to go on, either. All of them seemed to be local, anyway.

Erica said, "Call me corny, but I think Lily knew 'W' before he married Rose. After that, she heard from them jointly, and they were here for her during the war. Maybe they came here for reasons of safety. Many people went to the country, right?"

"Sure. 'W' and Rose got married. If there is anything truly interesting to that story, I can't imagine what it is."

"Me neither," concurred Erica, shrugging.

"Well, I say we eat something," suggested Graham, standing.

"What about the pictures?"

"Later. I'm looking for one picture in particular, and you've already said it isn't here."

"It isn't. I've looked at them repeatedly, even scanned them all. I'd know if it were here. I was just trying to give Lottie a little hope."

Erica was surprisingly hungry and Graham always so, so they fixed sandwiches and ate in the kitchen. They shared a bag of crisps, and drank lemonade that Fran had made up for them. The day was overcast, but pleasant, so he offered to show Erica around the property if she was up to it.

She was eager, so he showed her where the boundaries were now and where they had once been before Lily had sold off some of it. He told her stories of his childhood, like when he had fallen from a certain tree or had gotten in trouble for uprooting some flowers. "Grandmother doesn't care about flowers anymore. Love of flowers, especially roses, was something she and my mother had in common."

"I've seen the rose garden. It's still beautiful in its wildness," said Erica.

"Perhaps," he replied.

As he showed her around the southern part of the property, Erica asked about his parents and was mildly surprised when he was forthcoming about much of their history. Likewise, they talked about her upbringing in Nebraska, Graham asking many questions.

They were so interested in what the other was saying, neither of them noticed that rain was imminent. When it suddenly came down in a torrent, Graham grabbed her hand and dashed for the tack room entrance. Laughing, they burst in to find Kyle shaking water from his head and arms and collecting his rain gear. He grinned.

"I didn't see that coming."

"Neither did we," said Graham. Slightly self-conscious, he busied himself shaking the water from his arms. He wiped his shoes on the old carpet runner to keep from looking at Kyle, who for some reason made him feel self-conscious about being with Erica.

"I'm going to go ahead and put the horses in their stalls," said Kyle. "They're already huddled under the covered paddock. I'm glad I brought my car today. I'll just grab a piece of Fran's cake, if you don't mind, and then I'll finish up."

"Please do," said Graham. He was picking up on Kyle's knowing smirk, and it was making him uncomfortable. He was glad to hear the front doorbell ring to end the exchange.

Kyle and Graham both went through to the kitchen, but Erica stayed in the cozy atmosphere of the tack room. She found an old towel to dry her arms and face, and she wasn't disgusted when it smelled a little horsey. She, too, liked the combined scents of leather, linseed oil, and horse. It reminded her of home. It reminded her of her mother.

Whoever might have come to the door, Erica found she wasn't even slightly curious. She had intended to call

Andrea, but wasn't ready to share anything with her yet. She didn't feel a bit social, so she decided to curl up on the sofa until whoever it was, left.

She hadn't indulged in missing her mother to the fullest for a long time, and she felt she needed to be alone and think about her. She took advantage of the privacy and wallowed in the pain of losing her. It never really left her, and sometimes she had to give it her full attention.

Chapter Twenty

Graham opened the door to his ex-girlfriend, Jenny. His jaw dropped, as she threw herself into his arms. "Oh, Graham, I've been so worried about you. You haven't answered your mobile when I've called the past few weeks. I assumed you've blocked me, so I rang your office three days in a row. Your secretary said you weren't in, but she wouldn't tell me where you were."

"Good thing for her." Graham, extricated himself from her. "She must have wanted to keep her job."

"Well, then I realized you must have come up here," she explained.

"So you took the train rather than ring me here at the house?" he questioned suspiciously.

"How was I to know you might actually answer it," she said petulantly.

"Someone would have," he replied. "So, what are you doing here?"

"I said I was worried, didn't I, and it occurred to me that your grandmother might have been doing poorly."

"My grandmother has been doing poorly for the past four years, and you not only didn't offer to come up here and meet her, but you were pretty adamant that I shouldn't come, either."

"Well, maybe I just wanted to see you," she said, seductively.

"You were going out with someone. What happened to that?" He was unaffected by her feminine wiles.

"We broke up. I came to my senses and realized I had taken you for granted, and I wanted to give us another try."

"Are you sure he isn't the one that came to his senses? I'm sorry—that sounded cruel, but you must understand, we left things final. I've no intention of getting back together with you. I can't imagine what made you think otherwise. To have come so far. It's rather baffling."

"I wanted to show you I'd changed my feelings about your love of Cairnview. I just wanted to lend my support if your grandmother was doing poorly." She repeated her practiced line, having nothing else to fall back on.

"It sounds good, Jenny, but not coming from you. Sorry, but I think you came up here without ringing first to force me to offer you hospitality. Once embedded, you planned to work your magic and win me back by the time you left, but you've given yourself too much credit. Not only am I not interested, you aren't welcome to stay here. So, it looks like you'll be putting up at the inn or getting on a late train for Newcastle."

"That's not fair, Graham. I'm offering to start fresh," she said, pouting provocatively.

"It's no good, Jenny. I hope you told your taxi to wait for you." Graham opened the door slightly to see if there was a car outside, and seeing there wasn't, asked warily, "Where is your suitcase?"

"Just outside the door," she said. "Where else would it be?"

"Excuse me, for a moment," he said brusquely, leaving her there by the door and going quickly down the hall towards the kitchen.

Kyle washed down the piece of cake he'd eaten in record time and had made his way back to the tack room to put on his rain gear. Before leaving, he remembered to peek into the cozy corner to make sure he'd turned off the television. He'd turned it on when he'd first dashed in out of the rain to check the weather forecast. He was hoping this was just a burst of rain, not a system that intended to stick around for days. The television was off as he'd hoped, but he was surprised to hear Erica's quiet weeping coming from the sofa. He silently left her, hoping he hadn't disturbed her.

He was about to step outside, when he heard Graham calling him from the kitchen.

When Graham saw Kyle peek his head into the kitchen, he said, "Thank goodness! I was afraid you'd gone. I have to ask a favor. If I put the horses in, do you think you could give our unexpected guest a ride back to the station?"

Kyle's eyebrows shot up in surprise. "He just came from the station and is going back already?"

"It's a she, and yes, she is going back to Newcastle, tonight."

"Be glad to do it if you'll see to the horses for me. They won't be too happy with me tomorrow, though, if you forget to put them in."

"I won't forget," assured Graham. "Bring the car around front, and I'll bring her out. I owe you."

"Yes, you do," teased Kyle. "Say, I didn't mean to intrude, but Erica is in the tack room. Hope you aren't responsible for her tears."

"I hope not," said Graham uneasily. "Can't remember being rude—lately, anyway."

Kyle slapped him on the back. "I'll bring the car around."

It was still raining lightly, and it wasn't without drama as Kyle put Jenny's suitcase in the boot of his little car. She tried hysterics, since nothing else had worked, and it fell flat. Graham was immovable.

Kyle cleared his university books off of the passenger seat and quickly picked up as many candy wrappers and Coca Cola cans as he could in a few seconds from the floorboard to make space for her feet.

Graham opened the car door, and Jenny got in seething mad. "I won't be forgetting this, and I'll make sure that people hear about it, too."

"Terrified," he said flatly. "Have a nice trip back." He slammed the car door harder than he would have had to, and to Kyle, over the top of the car, he said, "I really do owe you."

"Yes, you do," said Kyle. He got in and sped off.

"Yes, I do," repeated Graham going back inside out of the drizzle. As he closed the door, he was aware of an exhilarating feeling. He felt curiously free and unencumbered. Poor Kyle, he thought.

He went to the kitchen to see what Fran had prepared for them to reheat for dinner. He was pleased to see that there was still some cake and more than pleased to see his favorite, shepherd's pie, waiting in the refrigerator to be heated in the microwave. He checked the clock and realized he still had about a half hour before he needed to prepare trays for the ladies upstairs.

As he went out and put the horses in for the night, he thought about what it would be like if he did his accounting work from Cairnview. He well knew that his grandmother had not long to live. He could sense it, and Joann's comments had only confirmed that. He wanted to stay until she passed.

When back inside, he got rid of his rain gear and made for the cozy corner to check on Erica. He found her sleeping, reminding him of the night before. He nearly jumped from the reaction it caused in him. The one thing different about her, was her hair. Having been out in the rain, it had curled again and looked just like it had the first time he'd seen her. It pained him to think how he'd treated her upon her arrival. If he'd had an ounce of empathy in him, he should have been able to tell that she was a girl at the end of her rope.

He turned to leave, knowing she would wake on her own, hungry for her supper. As he moved away, he heard her say, "I was hoping you'd wake me like you did last night."

In two steps he was standing over her and asked, "You knew. I mean, you remember it?"

"I must not be a very good kisser," she teased, sitting upright, "if you thought I hadn't noticed."

"I think you played with me today. My grandmother has worn off on you, because that is just the kind of thing she would do," he said, laughing.

"Well, I didn't know what to do. My motto has always been 'When in doubt, don't.'"

"Too bad I didn't meet you a couple of years ago. I could have saved myself a lot of trouble with my grandmother."

"That's all over now," she said. "You've got her back."

"Are you all right?" asked Graham tenderly. "Kyle thought maybe you weren't."

"I'm fine. I'm just missing my mom. You want to

know what I've been thinking?" She motioned to him to join her on the sofa.

"What have you been thinking?" He sat down beside her.

"That the memoirs have already accomplished much of their purpose. Imagine how your grandmother must feel, knowing that she had her mother's support all that time. Lily wanted all of this to come to light. She wanted to tell her daughter that she'd known about your father and understood, and I am absolutely convinced that she hid the picture of your grandfather to protect Lottie and George's marriage."

"Want to know what I think?" he asked.

"What do you think?"

"I think Lily won't rest completely until we find the picture of my grandfather, Elliot Gregory. I am convinced she hid it. She didn't destroy it. She wouldn't do that to her daughter."

"I think you're right. Should we look in the attic?"

"We'll ask Grandmother tomorrow. Can you guess what I want to know?" he asked tentatively.

"What?" she asked leaning into him.

"How you'd react if I kissed you again, right now."

337

"You should try it and find out," she said softly.

The next morning, Graham and Erica met in the kitchen early to go riding. There was a different kind of tension this morning, but to Graham's relief, they didn't have to pretend that there was nothing going on between them. They absolutely knew there was something there and had mutually decided to enjoy it and not analyze it too deeply at this point. That had been Erica's idea, and Graham had agreed, although somewhat reluctantly.

He had told her the night before about Jenny's unexpected appearance, and Erica was still trying to be completely rid of Dean. Each knew that they had to get their pasts cleared up before they could talk about what was happening between them now.

Fran was bustling about when they got back, and Joann had been down to breakfast and had already taken Lottie's tray up. Fran dished them up porridge and toast, and they ate across from each other, locking eyes, whenever they looked up from their bowls.

Graham moved his foot, accidently touching Erica's, and she almost upset her porridge, reacting to it. She knew their attraction for each other would not go unnoticed if they couldn't hide it a little better than they were doing, so far, and she telepathically sent the message to Graham across the table. He smiled.

On their way upstairs to shower and change, Erica whispered to him, "If we aren't going to analyze what's happening between us, it might be best if we don't broadcast it to everyone in the house."

"Are we doing that?" asked Graham chuckling.

Erica laughed. "I'm afraid so."

At the top of the stairs, Graham, replied, "Oh well," and then proceeded to take her into his arms and kiss her meaningfully. "You mean, like that?"

"That's what I mean," said Erica, pretending to scold. "Nothing—absolutely nothing—gets by your grandmother. You know that even better than I do."

"You're right. I'll try. After all, as we agreed, we have to clear up our past before we talk about us."

"Precisely," she concurred. "Let's try to remember that."

"Well, I say we make sure it's all right with Grams to really search the house for the pictures. I've been thinking that there must be more to Lily's stash, because, if you think about it, we are looking for not one, but two pictures now."

"True," said Erica. "Lottie said something about her mother's camera, too."

"Treasure hunt," said Graham eagerly.

Erica showered and made herself presentable. While straightening her hair, her telephone received a text. It was Andrea. **How r u? I've had no time to ring u. Falling in love. Please talk me out if it.**

Erica quickly texted back, **Sorry. Can't help u. Doing the same here. Need details. Talk soon.**

Graham and Erica appeared at Lottie's door just as Joann was coming out of it. "She didn't want to get up today. Don't stay too long unless she insists. She's pretty worn out."

"Of course," said Graham. "We'll just get her permission to do something."

"I'll stay out here," said Erica. "Go on in."

Graham entered his grandmother's room. Fear gripped him as he took in her extreme pallor. He went to her side and told her he would visit her when she was rested. She nodded. He kissed her forehead and slipped out.

Erica's heart fell when she saw him. "Graham?"

"She's doing very poorly. I've never seen her so, well, almost absent. It seems she's not really here anymore."

"Not time travelling?"

"Afraid not," said Graham. "More like crossing over. Maybe I should sit with her."

"Oh Graham, I'm so sorry."

Joann came out of her suite and saw them standing there indecisively. "I was just making my bed. Did I miss something? Does she need me?"

Graham said, "I just don't know what to do. Maybe I should sit with her. I don't want her to go alone."

"It's up to you, Graham," said Joann, "but sometimes just having family in the room is tiring. Sometimes, without knowing it, the dying wait to be left alone a moment, so they feel they can actually go."

"We were going to look for some things she'd like us to find," said Erica, taking Graham's hand unconsciously.

"Why don't you do that then," suggested Joann. "I'll keep a very close eye. She will know I'm nearby. She worries about you, Graham. I might be the one to keep watch for a bit. Go on."

"Come on, Graham," said Erica. "Let's go downstairs and talk about what we are going to do next. Joann will get you if need be." Turning to Joann, she said, "We won't leave the house. We'll be in the sitting room, kitchen, or the sofa corner of the tack room."

"Or maybe the attic," added Graham.

Joann nodded. She reached out and patted Graham's back, and said firmly, "It's going to be all right. You remember what we've talked about?"

Graham nodded and let Erica pull him away by his hand.

They went down the hall, and as they reached the top of the stairs, the house phone began to ring. Fran was there in an instant, and she answered, "Cairnview, this is Fran speaking." She listened, while Erica and Graham stood frozen at the top of the stairs.

Fran stiffened her back. "Mr. John, I'm not at liberty to say at the moment. I'll have Mrs. Hill return your call as soon as she is able." Without waiting for a reply, she hung up the telephone.

She looked at Graham at the head of the stairs and said, "That was your cousin, John. He wants to come up, bringing his sister. I thought you might like time to think about it before talking to him."

"I'll bet you anything," said Graham, as he stomped down the stairs, "that he has been calling my office to see if I'm there. Believing I'm here, he must suspect how badly Grams is doing. I don't want him here. Grams doesn't want him here. He's like a vulture circling the sky, waiting for his prize."

"What do you want to do?" asked Fran and Erica in unison.

"I want to find that picture. She needs us to finish this. I think that's what she's waiting for. She needs the closure."

"Should I see if Kyle can give us hand?" asked Erica.

"Are we going to search the house without grandmother's permission?" he asked horrified.

"Yes, we are," said Erica. "She told us not to turn the place upside down. That was her giving us permission. We have it. When she's rested and up to seeing us again, we'll have all the answers for her."

"That's a fine idea," said Fran, chiming in. "I don't know what you're looking for, but it sounds very reasonable."

"I'll run see if Kyle has class today," offered Erica. "We won't turn the house upside down, but we are going to do this as quickly as possible. The state of the house means nothing compared to the state of Lottie's mind. We want her to know that all is well, so she can go peacefully."

Erica dashed through the kitchen and out to the stables. Kyle was just getting into his car to go home. She caught up with him and said breathlessly, "Hey, do you have classes today?"

"No, do you need help with anything?" he asked. "How is Mrs. Hill?"

"Not good. It's almost like she's fading away."

"I'm so sorry to hear it," said Kyle sincerely.

"Even Joann thinks her time is very near. Lottie has been wondering what became of some things, and we want to find them as quickly as possible. We think the closure of finding them will do her good."

"I'll meet you inside then."

An old wooden chair was pulled up to the beat-up sofa in the cozy corner, and the three of them sat down to discuss the matter. Graham said, "This may sound frivolous, but we are looking for some pictures that have gone missing. Framed portraits of my grandmother and her mother seem to have disappeared. Also, we are looking for a smaller photo of a gentleman dressed in a World War Two army uniform. Kyle, it was you who gathered the letters for my grandmother and brought them down from the attic. It seems the smartest thing to do would be to see if something got missed. The large framed pictures won't be there, of course, but maybe the military photo, by chance. We are also looking for a Brownie camera. I'm thinking if we find one of these things, we may find them all."

"I'll start in the attic then, right?" asked Kyle.

"Yes, Erica and I will search the drawers and behind the books in the library. It would be pretty easy to hide things in a library."

"Someone really hid all of these things?" asked Kyle, in surprise.

"We think so, possibly," answered Erica. "Let's look for them with the idea that they may have been hidden for a purpose. It will make us more thorough. Oh, and Kyle," she added, "try to be as quiet as possible up there. We don't want to disturb Lottie's rest."

Kyle was eager to start. "I'll do my best."

Two hours later, the trio met in the library, and seeing how dirty Kyle had gotten from his maneuvers in the attic, they moved their meeting back to the tack room. Kyle and Erica went the shortest route through the garden room, but Graham went through the kitchen to speak to Fran.

"By the looks of things, you two didn't find anything, either," said Kyle, when he and Erica sat down on the old sofa.

"No, not yet," said Erica wearily.

"Sorry, but I came up empty, too, I searched the whole attic under the assumption that the pictures and camera had been hidden intentionally, and I don't think I could have missed anything. I searched the spot where I got all the papers, and it was clean. There weren't any other hidey holes like that one, either. I checked. I looked in every box, trunk, and drawer that was up there."

Graham had joined them by then. "Fran is fixing you a bag lunch before she leaves. We always eat late, but it occurred to me, you may have missed your lunchtime by a couple of hours. Thanks so much for helping. It meant a lot. I just wish we'd gotten lucky."

"Let me know if I can help with anything else," said Kyle genuinely. "Keep me posted on your grandmother, would you? She and I have become very good friends over the past couple of years, and I want to know what's happening, if I could ask that."

"Of course," said Graham.

Erica and Graham went back to the library to put a few things back in place. They stood by the desk, staring and thinking. Erica broke the silence, saying, "I think you're looking for a loose panel, just as I am."

Graham chuckled. "I will admit, I'm desperate. We simply aren't on the right track, yet. I mean, if the letters from 'W' and Rose have no meaning, why did she hide them? And though they seem unrelated to the missing items, they must fit into the puzzle, somehow. Let's go eat something. It's got to be close enough to lunchtime."

They found the kitchen shining like a new penny, just as Fran left it every day that she came. Erica said, "Fran is a prize, Graham. How long have you known her?"

"Oh, heavens, ages and ages. My whole life, really."

"So was she here already in '69 when Lily died?" asked Erica.

"I don't know. I wasn't born yet. I suppose we can ask her. If you are thinking she would have been told to hide anything, I think that's pretty far-fetched. She was always in the kitchen. When my mother came to stay with my grandmother, Fran was still at Cairnview most of the day, I think. We knew that Grams couldn't live alone anymore, so my mum came to stay and my dad commuted. Fran started coming in for fewer hours, as she was getting on in years, too. I was always close to her, because I was always in the kitchen looking for something to eat."

"I think we should have involved Fran in the search. I don't know why we didn't. I'm beginning to think she knows more than we do," said Erica, concentrating.

"Well, I can't imagine her hiding anything for anyone, but we can pursue it. I think we should look in the tack room. There are boxes on the shelves that separate the television corner from the rest of the room. I say we look there."

"Are you sure you aren't just trying to get me back to the kissing sofa?" asked Erica playfully.

"I'm not sure of anything, but if we get tired of searching, that's always an option."

"I'm all in," said Erica, laughing.

"What shall we eat?" said Graham, standing in front of the open refrigerator.

"Other than cake?"

Graham grinned at her. "Food, first, cake, second."

Chapter Twenty-One

By dinnertime, Erica and Graham were filthy, tired, and hungry. They had gone through many boxes. Everything seemed to belong to the males of the family. Every kind of tool, gloves, hardware, garden chemicals, motor oils, and horse paraphernalia were stored in boxes on the massive shelves. By the time they were finished looking, they were covered in grease and dirt.

Erica looked down at her filthy clothes. "Certainly all of this stuff didn't accumulate since you made this the tack room."

"No, it was just moved. Don't you know we never throw anything away?"

"Like Americans do? Is that what you're implying?" she asked, laughing.

"Everybody knows you Americans throw everything away."

"Right. Well, at least we could find something if we had to."

"Ouch," said Graham, laughing.

Erica had a smudge of grease on her face, and when Graham went to wipe it off for her, he just made it that much worse. The laughed and then embraced, unable to keep their hands off each other any longer.

They had enjoyed themselves as they'd worked, but they'd always found their way back to feeling the sobering urgency of what they were doing and also the frustration at their helplessness in the situation.

After showering, they sat across the kitchen table from each other, as they'd done so many times since their first meeting there. Graham dished up Erica's food, because she'd overdone it in her exertions. She was visibly exhausted, and Graham scolded himself that he should have been thinking of her, instead of fixating on the pictures he was so determined to find.

As if reading his mind, Erica said, "I'm perfectly fine, Graham. I personally want to find the picture of your grandfather, especially, so that Lottie can put to rest the possibility that your Granddad George was the one who discovered it. I know that's pressing on her mind."

"I feel the same," said Graham. "But would we really be able to tell? She really needs this closure. I sense it."

"I believe that *where* we find the picture will tell us who put it there. Does that make sense?"

He said, "*If* we find it, that is."

When Fran came in the next morning, Erica was waiting for her. She followed her around the kitchen, trying to be useful, but mostly getting in the way.

Finally, Fran said, "You'd better sit down, or I'll never get this breakfast made."

"Can I ask you some questions about the family? Graham has given his permission for us to discuss some things."

"Well, I don't talk out of school. It's not my way."

"I know. You are very faithful that way. I knew that about you, right away. And I know you are concerned for Lottie."

"These trays are for Nurse and Mr. Graham. Poor Mrs. Hill isn't eating anything anymore," said Fran, wiping her eyes with her tea towel.

"I know." Erica didn't know how to console her. "We know her time is near. For her sake, we are looking for some things that are important to her. We had no luck finding them yesterday and thought you might be able to help us. I understand you were always in the kitchen, so you might not be able to help anyway, but you have been here longer than anyone else. You are our last hope."

"All right, I'll help if I can," she said, returning to her work of making up the trays.

Erica was relieved that Fran was willing. "When Lily Jackson died, did you help at all with going through her things?"

"I did, because Mrs. Hill didn't trust the daily we had coming in. I helped her go through the clothes to give away. She even gave me a few things to remember Mrs. Jackson by."

"So everything was disposed of?" Erica felt her hope waning.

"All but the boxed items," said Fran.

"What boxed items?" Erica's hope surged again.

"Well, there were quite a few. My Ben was supposed to come help tote the boxes to the attic, but he'd fallen and broken his arm, so we just stacked them any old way."

"Where?" asked Erica, dying from suspense.

"We just pushed them across the hall."

"Into Nurse's sitting room?" Erica's hope was rising and falling like a roller coaster.

"It wasn't used at the time," explained Fran. "You

see, when we did all this, Mrs. Hill was moving into Mrs. Jackson's old room. Mr. Hill kept her awake at night. He had trouble sleeping and hated disturbing her all the time."

"What happened to the boxes when Nurse came?" asked Erica.

"Mr. Hill's things had been added to it, too, when he'd passed. His room then became the room that Mr. Gregory and his lovely wife—I called them Mr. and Mrs. G to save confusion—stayed in when they came to visit. They came more often to check on Mrs. Hill after that, and later, Mrs. G came to live here and Mr. G came on weekends. Mrs. Hill decided to have your bedroom all done up about that time, putting in the en suite, because the master bedroom was in pretty bad shape, too. She wanted Mr. and Mrs. G to have a nice accommodation. Of course, more boxes went into the dressing room. We always said it was lucky we had that room to shove everything into."

Fran paused at the memory. "Those were happy days," she said wistfully.

"Then there was the terrible accident that took Graham's parents."

"Aye, we didn't think Mrs. Hill would ever get

over it. She never really did, did she?"

"Is that when a nurse was needed full time?" asked Erica.

"Aye, Mrs. Hill was never the same after that. She knew she'd need help, so she immediately ordered the master bedroom remodeled for her first nurse. Joann is her second nurse."

"I didn't know that. So what happened to all the stuff in the dressing room?" Erica asked, bringing them back to the subject.

"I have no idea," said Fran. "I think they took it all down to the governess's old bedroom. That's what they called it—the one Millie stayed in. I had some problems myself after those dear people died. It was just too much for me. I took a leave of absence for a few months to get myself well again. My Ben wasn't supportive, at first, of my coming back to work when I did, but I won him around. I wanted to come back and serve Mrs. Hill, so I did, and I've been here ever since."

"Thank you for telling me, Fran. Let me take the trays up."

As Erica was leaving the room, Fran asked, "Did Mr. Graham remember to telephone that pesky Mr. John?"

"He did. He stalled him."

"That's good, then. I'll be leaving right away today. I put something in the crock-pot for you."

"Thank you, Fran. I'll tell Graham."

Graham had been sitting with Lottie since very early in the morning. Joann tapped on his door to wake him, so he could take over the watch. He'd asked her to wake him when she needed to rest.

When Erica went in with the tray, she found Joann resting in her bed. She wasn't sleeping, she assured Erica, but she had gotten some good sleep when Graham had taken over, and she was ready to relieve him now, whenever he wanted her to.

Erica arranged her tray. "We'll get you if we need you."

Joann smiled appreciatively. "I'm glad you two are here. It makes things much easier for me. When was the last time I had breakfast in bed, I wonder?"

When Erica entered Lottie's room, she was startled by the absence of energy that the room had always exuded. A powerful force was slipping out of the world, she knew, and by the look on Graham's face, he knew it only too well, also.

"Here you are," she whispered, putting his tray on the stand. She stroked his mussed hair. "May I sit with her a while after you eat?"

"I don't know." Graham looked like a lost little boy. "I hate to leave."

"I know," said Erica sympathetically. She watched on as he ate his breakfast mechanically, his mind obviously far away from what he was doing. After eating as much as he could, he set the tray stand aside and leaned back in his chair with his coffee.

"Did you learn anything from Fran?" he asked in a whisper.

"She was here when some of Lily's things were put into Joann's sitting room."

Graham rubbed his eyes. "At that time it was the dressing room, I remember."

"Yes. When your granddad died, his stuff was added to it, so that your parents could come and stay in his old room. Eventually, the room I'm in was updated for them, so they could stay more permanently. More stuff went into the dressing room and later to the governess's room, Fran said. When your parents died, Fran went home for a few months to get well."

"I didn't know that and I should have. I should have checked on her and shown concern."

"You weren't able to, Graham. You did the best you could. Anyway, everything just got shoved from room to room…..oh, Graham, I just realized something."

They looked at each other wide-eyed. Graham said, "How could I have been so stupid? I've been tripping over the stuff for days. Why didn't I think of it?"

"I don't know. I feel just as stupid. I think it's because we had it in our heads that it was hidden." she whispered excitedly. "Come, let's go find it now. I'll get Joann."

Erica bolted into Joann's bedroom again, saying, "Oh Joann, we think we know where the lost items are."

"I'm finished eating. I'll come sit with her while you look," said Joann, getting up and grabbing her robe.

Graham and Erica hurried into his bedroom and closed the door. He pulled her into his arms and said, "You figured this out. It will be all to your credit!"

"Let's find it before you give me too much credit. Lottie won't know if we tear the place apart, as she put it. I say we do it the messy way."

"I agree," said Graham, already moving boxes.

They worked frantically for several minutes, opening the boxes like it was Christmas morning. Finally, Graham exclaimed, "It's here! Look, Erica."

In a small box within another box, were the framed pictures of the women. Erica gasped when she saw the picture of Lottie. "Oh, so young and alive!"

Laying the picture frames flat on the bed, Graham dug into the box further, coming up with the missing Brownie camera. He looked again, and seeing nothing else but a few strands of cheap beads, he was devastated. "No photo."

"No?" asked Erica, disbelieving. "It must be here." She looked herself but found nothing.

Graham picked up the camera and opened it, hoping against hope that he'd find the photo tucked inside it, but he was wrong. Having his hopes dashed so completely, he was frustrated to the point of anger. "I just don't understand! I was so sure."

"Go ahead and get dressed, Graham. I'll go sit with your grandmother. We'll show her these pictures the next time she is awake. We can look through the rest of these boxes later."

"There's no sense," said Graham. "This is where everything is. It should have been right here."

The doctor came early that afternoon, and Graham waited nervously in the hall for his appraisal. When he came out of her room, he said, "She's awake and pretty lucid right now, son. It might be the time to say your goodbyes and call in any family. She doesn't have long now. Today may be her last rally."

Graham and Erica entered the room with the framed portraits. Joann left, so they could have their time with her. Approaching the bed, Graham said, "Grams, we found your portrait, and we found your mum's with it." He held one of them up and Erica held the other one for her to view. "Can you see them all right?"

"Just move out of my light a bit," said his grandmother weakly. "Where are my glasses?"

When Graham lovingly put her glasses on her face, and she attempted a smile. "Well done, my children!"

Graham and Erica looked at each other fondly. Graham began to explain that they had yet to find the photo of his grandfather, but before he could, Erica nudged him.

He looked at her quizzically, and she pointed excitedly at the backs of the frames. He saw that the easels of each of the frames were missing one of the screws, but failed to see the significance and shrugged questioningly.

"I'll get Nurse," she said. "I'll be right back, Lottie. Graham, help her take off her glasses."

Erica came back in with Joann and told Lottie that they needed the pictures for just a minute, but would bring them right back. Tucking the frames under her arm and grabbing Graham's hand, she dragged him down the back stairs, through the garden room and into the tack room.

"What are we doing, darling?" Graham was exasperated. "I've got to stay with Grams. I have to be with her."

Erica set the frames face down on the workbench. Grabbing a screwdriver, she excitedly bent back the metal tabs that held the backs of the frames in place. She carefully lifted off the back of Lottie's frame, revealing what she knew would be there. Attached with scotch tape to the back of the portrait was the photo of what could have been Graham in a uniform. There he was—Graham's grandfather, Elliot Gregory.

Graham gasped at the discovery. They carefully

peeled the tape back, releasing the photograph, and he took it to the nearest window to see it more clearly. Erica looked at him fondly, only imagining what he was feeling. He was obviously emotional, so she determined to leave him alone and press on by herself. Following her instinct, she pulled off the back of Lily's picture. There, taped to the back of her portrait, was a picture of a fine-looking officer. She held it up and whispered, "Hello, 'W.' I am so glad to have found you."

She carefully took out the photo and gazed at it, willing it to give up its secrets. He was very handsome and wearing the uniform of the First World War. Suddenly, a chill enveloped her as she slowly turned it over. On the back, it read, "For my most darling friend, If only, from William, 1917."

Erica began to weep. She couldn't contain it. Finding the answers for Lottie had become personal for her. In finding answers for Lottie, she had been, simultaneously and unknowingly, finding them for herself. She felt an amazing relief, but also a release from the emotional bondage that had always had so much power to hurt her. She had broken free from Dean, from her father, and most of all, from the debilitating pain of her mother's death. The perspective she'd so badly needed had been given to her in small doses since her arrival at Cairnview, and now she had been freed by it.

Graham joined her, putting his arm around her. He stared at the back of the photo in her hands. "William, 'W.' How did you know?" he asked incredulously.

"I'm not sure," she admitted shakily, turning the photo over. "I didn't figure anything out, Graham. Lily took the screws out deliberately to lead us to the pictures. When that dawned on me, I knew the search was over. I knew what to do. I felt as if I was being guided. I think we all were."

"So my great grandmother was obviously in love with this man, but he must have married someone else," said Graham, staring at the photo.

"Officers stayed here at Cairnview during the Great War. I remember that Lottie said her mother was noticeably happier during the war. She'd found a friend in him, but she wasn't free. They stayed friends, Graham. He finally married, and then he and his wife, whose name was probably Rose, were still Lily's friends. When Lily's husband died, it was too late for them as a couple, but he didn't desert her. I think Rose knew about their friendship—their story—I really do. I think she understood and approved. Like your grandmother said—there are different kinds of love."

"It's so amazing. You really did figure it all out."

Erica talked excitedly. "We have no reason to say whether or not Lily and William were lovers. It is simply none of our business. Nothing in the papers even suggests it, but when Lily wrote the letter to Lottie, she wanted her to know that she truly understood about love. She wanted Lottie to know it all, but she feared if she acknowledged Lottie's secret—or her own—her daughter's happy marriage with George might somehow be threatened. She couldn't risk it. She couldn't risk her daughter's happiness, so she waited."

"Until now," finished Graham. "Let's try to tell Grams while she's having a good day. I hope she can take it in."

"I don't doubt it for a minute," said Erica with certainty.

When they entered Lottie's room, she sensed their presence and opened her eyes. Joann motioned for them to come in, and she slipped out quietly. They stood beside the bed, and without saying anything, Graham carefully put his grandmother's glasses on her again and put the photo in her hand.

She inhaled sharply and stared at the photo of the wonderful man she'd been forced to forget. Tears rolled down the papery pale skin of her aged face, and seeing this, Erica and Graham couldn't keep their tears at bay, either.

Finally, Graham said tenderly, "We found out who 'W' was, Grams."

She looked at him blankly.

"The little notes and letters from 'W.' It stood for William. Your mother met an officer during the first war. He probably stayed here for a time. Erica told me that you remembered there being officers here."

Lottie nodded.

"Your mother put Elliot's picture behind yours in the frame. And behind her own picture, was this. He signed it, *For my most darling friend, If only, from William, 1917*."

Lottie took the second picture in her shaking hand, but she couldn't hold it still enough to see it. Graham took it from her and held it up for her. She smiled weakly and said haltingly, "I knew him. I called him Uncle Bill, although I always knew we weren't actually related. He looks much different here than I remember him. I haven't even thought of him in years. He came to visit my mum in her final years. His coming made her very happy. I remember that now."

Erica explained, "We think that your mother and William agreed to be friends, since nothing else was possible. If things had been different, I'm sure they would have married. Lily knew she couldn't get a divorce. He must have married someone with Lily's blessing, maybe Rose, and they all remained friends. Quite a remarkable story, I think."

"Uncle Bill came to my mother's funeral. He came alone, I remember. I do, quite distinctly."

"We believe you, Grams," assured Graham.

Finding it difficult to speak, Lottie said, "My mother really did understand love, and she wanted me to know it. That was the treasure she wanted me to find. Oh, dear children, I couldn't have done it without you. I couldn't have done it at all. Thank you for coming, Erica. Your coming was divinely set in motion."

"If you'd seen the kind of day I had getting here, you might question that assessment, but I don't. It was meant to be. I've loved being here."

"Don't you dare go away. We aren't done yet," said Lottie, trying to sound like her normal, incorrigible self, but unable to pull it off in her weakened state.

"You look very tired, so you must rest, Grams," said Graham lovingly.

"Thank you, my children. Thank you so very much," she whispered.

They each kissed her in turn, and this time she didn't tease them. Instead, she said, "I love you two, you know. Now, let me see you ride out on those horses together. Get along."

"I can't leave you, Grams," pleaded Graham. "Please, don't make me."

"I'm sorry, darling Gram, but you must."

Two hours later, when the riders returned, Joann met them at the kitchen door and, by her expression, they knew that Lottie had passed. Joann wrapped her arms around them both. "She was an amazing woman. I feel blessed to have known her. I was right there with her when she passed. She made me lift her up to see you ride out. She passed moments later. Things have been set in motion, so there really isn't much for you to do at the moment, unless you want to come up and see her before they come for her. If you don't mind me saying, though, I think she would rather you didn't. She doesn't want a public viewing, either. She isn't there anymore. Remember her as she was."

Nodding their agreement, Erica and Graham clung to each other for strength.

"What you could do is let her friends Kyle and Fran know right away," suggested Joann. "It would mean a lot to them to be the first to know."

Chapter Twenty-Two

The funeral was attended by many, most of whom Graham knew well. John and Elizabeth traveled together and had made it only as far as Edinburgh the night before. John tried to take control of the proceedings upon his arrival that morning, but everything had long been set in motion, so there was nothing left to decide.

Fran had been in charge of the tea after the funeral, but a catering group was brought in to carry it out. She had taken Lottie's death very hard, and her husband was worried about her. They were at the funeral together, and when back at Cairnview, Graham settled them in comfortable chairs in the sitting room and brought little plates of food to them. He checked on them often to give them more tea and to make sure they were comfortable. Erica smiled as she watched his attentiveness to the elderly couple.

When Joann came downstairs, he did the same for her. He insisted she keep her accommodations until she had firm plans, and she accepted gratefully.

Kyle was there with his family, and Erica spoke to them like old friends and took Kyle aside to tell him they'd found the missing pictures before Lottie had passed. He was very pleased, as she knew he would be.

Erica knew the doctor, the Smiths, and the people from the inn, so she spoke briefly with each of them, too.

Graham's work associates from Newcastle came, and of course, Lottie's solicitor, Mr. Warren Adamson, was there. He kept looking at Erica, and since Graham had pointed him out to her earlier, she went over to introduce herself. He already knew about her. He'd talked to Mrs. Hill, and she had sung her praises, he said.

"I don't know what will become of her memoirs, now," said Erica.

"You will know what to do. Now isn't the time to fuss. It's a day to remember," he said kindly. "Have you met Mr. and Mrs. Paul Davies?"

"Are they here?" Erica was surprised. "I work for him, as you probably know, but we've never met."

"They just came in. Graham is talking to them."

"Thank you for pointing them out to me, I'll speak to them now."

As she turned to go, he said, "You are to be at the reading of the will tomorrow, Miss Sinclair. Did Graham tell you, yet?"

"We've hardly bumped into each other all day. I can't imagine why I should be there."

Mr. Adamson smiled kindly. "Because Mrs. Hill requested it."

"Of course."

She joined Graham and was introduced. The Davies seemed especially glad to make her acquaintance. "We'll have to get together when you get back to London," said Mr. Davies.

Dreading the prospect of London, Erica nodded politely. "Thank you. That would be nice. This was a wonderful opportunity for me. I'm so glad to have had the chance to know Mrs. Hill."

As Graham, John and Elizabeth were tied up with the other guests, Erica wandered outside to the horses. Fancy came up to her to comfort her, and Erica said to her, "I think it's just you and me again, old girl."

She buried her head in the horse's neck and let the tears flow. It felt good to let it all out. She felt like she'd lived two lifetimes in the past month, and her emotions, having stayed ever close to the surface, seemed to lay in wait for any moment of weakness. When she was able to catch her breath, she heard footsteps coming up from behind her, and she turned to see Millie and Henry approaching her. She threw herself into their loving arms.

"I didn't think you would make it," cried Erica.

"We did the best we could. We'd have made it to the church, too, if the train had run on time," said Millie.

"You're here now, and that's all that matters," said Erica, wiping her tears. "Come inside and have something to eat. Fran will be happy to see you. She's in the sitting room today, not the kitchen, and Joann looks a little lost. She will be so happy to see you, too."

When she'd taken Millie and Henry to see their many acquaintances in the sitting room, she found them something to sit on and went to get their refreshments. After that, she kept herself busy filling tea cups and seeing to the guests' needs until the last one was gone.

She knew that Graham's cousins had gotten as far as Edinburgh the night before and had stayed there for the night. If they were staying the night at Cairnview, she assumed she would need to vacate and prepare her room for one of them and get the other little bedroom readied for the other. She would curl up on Lottie's bed.

She was finally able to get Graham alone and asked him about the arrangements for his cousins. He said,

"That's for them to figure out. If anyone goes to the inn, it can be them."

"But they are family," argued Erica.

"If they are, then they figure out where to sleep and make up their own beds."

Erica wanted to argue the point, but John was now approaching them. She hurried back to the kitchen to avoid hearing their conversation.

John did have the expectation of rooms at Cairnview, and an intense conversation ensued. Graham explained that with the nurse and Erica still there, he and his sister could have the sofas or go somewhere else.

In the end, Elizabeth joined the conversation, saying, "Oh, I think we definitely should go to the inn, John."

Although he acquiesced to his sister's wishes, John made sure everyone knew he was not pleased.

When the house was finally empty, Erica and Graham met in the kitchen. They'd hardly eaten a thing all day.

Pulling things from the refrigerator, Graham remarked, "Looks like the caterers left the kitchen clean enough for even Fran's high standards."

"Is she coming back to work?" asked Erica in surprise.

"No, she's just coming tomorrow for the reading of the will. You are to be there." Graham looked at her meaningfully.

"Mr. Adamson told me, although I was a little surprised. I hope it's about her wishes for the memoirs." Changing the subject, she looked at him askance and said, "It looks like the inn will be full-up tonight."

With a gleam of mischief in his eyes, Graham answered, "I did offer Millie and Henry the small bedroom, but they insisted they go to the inn."

"Shame on you! That would have made John furious," said Erica with mock severity.

"I know, but I'm glad we're alone tonight, because I want to show you something."

"Oh?"

"Aunt Dede gave me an envelope containing a single sheet of paper."

Erica looked on expectantly as Graham pulled the paper from his jacket pocket. He handed it to her.

Upon seeing the heading, she exclaimed, "The Christmas Blitz!"

From the first glance, she knew it was the list of those buried after the bombing. Scanning the document, she saw, "Elliot Gregory, of Inverness, Scotland—interred in Toxteth Park Cemetery in Liverpool.

Her eyes met Graham's. "Dede knew?"

"She had to have. Remember, she shared a room with Grams at the school. Apparently, she knew far more than she ever let on. I suppose she couldn't explain it to me, in the event I didn't know, so she just handed me the envelope and said that it should be kept with my grandmother's things."

"I wonder if Paul used the tools at the paper to discover it for her," marveled Erica.

"She's probably had it for decades, but couldn't let on that she knew until Grams told her about it, which she never did. I can do what Grams never could, Erica. I can visit my grandfather's grave."

"Oh, Graham. I'm so happy for you," she cried, throwing her arms around him.

After the exhausting day they'd had, they tried to watch a movie together but were asleep on the sofa within minutes. When they awoke, it was morning.

Graham said playfully, "I'm afraid we just slept together."

"Oh, Graham," exclaimed Erica, "my mother would not approve."

He replied, "Nor would my grandmother, but as we are completely innocent, I think we can rule out guilt."

Erica smiled brightly."What a fine idea."

The reading of the will took place in the sitting room, where the extra chairs for the funeral still sat about. Those invited included Joann, Fran and her Ben, Kyle, and Kyle's predecessor, a man by the name of Weylan Wallace. Others there included John, Elizabeth, Paul and Dede Davies, and of course, Erica and Graham.

Erica saw hostility in John's eyes as he looked around the room. She could guess he was wondering how much of his inheritance would be divvied up among those present. Everyone else was conversing amiably. Erica didn't know why she had been invited, but assumed it had to do with Lottie's final wishes for her memoirs.

With the help of Millie and Henry, Fran and Ben had made little sandwiches, cakes and tea to be served after the reading. They had it beautifully prepared, ready for Millie and Henry to set out on the dining room table at the right moment. It was Fran's final act of service for Lottie, and she had been adamant that she be able to do it. When all was to Fran's satisfaction, Millie pushed her and Ben into the sitting room with the others, promising all would be well.

When John had thought enough small talk had taken place, he cleared his throat and took it upon himself to open the meeting. "Ladies and gentlemen, we have met for the purpose of reading of my grandmother's will, and I think we should do that now, so that Mr. Adamson need not be detained further."

Mr. Adamson, who had just started up a delightful conversation with Fran and her husband, frowned at the implication that he couldn't wait to leave. He stood reluctantly, reached for his folder and faced the group. He cleared his throat, and each listened attentively to the final wishes of Mrs. Charlotte Hill.

As Mr. Adamson read all the preliminary legal jargon, all present listened attentively, whether they understood it or not.

As he began the bequests, the room was as silent as a tomb. It began with Fran, who was to be given a gift of money and a generous monthly pension. She wept silently as her husband helplessly patted her back.

Joann was given a large sum, which would enable her to retire whenever she was ready to do so, and although she remained silent, her face registered complete surprise.

Mr. Wallace, the retired stable hand was already receiving his pension but was given an additional gift of money. Feeling emotional, he hid it behind a contrived cough.

Kyle was given a gift of money, enough to cover his education. He was so stunned, he put his head in his hands until he had his emotions in check.

The last bequest was a sum of money for Mrs. Dorothea Davies, which made her shake her head in wonder.

After these bequests were announced, there was a moment of complete silence, and then Mr. Adamson requested that those already mentioned go on into the dining room where the refreshments were being laid out.

When the others had filed out, Mr. Adamson closed the tall double doors to the sitting room. He returned to the remaining four and said, "Mrs. Hill asked that this portion be read only to you still seated here."

John asked, "Why is the journalist to remain with the family?"

Mr. Adamson said, "Because your grandmother requested it, Mr. Hill. She also wanted the family to understand that what transpires here is final. She has expressed that as her gifts are extremely generous, there is no room for quibbling.

He read, "To my trusted friend, Erica Sinclair, I leave the sum of fifty thousand pounds." All eyes were on her, as she tried to take it in. She was embarrassed being watched and felt the inevitable tears coming to the surface.

Oh Lottie, I don't deserve it, thought Erica.

She was sure the same thought was racing through John's mind at that same moment and dared not look at him.

Mr. Adamson read on, "To my granddaughter Elizabeth, I bequest the sum of three hundred thousand pounds. As she is of age and has shown herself to be sensible, she can use it when she sees fit and how she sees fit."

Everyone now looked at her. She was openly shocked and touched by her grandmother's generosity.

"How kind," she whispered.

"To my grandson John, I bequeath one hundred fifty thousand pounds, as he has previously claimed the larger portion. This amount is to be given to him in three equal increments on the first, second, and third anniversaries of my death to teach him patience and frugality, which are important lessons that have more value than the actual gift of money.

John was observably agitated, but said nothing. His face turned slowly red, indicating embarrassment, or anger, or both.

Mr. Adamson continued, "To my grandson Graham, I leave the remainder of my estate, which includes Cairnview and all my other assets. He has proven himself worthy of this responsibility, and although unencumbered with debt, the estate is still cumbersome in its scope. He loves Cairnview as I do, and I know he will use the resources at his disposal to keep it maintained and, more importantly, lived in."

The stunned group was silent as the rest of the document was read. When finished, Graham stood. "Let's all adjourn to the dining room. I think we all would like to drink a toast to our grandmother and friend, who has treated us so generously."

John got up angrily to storm out. Graham caught him at the door and said sternly, "She has been very generous, John. Don't spoil anything."

"How am I supposed to know what you are getting?" asked John angrily.

"I think if she'd wanted you to know that, it would have been part of the will," said Graham. "If it makes you feel any better, I don't know how much it is, either. You would have sold Cairnview immediately, you remember. She knows I won't do that."

"You were up here influencing her. That's why you stalled us, so that we couldn't even say our goodbyes to her."

"Please remember, you haven't been here in four years, John," said Graham. "I must see to my other guests, now."

Graham's cousin Elizabeth caught up with him after the toast and said discreetly, "I'm so pleased that Cairnview won't be sold. I would like to come back for a real visit sometime, if you will have me. It's so lovely. I can't imagine why we didn't visit more often when I was a child."

"Of course," said Graham. "Cairnview will always welcome you."

That night, although Joann was still occupying her apartment upstairs, Erica felt suddenly awkward being there alone with Graham. There had been a telephone call for him, so she had wandered into the library, where she had so often found comfort. She touched the smooth surface of the desk, where she had learned so much about life and death, but most importantly, love.

Through Lottie, she had learned that there are many kinds of love. Above all, she'd learned that her giddy feelings of pleasure and excitement that she'd felt for first Andrew, and then Dean, did not qualify as love at all. Acknowledging that, she wondered if she could ever trust her heart to get it right.

She felt overwhelmed by the generous gift that Lottie had given her and entirely at loose ends. She didn't know what was to come next. She wondered why Lottie hadn't specified what she wanted done with her memoirs, and Erica berated herself for missing her chance to get detailed instructions. Time had run out so very quickly, and there were so many unanswered questions. She missed

Lottie terribly, and the house seemed empty and hollow without her.

Suddenly she had doubts about Graham's feelings towards her. She wondered if she'd read too much into his attentions, assuming too much. She moved to the window and stared out over the dusky landscape.

Am I doing it again? Am I falling in love too quickly? she wondered.

Graham found her there after he'd ended his telephone conversation and had secured the house for the night. He came in, announcing happily, "That was my solicitor, Giles, on the telephone. He wanted to convey his condolences. He spent much of the day on the telephone with a colleague of his from London. Giles's colleague is going to represent Dean in his present troubles, provided he drops the nonsense about you owing him anything. He accepted the offer readily, so Giles wanted to let us know right away."

Erica turned to him and smiled gratefully. "Oh, that is a relief. Thank you so much for that, Graham." She turned back to the window as tears filled her eyes.

Sensing something, Graham approached her. "What's the matter, darling?" he asked tenderly.

Full of self-doubt, she turned to him, and smiled shyly. "This has been such a memorable time. I won't know how to go back to regular life. I won't go back to London. I can't imagine being able to stand it."

"You're not talking of leaving, are you?" asked Graham in dismay. He lifted her chin to force her to look him in the eye. "What's going on in that pretty head of yours?"

"I think perhaps my confidence died with your grandmother. I suppose I'm afraid of being hurt, and I honestly don't think I trust myself."

"May I make a suggestion?"

She nodded timidly.

He took her gently in his arms. "Let's have trust in the things my grandmother taught us. She experienced it all. She handed us her wisdom and said, "Here, learn from it.'"

"I know, and I am. But, what about right now? I can't stay on indefinitely, can I? I can't make that mistake again."

"Erica, now that I've found you, I can't let you go." He tightened his arms around her.

"We can't be impulsive, though, can we? It isn't

like it was for your grandparents during the war. For them, there was such an urgency to live every day as if it might be their last."

"The war simply made them aware of the value of each and every day—to live it fully. They had it right. Every day should be lived as if it's the last. I haven't told you, but you must know it—I've fallen in love with you, Erica. You may not believe this, but I think I've loved you since the first time I saw you."

"Oh Graham, I love you, too. What would you have us do?"

"Well, although we did sleep together last night, I'm not asking you to move in with me, if that's what you mean," he teased.

"But, I'm already living with you," argued Erica.

"We're not here alone. Joann is still here. Besides, Grams gave us her blessing."

"Did she?"

"Of course she did. Will you marry me, Erica?"

Oh, I want to, but I'm afraid. I think I need Lottie's approval. What if she thought me a gold digger? How was I supposed to know she was leaving you a fortune? How do we know she'll approve?"

"Because she told us, remember?" soothed Graham.

Nodding, Erica said, "She did, sort of, didn't she? Yes, I think she did. Oh, I'm going to miss her, Graham."

"I know. I miss her terribly already. I didn't get to keep her long enough, and you are the only one who understands what I mean by that. Know what else I've missed the last couple of days?"

"I know what I've missed," she said, putting her arms around his neck.

After a long and tender kiss, Graham led her by the hand to the cozy corner of the tack room. Settled there, she leaned into the crook of his arm. "We never got to take Lottie for her ride in the country. I wanted to so badly. Oh Graham, our children will never know what it's like to have caring grandparents."

"I know how you feel exactly, but did you know that Grams left Millie and Henry a bequest, as well? Millie told me before they left today."

Puzzled, Erica asked, "She did? Why weren't she and Henry at the reading of the will, then?"

"Because Grams didn't have to put it in writing. She bequeathed us to them. The day that Millie and Henry came to take you sightseeing, she asked them to be our family."

"But that was days before we even knew ourselves," marveled Erica.

"Is that really so surprising?"

"She really did give us her blessing, then." said Erica in awe. "It seems she thought of everything. Oh, I'll miss her so."

Taking Erica in his arms, Graham said lovingly, "She's free now, my darling. She stayed here only as long as she had to. I truly believe that once she'd found the answers she'd longed for and accomplished all she'd set out to do, she was able to quietly, almost regally, slip away."

Erica whispered reverently, "And so she did."

Epilogue

In late September, Graham and Erica were married quietly amongst their most intimate friends and neighbors.

Andrea came from London to act as Erica's maid of honor, bringing Steven, her significant other, and Kyle stood up with Graham as his best man. Millie and Henry came, as did Graham's cousin Elizabeth and a many of their local friends, as well as colleagues of Graham's from Newcastle.

Erica's dad did not come for the wedding, but provided copious bouquets of hothouse roses in yellow and white. Touched that he remembered her passion for yellow, Erica had renewed hope for a meaningful relationship with him in the future.

The marriage was solemnized in the village kirk, where Henry had the honor of giving away the bride. Erica wore a simple ivory gown that drew attention to the glorious, cathedral-length, vintage bridal veil of ivory lace that Millie had worn at her own wedding.

The reception was held in Cairnview's old garden room, which had been painted a pristine white and decorated with the abundant roses. The spotless windows invited the show of autumn colors that surrounded the estate. Fran insisted on making the glorious three-tiered wedding cake herself, but allowed a local catering group to handle the food. It was a great success, and more than once, Graham and Erica felt Lottie's presence. They knew she was celebrating with them.

After Christmas, Graham and Erica decided to proceed with the memoirs that had been so important to his grandmother. Although still unsure how to deal with all the delicate information at their disposal, they decided to cross each bridge as they came to it, trusting they would somehow be guided.

Sitting down together in the cozy corner of the tack room, they read the introduction to the memoirs that Erica had written just days before Lottie's death.

Asked to assist Mrs. Charlotte Hill in the writing of her memoirs, I found that as the work progressed, so did my perspective. It has been my unique privilege to hear her story in her own words and from her own mouth.

In the beginning, as a stranger, I was only able to peer timidly into her life. This evolved quickly into a sense of experiencing some of the events of her life, as she took me back in time with her. My feelings began to echo her feelings, and her pain became my pain. As she described the terrible human tragedies of war, there were times when she had to stop her narrative to console me.

In interviewing Mrs. Hill, who will celebrate her one hundredth birthday on Christmas Day, I found her to be in possession of great wisdom, only accrued through vast time and broad experience. That may sound like meaningless words to the casual reader, but to me they are much more than that. I stand in awe of her character, her strength, and her legacy. I feel like a time-traveler, who fears he will not be entirely credible upon his return to his own time, so great is my desire to share what I believe will be of great benefit to those who will listen, or in this case, read.

Sequestered as we were at the Cairnview Estate in Stirling, Scotland, there was almost a shipboard atmosphere, where the hands on the clock meant very little. The players included Mrs. Lottie Hill, herself, mostly bedridden and yet living a full life from her bedroom on the upper floor; her kind and sensible nurse, whose experience taught her that the life well-lived is the only real goal; their intuitive cook, who has been with the family for years; and a handful of generous neighbors, who have been in the area for generations.

Add to the mix the part-time stable hand/law student; a kindly doctor, who still makes house calls; a caring grandson, who commutes miles to be with her; and then me, an American journalist.

I inevitably bring my own perspective to the project, but you will see for yourself as you turn the pages of these, her memoirs, that she has a remarkable story to tell. She has asked that I write them for her, as she cannot do it for herself, but fear not, her essence and perspective is woven everywhere throughout.

I have felt like a trespasser many times since the beginning of this project, but I have become more than a record keeper, more than a scribe, and more than an observer. I have become a beneficiary of her great wisdom and perseverance, garnered from the rich experiences of her life. She has survived almost everyone she has ever loved, and yet she presses on. She has fought the fight, and she is the victor. She stands like an ancient oak that has weathered many a storm and is all the stronger for it. I present to you the memoirs of Lottie Hill.

The End

About the Author

Meredith Kennon was born in South Dakota, in 1951, and spent her childhood years on a farm, enjoying all the blessings that such an upbringing affords. Her husband's work allowed the family to see much of the United States and enjoy its diversity. The children now grown, she and her husband live in a small town in southeastern South Dakota, where they enjoy their country life. They have been married forty-four years, have six beloved children, six amazing children-in-law, and twenty-five beautiful grandchildren.

If you liked the character Kyle Johnson, watch for the release of *Tia's Retreat* in the coming year. Meredith's writing reflects her values and her passion for all things rural and domestic. Her books are a throwback to simpler times, even old-fashioned, for which she makes no apology. She believes that many readers retreat to their books to find respite from a hectic, modern world, and she writes to that end. If you enjoyed this book, please give it a rating at Amazon or other book websites. Your comments are always welcome on her Meredith Kennon Facebook page and also on her blog, meredithkennon.blogspot.com. Thank you for reading.

Printed in Great Britain
by Amazon

82142412R00226

The Cat
Who
Taught Zen

The Cat
Who
Taught Zen

James Norbury

MICHAEL JOSEPH

Also by James Norbury

Big Panda and Tiny Dragon

The Journey: A Big Panda and Tiny Dragon Adventure

For the animals.

Teachers, messengers and most of all, friends.

Far from here, there was a city.

It sat upon the shores of a great river.

And was home to many thousands of people.

But this story is not about people.

This tale is about a Cat.

And on this cold autumn night, he is sheltering from the rain
with his very good friend, the Rat.

Rain spilled from the rooftops and bubbled down the gutters.
The people of the city hunched their shoulders against the
downpour and hurried to their homes.

The Cat watched them.

After a while, he turned to the Rat and said,
'I have been searching for many years.
But there is still so much I don't understand.'

'And what is it you're looking for?' asked the Rat.

The Cat sighed.

'I wish I knew.
Peace?
Acceptance?
Perhaps a way to make sense of the world . . .'

'Nothing too difficult then,' said the Rat, smiling kindly.

'But maybe I can help – I have heard that far from here,
deep within the maple forests that shroud the valley,
there is a single ancient pine tree.
And one who sits within its boughs will attain
a peace and understanding like no other.'

'Really?' asked the Cat.

The Rat nodded.

'Then my path is clear, I will leave at once.'

And bidding his friend farewell, he dropped soundlessly from the wall and followed the old road that led out of the city and towards the valley.

The Cat travelled for many hours.

As dusk fell across the land, he saw the glow of firelight
coming from a distant cave.

He was sodden and cold and decided to take a chance.

The Cat peered cautiously into the cave.

To his surprise, a Hare was drying himself by the fire.

'Oh . . . hello,' said the Hare, a little startled.
'Come and join me. What brings you out here?'

As the last of the light faded,
the Cat gratefully seated himself by the fire.
'I am a spiritual traveller,' he said.
'I seek the ancient pine that grows amongst the maples.'

'Really?' said the Hare.
'And what brought you to follow this path?'

The Cat thought for a moment.
'I suppose it started many years ago, when I was just a kitten.'

'Once a year, a wise Dragon would visit the village where I lived.
The Dragon would talk with anyone who came to see him, and offer
guidance and wisdom.'

'I loved to visit him, every day.

But back then, I was mischievous and each time
I went to see the Dragon, I couldn't help but steal something
– a plum, some incense . . .

And on one occasion, I'm ashamed to say, his beautiful,
treasured bell.'

One day, when I went to see the Dragon, he was gone,
and in his place there was a small scroll with my name on it.'

Dear Kitten,

I very much enjoyed our conversations.

I know we will meet again.

Please don't forget to oil the bell now and then.
It will rust in this misty valley.

Ever your friend,
Dragon

'Well, as you can imagine I was overcome with guilt, but more importantly,
I couldn't believe how kindly the Dragon had treated me,
even though he knew all along I had been stealing from him.

This act of forgiveness had a profound effect on me.

It showed me how, without preaching, another's actions can inspire
change in those around them.

I became determined to continue the Dragon's good work.

That is how I came to follow this path.'

'I see,' said the Hare.

'So what did you do to start following the teachings of the Dragon?'

'Well, I started slowly,' said the Cat, 'and I made many mistakes,
but I think there are a few things which have made a real difference to me.'

'Please share,' said the Hare.

The Cat pondered a moment.

'Well,' he said, 'I still visit the Dragon every year, and each time he
shares something with me that changes the way I think.

So I would have to say the first thing would be to . . .

. . . keep learning.

New ideas can help us grow and avoid
repeating the same mistakes.

It's easier to learn when you realize
life is always trying to teach you something.'

'Spend time in silence,

appreciate nature,

be mindful and seek peace.'

'Nature has no words

but it is trying to tell you something.'

'I once heard someone say,
it was not the journey or the destination that mattered most,
but the company.'

'Spend time with those who bring out the best in you.'

'What if you have no one?' asked the Hare.

'Wherever we go, we are our own companion,' said the Cat.

'And that is why we must try to be a good
friend to ourselves and treat ourselves with gentleness.

After all, we are the one we spend the most time with,
and we have a habit of taking our own opinions very seriously.'

'Kindness and gratitude are two qualities
I found difficult to learn, but they can help us in so many ways.

They cost nothing,
but their value cannot be overstated.'

'If you knew how much kindness could change your life,
you would practise it at every opportunity.

And, of course, if your kindness does not include
yourself or those you find difficult, it is incomplete.'

The two animals spoke long into the night until, at last,
they fell asleep around the dying embers of the fire.

Morning broke across the mountains, but when the Cat finally awoke,
the Hare was gone.

In his place, there was some food carefully wrapped in a leaf.

The Cat smiled and gratefully ate the Hare's generous gift.

The morning sunlight had burned off the mists and
the Cat, stomach full, headed out along the mountain trail.

He had only been travelling for a few hours when a raucous cawing
broke the stillness.

Looking up, the Cat saw a Crow perched in a dead tree,
screeching and flapping its wings.

'Crow,' called the Cat.

'What is the matter?'

The Crow flew down to a low branch and eyed the Cat
with a tilted head.

'The nerve!' she squawked.

'Someone has stolen my shiny thing. I had a great deal of trouble
getting it and now someone has stolen it. I am furious.
I was going to use it to impress a friend!'

'Perhaps it's not the disaster you think it is,'
said the Cat.

'Pah!' scoffed the Crow. 'What would you know?'

'Well,' said the Cat, 'allow me to tell you a story about a little dragon I once knew, a descendant of the Great Dragon who used to visit my village.'

'His name was Tiny Dragon, and one day, while on a journey to meet
his friend Big Panda, he found the most exquisite thing;
a large, sea-green crystal that when gazed into, seemed to hold
all of the mysteries of the world.'

'But so absorbed did Tiny Dragon become, looking into the crystal as he walked along, that he stumbled and dropped it on his delicate dragon foot.'

'Well, needless to say he was in agony. He thought the bones
had been broken and was forced to halt his journey,
limping his way across the bridge to an abandoned hermitage.'

'Tiny Dragon, feeling sorry for himself, sat down on a rock.
It would probably take at least another day before he met
with Big Panda.'

'Hours passed and Tiny Dragon was wondering if it might be possible to walk on his injured foot when the skies opened and rain fell in torrents.'

'The storm raged.

Thunder and lightning wracked the skies and the earth shook.

Tiny Dragon huddled up in the corner of the hermitage and
hugged the crystal tightly to his chest.'

'When the storm had finally blown itself out, Tiny Dragon cautiously peered outside.

To his dismay he saw the bridge had collapsed.

He felt very unstable on his injured foot and decided he couldn't risk picking his way through the rubble.

Resigning himself to staying here overnight, he sat on a mossy stone and watched the bamboo swaying in the last whispers of the storm.'

'It was truly beautiful.'

'Night fell over the forest, and Tiny Dragon limped back
to the shelter of the hermitage.'

'As he sat staring out into the darkness, something was moving
amidst the trees.

Tiny Dragon felt a cold sense of dread.

But instead of hiding and despite his fear, Tiny Dragon watched
as a great beast, heavy and powerful, stepped into the moonlight.
He had never seen such a thing before, but knew from Big Panda's
stories it must be a Stag.

It paused for a moment, majestic and wild.

Tiny Dragon was overwhelmed to see such a magnificent sight.'

'Through Tiny Dragon's bravery,
darkness had been transformed into beauty,
and fear into wonder.'

Tiny Dragon watched until the Stag became one with
the leafy shadows. If he hadn't hurt his foot he would never
have seen one of the most incredible sights of his life.'

'Tiny Dragon climbed into his little makeshift bed
and thought to himself . . .

I wonder what wonders tomorrow will bring.'

'When morning came, Tiny Dragon decided his foot
was strong enough to continue.

But the crystal was becoming so heavy to carry that despite
how much he adored it, Tiny Dragon decided he would swap
it with a passing trader.'

'But the trader shook his head. "This is very common,"
he said, "and completely worthless."'

'But when Tiny Dragon thought about the experiences he'd had after finding the crystal

the beauty and the suffering,

the fear and the joy,

he was not so sure it was worthless to him.'

'So was the crystal beneficial?' mused the Cat.

'Who knows.

The way Tiny Dragon chose to look at it . . . perhaps.

My point, friend Crow, is that sometimes what we think is
bad ends up good, and something we have always wanted,
ends up harming us.'

'Flowers can bloom in the most unlikely of places.'

'I think I understand,' said the Crow.

'Fate leads us on a winding path and despite how bad a situation
may appear, we can never really know how it will turn out.

I'll try to remember that, then maybe I won't get so
upset when things don't go my way.'

The Crow nodded to the Cat, and with a beat of her great black wings,
took to the air.

The Cat watched until the Crow had disappeared into the mists.

At last he continued on his way, but before long,
gnarled oaks closed in and the Cat found himself in a dark,
tangled forest.

A rustling broke the quiet and from the brambles emerged
a solitary wolf cub, looking a little forlorn.

'Hello,' said the Cat, 'why are you out here alone?'

'The adults have gone hunting,' replied the Cub.
'They won't let me go – so I have to stay near the den.
I tried to sleep but I've had a very strange dream.'

'Would you like to tell me about it?' asked the Cat.

The Cub was reluctant at first, but with nothing better to do,
and feeling confused by the dream, he settled down next to the Cat.

'In the dream, I'm being chased by a big dog.
I'm scared and I wish I was strong and powerful
like our pack leader. Then I wouldn't need to be scared of dogs.

And suddenly I'm magically transformed into a huge fearsome wolf.'

'So I chase the dog to scare it off, but quickly I feel hot and tired.

And then I see a river. It's flowing fast and cool across the land
and I really wish I could do the same.

Then suddenly . . .

I'm a river.'

'I flow fast and free, but very soon I merge with the ocean
and the excitement of being a river is gone.

Now I am still and deep, but I feel trapped and I'm getting bored.

I look up and see a great eagle soaring through the clouds. I think
how wonderful this would be and no sooner have I thought it than . . .

I'm an eagle!'

'Yet although I'm great and powerful, I am old and my life is nearing its end. Below me I see a wolf cub playing with her brother and sister, and I think about how much fun she's having, how she has her whole life ahead of her.

And then I wake up . . .'

The Cat listened in silence and when the Cub had finished he asked,
'So, what do you think it means?'

The Cub thought for a moment . . .

'Maybe,' he said quietly, 'we each have our own gifts to offer the world,
and we should celebrate them, rather than wishing we had
someone else's.'

The Cat nodded and smiled.

'Thank you,' said the Cub.

'I didn't do anything,' said the Cat.

'You listened,' said the Cub,
'and that made all the difference.'

The Cub ran back into the forest and the Cat continued along the path.

It was not long until the trees gave way to the grounds
of a great temple.

The Cat was walking along the shore
of a lake when he began to hear strange, garbled noises.

As he got closer, he saw a Monkey on a stone lantern
nervously chattering to himself.

When the Monkey spotted the Cat he peered at him intently and
started to bombard him with questions and nonsense.

'Who are you?

I'm hungrier than I was.

Do you want something from me?

It's going to rain soon . . .

Why are you here?'

'I am here,' said the Cat, 'because I seek the ancient pine.
It is said that those who sit within its boughs
will attain the greatest peace.'

'Peace!' said the Monkey. 'If only I could have a little peace.
My thoughts – they're driving me crazy.'

'Come and sit with me,' said the Cat.

'This lake,' he continued, 'is fed by a river.
If you listen very carefully you can hear it.'

The Monkey tipped his head to one side and listened.

But he could hear nothing.
He focused harder, straining his ears for
even the faintest sound of running water.

'It's no good,' he said eventually, 'I simply cannot hear it.
Maybe I need big long cat ears like you?'

'Whether you could hear the river or not doesn't matter,' said the Cat. 'But tell me, for those last few moments, how busy was your mind?'

And the Monkey realized, for the first time in as long as he could remember, that his racing thoughts had calmed.

'For a moment there,' said the Cat,
'you were so focused on listening that the past, the future,
and all your thoughts about them ceased to exist.

It was just a glimpse, but you have seen the peace that is within us all.'

The Monkey didn't move, he didn't speak.

He just watched the swallows skimming the water and
felt the autumn breeze against his fur.

The Cat left him to enjoy his peace and
walked on through the temple gardens.

Nestled in the grass he saw an ancient Tortoise, hidden in her shell.

The Tortoise's head slowly emerged.

'Hello,' said the Cat. 'This place is beautiful.'

'It was,' said the Tortoise.

'But I tire of its cherry groves and am weary of the motionless lakes,
the incessant babbling of streams and the relentless drone of the wind
in the trees.

The buildings never change and each day brings the same
sun and rain and clouds . . .

and so it goes on . . .

and on and on.'

'You are tired of life,' said the Cat.

The Tortoise nodded.
'With any luck, my time will come and I can leave this tiresome world.'

'I have something which might help you,'
said the Cat, dipping his paw in the damp ash of a temple lantern.

He then wrote upon a large flat stone.

Each moment is a unique place
in the world just for you.

Savour it now,
for you can never visit it again.

The Tortoise peered at the Cat's words,
and taking her time – as Tortoises do – turned to the Cat,
a tear on her cheek.

'I had never thought of it like that,' she said.

'All I wanted was for this moment to be over,
hoping the next would be better and somehow fulfil me
. . . but it never happened.

And now I read this – I see why.'

'I have seen a lot, friend Cat.
A hundred summers, a thousand temples, a million stars,
but have I ever really, truly smelt a flower?
Well . . . I cannot wait to do so.

Thank you.'

And as the Cat walked away, the Tortoise was left
not just with her flower, but with a sense of hope.

The Cat felt something powerful stir deep within him,
for he felt he had done more good since leaving the city
than he had in years of being shut away, focusing on himself.

The light was fading.

The Cat was just beginning to think about stopping for the night
when an explosion of teeth and claws burst from the trees.

The Tiger raised its massive claw and snarled.

'Ah,' said the Cat, 'here opens the gateway to suffering.'

'What!?' roared the Tiger. 'You should be terrified.
I could kill you here and now.'

The Cat eyed the furious creature for a moment.
'You are creating your own pain, friend Tiger.

You think that by besting me you will feel mighty and strong,
but it will not bring you the satisfaction you are seeking.

It will never be enough, and you will live angry and unfulfilled.

If I am mistaken, do tell me, but I imagine the last time
you did this your victory was hollow and short-lived?'

The Tiger paused.

He thought back to the countless times he had done this same thing,
relishing his power and ferocity and the terror in his victims.

But just like the Cat said, it had never lasted,
and he had quickly set out to find more ways to strike fear
into the creatures of the forest.

The Cat watched the Tiger's fury dissolve.
His claws and fangs retreated and his eyes softened.

An expression of confusion and even curiosity spread across his face.
For what the Tiger had been so sure of just a few seconds ago,
he was no longer certain about.

'Ah,' said the Cat, 'here opens the gateway to peace.'

The Tiger made no sound. He looked at one of his great paws, sheathing and unsheathing its dagger-like claws.

'Maybe I was wrong,' he said. 'I have been angry for so long. I thought that being better than those around me would somehow make me feel good.'

'Just the idea of not trying to be the best feels so good –
so calming – I somehow feel I have come back to myself.'

Fascinated by what the Cat had said and
the peace that had settled over him,
the Tiger asked if he might accompany the Cat for a while.

The Cat agreed, and after spending
the night in the boughs of a great oak,
they were ready to continue towards the valley.

The next morning, mist had fallen across the land and the Cat was
concerned he would become lost. But the Tiger knew the area well.
'Sit on my back,' he said, 'we will make good time.'

'Have you always travelled alone?' asked the Tiger.

'In my heart, yes,' answered the Cat.
'But I am learning to change.'

'I have never had a friend,' said the Tiger.
'How odd that we two strangers should get along.'

'Our souls are not so different,' said the Cat.
'Deep down, we need the same things.'

'It's strange,' said the Cat, 'I was talking with a crow yesterday about how you never know how things are going to turn out.

There is every chance I could have been your dinner last night, and now, here you are, helping me on my journey.'

'True,' said the Tiger, 'but your actions are motivated by kindness, and I think perhaps the universe is looking out for you.'

This made the Cat pause, and again, he thought back to his time in the city and how much he had been focused on himself and his path.

'Maybe,' he said after a time.

'But one thing I am certain of,' said the Cat, 'is that the more I have gone out of my way to help others, the richer my life has become.'

'Like sowing seeds,' said the Tiger.
'A little work, perhaps, but so much to reap.'

They journeyed on for much of the morning until they came to
a fork in the road.

One path rose sharply upwards, the terrain rocky and treacherous.

The other, broad and devoid of obstacles, continued through the mist.

A signpost stood in the fork.

'That way to the Great Tree,' said the Tiger, gesturing
to the more difficult route.

'The obstacle is often the path,' thought the Cat.

The Cat and the Tiger sat down in the long grass. The Tiger turned
to the Cat and said 'I can't stop thinking about your words.
I can feel something has started to change inside me and
I want to walk a new path.

But I am not "quite" ready to begin.

I have seen the monks at the temple, and they have special cushions
and incense and candles. They also have books brimming with wisdom.
I shall need to acquire these things before I start.'

'That signpost,' said the Cat 'is not the destination.
It simply points to it . . .

Likewise, the books are not the way, although
they can help you find it. Just like the signpost,
if you spend all your time studying it you will
never get where you're going.'

'Let me tell you a story.

There was a lady with no money, who each day would sit on the side of the road and hope that strangers would give her coins so that she might eat. She lived that way for many years. I would often visit her.'

'Although we didn't speak

we understood each other.'

'One day I noticed that the box she always sat on was cracked,
and inside I could see the glimmer of coins.

Well, I knew these would really help her so I nudged the box
with my nose, but she just smiled and stroked me.'

'Each day I nudged at the box and mewed until one day
she became curious and looked more carefully.

When she spotted what was in it she was overwhelmed.'

'The first thing she did was rush out to get me food and a blanket.
She was so very kind.

She doted on me, as though I was the source of her good fortune.

But I was only the messenger.'

'The lady had possessed the treasure all along.
She just needed someone to show her where to look.

And even though she was no longer poor, she did not change.
She was simply able to do more of the things that were important
to her.

She helped those who needed it, for she was wise and she knew that
was where happiness dwelt.'

The Tiger sat in thought for a while then turned to the Cat.

'So you are saying that I should start walking the path right now,
even though I don't feel ready?'

'It is better to begin the journey, make some mistakes and correct your course, than to wait until everything is perfect and never even start.'

'I understand,' said the Tiger.
'And so I think it is time to walk my new path alone.
Thank you, Cat.'

'So which path will you take?' asked the Cat, looking at the two routes.

'Neither,' said the Tiger, turning towards the forest.
'I will walk my own path.'

The Cat watched the Tiger disappear into the leafy
shadows and smiled to himself.

The way ahead looked treacherous and difficult and
despite his eagerness to get to the ancient tree,
he decided to rest and continue in the morning.

It was raining when the Cat awoke, but he pressed on regardless.
The icy downpour soaked his fur, chilling him to the bones.

But few things can deter a cat once it has made up its mind.

By midday, the Cat had reached the higher slopes
of the valley and he was sure he could see the tree the
Rat had spoken of.

Its thick, gnarled limbs towered above the rest of the forest.

The Cat felt a surge of excitement.

He made his way down the mountain and into the maple forest.

The Cat paused for a moment to listen to the sound of the rain
pattering on the canopy.

This was indeed a magical place – he could feel it.

Up ahead the Cat noticed something moving in the path.

As he got closer he saw it was a Kitten
utterly absorbed in chasing autumn leaves.

The Cat moved closer until the Kitten, despite being intensely focused on a particularly badly behaved twig, noticed the Cat, and dived under a pile of leaves.

'Hello,' grinned the Kitten. 'What are you doing out here?'

'I am on an important task,' said the Cat, without slowing his pace.

'You have the eyes of someone who is searching for something,'
said the Kitten, bounding after him.
'Are you hungry? What are you looking for?'

'I don't think you would understand,' said the Cat,
eager to be on his way.

'Try me,' said the Kitten, optimistically. 'I'm smarter than I look.'

'I am very sorry,' said the Cat, 'maybe another time.'

'But where are your friends?' asked the Kitten.

'This is not a journey where I need friends,'
replied the Cat, a little impatience breaking into his voice.

'I am quite happy on my own.'

'But friends are like magic,' said the Kitten.
'When you share something good with a friend,
you somehow get more than if you'd kept it to yourself.'

'And if something isn't right, just telling your friend can make it seem
better, even though they might not know how to fix it.'

The Cat looked down at the Kitten,
who was clearly enjoying himself, and sighed.

'If only it were that simple. But if you will please excuse me,
I must be on my way, and for this particular "magic",
solitude is necessary.'

The Cat increased his pace, leaving the Kitten to his leaves,
and continued along the trail.

He slightly regretted his brusque treatment of the Kitten, but this
was important. There would be time for that kind of thing later.

And then . . .

finally

rising from the forest floor was the most magnificent tree
the Cat had ever seen.

It was everything the Rat had spoken of.
A magnificent specimen and older than the forest itself.

The Cat could sense a powerful spiritual energy.

He approached the tree and with the utmost care, climbed up into
the low-hanging branches.

He carefully selected a dry spot and sat down to meditate.

'Ah . . .' thought the Cat to himself, 'this is it.
This is what I have been searching for.'

He closed his eyes and allowed the power of the tree to work upon him.

At first the Cat was sure he could feel something, an energy,
a spiritual power, but as he sat there, he began to think the feeling
was no different to when he sat under the old ash tree
that grew outside the city.

'Perhaps it just takes a while,' thought the Cat to himself.
'Maybe my mind is not empty enough.'

But time passed, and still the Cat felt nothing.

Until, suddenly . . .

With a crash of pine needles and dead wood,
something sodden and furry fell from above,
slamming into him and knocking him off the branch.

The Cat leapt backwards, hissing and spitting.

'How dare you disturb my time of peace and calm!'

But the Kitten simply rolled onto its front and clumsily stood.

It showed no fear and no complaint.

As the Cat watched the Kitten, something began to change within him.

And it had nothing to do with a magical tree.

And he smiled a broad, sincere smile.

A smile he had not known for many years.

And as the Cat sat in the rain, watching the wet Kitten
playfully chasing leaves across the forest floor,
he finally understood why he was here and what he was missing.

He realized that through all the years of
solitary practice he had been focused only on himself.

And he thought back over his journey and all the creatures
he had helped to bring a little peace to:

the Hare, the Crow, the Tortoise, the Cub, the Monkey and the Tiger

and he realized that this was never about a tree.

This was about taking all the things he had learned over his life,
all the gifts he had been given, and sharing them.

And that the small things he'd ignored were in fact
the things he should have been paying the most attention to.

A sense of deep caring for the little Kitten spread through him and
he felt truly at peace for the first time in many years.

No yearning.
No desire to search outside himself.

Who would have guessed it would have taken a clumsy,
bedraggled kitten and its gentle, unconditional kindness
to show him the way.

It was not lost on the Cat that just yesterday he was talking about
how you never knew what would end up being good and bad for you.

'Thank you,' said the Cat. 'You teach what words could never explain.'

The Kitten tried to grab its own tail and, slightly disappointed,
turned to the Cat. 'I don't understand,' he said.

'Your willingness to not understand – that's your strength,'
said the Cat.

'Here I am trying to understand everything, trying to seek the truth.

And you're the one who is joyfully in this moment, not questioning why – seeing the value in the simple things around you and trying to build friendships.'

The rain gave way to mist and the sun hung low in the sky.

'I'd love to be your friend,' said the Kitten.

'And I yours,' said the Cat.

They sat under the shelter of the great tree for a while.
Then the Kitten turned to the Cat.

'So, did you find what you were looking for?' he asked.
'I think so,' replied the Cat.

'I've learned that what we want is seldom what we need.
And what we need is almost never what we want.'

The Kitten looked at the Cat, confused.

'Well,' said the Cat, 'the things we don't want can challenge us and frustrate us. Often we wish there was a "magical" solution that would fix all our problems.

But sometimes, it's these problems and the struggles that force us to face ourselves, and in the process of doing this, we learn about ourselves, we become stronger and we start to see what is truly valuable.

Then we can look at the world with new eyes.'

'Of course,' said the Cat, 'life doesn't always go to plan,
and we don't always have the presence and wisdom to
learn from our problems.'

'But the fact that you don't always know how things may ultimately
turn out can bring light to dark places.

The idea that the problem you are currently facing could end up
having something positive hidden within it can help you through
the experience.'

The Cat got up, took one last look at the ancient pine,
and prepared to leave.

The Kitten's face fell as he thought of his new friend leaving him,
but perhaps the Cat was right. Maybe there might
be a hidden benefit to being alone again.

'Are you going home now?' asked the Kitten quietly.

'I came here because there were things I did not understand,'
said the Cat, 'and despite what has happened here,
I'm afraid I still have much to discover.'

'But one thing I do know, friend Kitten,
is that whatever lies ahead,
it will be better with you alongside.'

'The secret to a beautiful life is not just
in an ancient tree or a star-filled sky.

It is in the leaves and the mud and the rain.

In you and me and in the bustling city I left far behind.'

The End

Afterword

Zen can be a confusing idea. It can conjure up a range of images from white, minimal apartments to solitary monks sitting in silence. To me, it is simply the cultivation of a way of being which brings more peace and wisdom into our lives.

One of the most fundamental aspects of zen is that it is almost impossible to explain, much like the taste of a peach, and the simplest way to understand it is to experience it. Unfortunately, its deeper meanings can be elusive to most of us.

In this book I have tried to approach zen in a more practical way that takes some of its ideas and stories and makes them more accessible and useful on a day-to-day level. To do this I have selected a number of traditional zen stories which have been used for hundreds of years to point towards ideas without literally explaining them.

I spent a great deal of time studying zen stories before settling on a selection I thought would work well in the book. Some of the tales are new and although I hope they capture the spirit of zen, are of my own devising.

I chose the stories I did mostly because they have ideas which you can immediately integrate into your own day, irrespective of what you are doing. For example, in the Monkey's story, he realizes that just by shifting his focus for a moment, the whole world can change – this is something we can experiment with at any time. Likewise, I'm sure many readers have felt like the Tortoise, but I find the idea that this moment that I'm in right now will never be repeated helps to add something deeply profound to our everyday, mundane experiences. You could consider it right now while you read this.

Many of us feel hesitant to start something new and tend to wait until the time is right, just like the Tiger. I feel this way when I start to create a new picture or book or write an afterword, but I have learned to give myself permission to start messily with no expectation and somehow, each time, things just seem to work themselves out.

I have also allowed zen philosophy to influence the art of the book. Although many of the images are in a traditional style, some use a technique called sumi-e which was used centuries ago in East Asia and involves painting with black ink on special papers. This type of work is extremely spontaneous and instinctive and does not really allow the artist to be fussy and overly detailed. The rich black brushstrokes on the delicate rice paper are supremely enjoyable and the way these materials work together creates all kinds of random yet wonderful patterns and effects.

Nature really is contributing to the final image, and it really teaches you to relinquish control (another wonderful zen concept). The pictures on pages 15, 17, 19, 21, 46, 53, 59, 89, 106, 109, 110, 124 and 169 use this technique.

Aside from retelling these stories, I also wanted to have an overarching tale which not only unified the stories into a single narrative, but also showed an individual's journey and the struggles they experience trying to follow a spiritual path.

During the Cat's travels he meets many animals and although he aids each one by sharing a version of an ancient zen story, he is also helping himself, for all life is connected, and when we benefit others, we cannot help but benefit ourselves.

The Cat finds it very easy to offer these creatures advice, but not so easy to apply it to himself and even starts to become annoyed towards the end of the story when he sees the Kitten as an obstacle to his enlightenment. But as the old expression goes:

The obstacle IS the path.

The Kitten was the last thing the Cat wanted, but the one thing he really needed.

During my own work day, one of my cats likes to pace back and forth across my work area, blocking off my monitor, walking on my paintings and generally doing anything she can to get attention. I am very tempted to shut her out of the room – I've got important work to do! But this is exactly the messenger I need – she reminds me to stop and stroke her and appreciate her tiny feline form. And one day she'll be gone, and I don't want to recall all the times I shut her out the room because I was too busy.

So where is the zen?

Much like the Tiger, it's easy to become seduced by the idea that the path to peace requires retreats, meditation, gurus and incense. Of course, these things can certainly help, but one of the things I like most about zen philosophy is how empowering it is to the individual. You can start on your own, right this second.

There is something beautiful in the drone of traffic or the stained concrete of an old tower block. As Big Panda says, 'There is beauty everywhere, but sometimes it's difficult to see.'

If you can take just thirty seconds to really feel the fabric of your clothes or listen to the noises outside your window, you can, like the Monkey, be transported to another state of mind. If, just for a second, your mind stops and the experience takes over, then you have encountered zen.

If you can practise this whenever you remember it, it may start to bring a little more peace into your life. Even zen monks do not spend all day in meditation, the majority of their time is spent doing tasks, but they attempt to do them with a deliberate, aware-mind state.

If you could take one thing away from this book, I would ask you to try and remember that good things often come out of seemingly bad things.

Lotus flowers are significant in Buddhism – in part because they grow out of filth.

If you can embed this idea in your mind, I think life can become more joyful as it can take the sting out of the negative experiences that visit us daily. This is not always easy, and some experiences are so overwhelmingly painful that trying to see the good in them is simply not always possible, but if you start small and try to develop it as a habit it can start to change the way you see the world, and ultimately increase your own happiness.

And if you feel uncertain about any of the ideas in this book, that's good – just like for the Tiger in the story, confusion is the first sign you are about to change.

MICHAEL JOSEPH

UK | USA | Canada | Ireland | Australia
India | New Zealand | South Africa

Michael Joseph is part of the Penguin
Random House group of companies
whose addresses can be found at
global.penguinrandomhouse.com.

Penguin
Random House
UK

First published in Great Britain by
Michael Joseph, 2023
005

Set in Bauer Bellefair

Colour origination by Altaimage, London
Printed and bound in China by C&C Offset Printing Co., Ltd.

A CIP catalogue record for this book is
available from the British Library

ISBN: 978-0-241-64015-9

www.greenpenguin.co.uk

MIX
Paper | Supporting
responsible forestry
FSC® C018179

Penguin Random House is committed to a
sustainable future for our business, our readers
and our planet. This book is made from Forest
Stewardship Council® certified paper.